# Afrekete

*Anchor Books*

DOUBLEDAY

*New York London Toronto Sydney Auckland*

*An Anthology of Black Lesbian Writing*

# *Afrekete*

*Edited by*
*Catherine E. McKinley*
*and*
*L. Joyce DeLaney*

AN ANCHOR BOOK

PUBLISHED BY DOUBLEDAY
a division of Bantam Doubleday Dell
Publishing Group, Inc.
1540 Broadway, New York, New York 10036

ANCHOR BOOKS, DOUBLEDAY, and the
portrayal of an anchor are trademarks of
Doubleday, a division of Bantam Doubleday
Dell Publishing Group, Inc.

Acknowledgments for individual pieces
appear on pages 315–17.

*Book design by Jennifer Ann Daddio*

Library of Congress Cataloging-in-Publication Data
Afrekete: an anthology of Black
lesbian writing / edited by Catherine E.
McKinley and L. Joyce DeLaney—1st Anchor Books ed.
p.    cm.
1. Afro-American lesbians—Literary
collections.   2. American literature—Afro-
American authors.   3. Afro-American lesbians
—Social conditions.   4. American literature—
Women authors.   5. American literature—20th
century.   6. Lesbians' writings, American.
I. McKinley, Catherine E.   II. DeLaney, L. Joyce.
PS509.L47A38     1995
810.8′09206643—dc20                         94-39560
CIP

ISBN 0-385-47354-0
ISBN 0-385-47355-9 (pbk.)

*With love for my family,*
*who taught me to believe in the work.* —C.M.


*To my sisters, Stacey and Maisha.*
*And to my mother.* —J.D.

# Editors' Acknowledgments

We owe so much to Marie Dutton Brown, our agent, who encouraged and supported this project from its uncertain beginnings, and who allowed her office to become an outpost, as is her spirit —although perhaps against her better mind; and to Arabella Meyer, our editor, who asked the right questions and helped to make the work fly. Julie Grau, Sapphire, and Emily Heckman, who lent their exceptional editorial skills to sections of the manuscript, also cannot go unrecognized. Deep gratitude as well to Charlotte Sheedy and Simon Watson for their belief in this project and their generous assistance in securing rights to some of the work included herein. And to Herman Beavers, who opened a dialogue that became this book.

I must add a note of personal gratitude to Marie Brown, who has been a professional mentor and "other-mother" over the past several years, and who has pushed and supported important growth. The love and faith of my parents, Elizabeth W. McKinley and Donald S. McKinley, and my grandmother, Elizabeth R. Wilson, have also been a mainstay. Thanks also to Kai Jackson, my very *best* sister-friend, who keeps reminding and insisting. And to Hawley Russell and Sir Jimmy, my soul mates and fellow itinerant wanderers. I love you two divas! Finally, big shouts and love to Alicia Batista, Beverly Green, Rebecca Walker, Sapphire, Jackie Woodson, Neeti Madan, Andrea Kincannon, and Jill Jackson, who provided inspiration and essential support in seeing this project through. —C.M.

Much thanks to my mother and father, James and Jeanette DeLaney. My sisters, Stacey and Maisha. My brother, James Rashad. My grandparents, Anne and Johnnie DeLaney, may they rest in peace. And my family from L.A. to LA.

A special thanks to the girls, Liz, Vandalyn (wherever you are), Delphina, and Leslie. To Pat Healey, for helping me to put the pieces back together. To Suzanne Hoover, for being there. And Gloria Ruiz, for keeping the faith. —J.D.

# Contents

*Contents*        x

# Introduction

Editors' disclaimer: This is the hardest part—the task of contextualizing the work, the seeming obligation to speak "authoritatively" about the project we have chosen. When the opportunity to edit this book was presented, we thought primarily of the chance to collect good writing—narratives we would want to read. We did not contemplate too long the specter of political debate that the writing would meet. We take on these debates every day in everything we do. It is tiring. It mutes our passion. Identity politics bind and frankly bore us. We return their hostility. And though we have academic training as literary theorists, we most often wish to be neither authorities nor critics outside our local debates. We are artists primarily and it is through our creative work that we wish to take on this struggle. We are two girls looking for our stories.

This is a story at once familiar and new. You may find yourself in it.

*I first discovered Audre Lorde's memoir* Zami: A New Spelling of My Name *(1982) at the end of my first year of college. I took this book home for summer vacation with the other artifacts of what seemed a freshly exhumed life—relocated and resurrected from small-town late-1960s-forged-and-1980s-weaned "mulatta" to urban Black woman intellectual.*

*My collection of books by Black female writers, particularly Black feminist texts, was now substantial and I righteously deposited all of my "white" books in the crawl space in the wall adjoining my room and my brother's. The volumes that replaced them were proudly displayed as both an altar and a gesture of defiance against my sur-roundings: the small, predominantly white and Roman Catholic New England factory town in which I was raised.* Zami, *however, because of its clear identification as a "lesbian" text, remained stashed in the bag that I carried to the nursing home where I worked, the lengthy shifts consuming my time as much as my loneliness did outside of it. I read* Zami *three times that summer, hiding out in patients' rooms until I could return home and retreat to my tiny, hot bedroom.*

*I spent that period mourning my lost freedom and proximity to New York City. I was burning with a nascent and fiery sense of myself as a Black woman, able to express for the first time a resistance to the condition in which I found myself—one that previously seemed intrac-table, inarticulable. I could not acknowledge my growing sexual pas-sion for women. Blinded to aspects of myself by a weighty preoccupa-tion with race, it would take several years before I would come out.*

Zami, *like those other texts, became symbolic of this newfound racial and gender consciousness. I identified deeply with Audre's childhood and adolescent experiences. And so simply, the title itself asserted what I saw as both a link to Afrocentricity at the beginning of what became a popularly recognized cultural movement in the mid and late 1980s; and a clear affirmation of Black femaleness. I was able to overlook the meaning of the word "zami" itself,[1] as well as the cover photo of Audre Lorde with her shorts and black-socks-clad white lover, and focus on its "Africanness."*

*At the same time,* Zami—*perhaps not ironically—offered a critical perspective that pointedly called this way of reading (the narrow nationalism, the strangling prescriptions of Black womanhood, and by extension, the homophobia endemic to the Afrocentric movement) into question. It would, however, take some time before Lorde's influence on my changing consciousness would fully manifest itself. I read with the furtiveness of my childhood, when I would stuff things in the gaps of the frame of the door to hide the light as I stayed up beyond decent hours, listening for my mother's footsteps; feeling aroused and ashamed. I used a pen to highlight important text, often skipping over the explicitly "lesbian" passages. Unless sex was involved. Rereading* Zami *today, the places where there is an absence of markings is a truer mark of the book's value for me.*

This story is a part of *Afrekete.* What shaped her in measure. And this is Afrekete:

Afrekete, in *Zami,* is Audre's last embrace. Afrekete is a child of the South, a migrant to Harlem. She is someone you may know. She is both wonderfully common and of the substance from which myths are spun: 'round the way girl, early banjee,

1. Audre Lorde describes "zami" as a name for "women who work together as friends and lovers," originating from her parents' native home of Carriacou. It is also used with slightly altered meanings in other Caribbean nations, such as Trinidad and Tobago.

roots daughter, blues singer. Together, these two women—who are at once a part of and outsiders in a post–World War II community of Black people whose lives and sense of communal identity are in flux—create a place of loving. Afrekete comes into Audre's young life briefly, helping her to collect the "journeywoman pieces of herself"—her converging experiences and identities—which allow her to chart a course for living. When Afrekete disappears as unexpectedly as she came, she leaves for Audre, as for the reader, "an emotional tattoo." This psychic mark permeates much of Lorde's work. Afrekete's mythic self becomes an icon both in Lorde's other writings and in the early critical discourse concerned with fictional representations of Black lesbians.

For too many readers, this was the first representation—or at best one of the very few—of a Black lesbian life drawn by an out Black lesbian writer. We chose this title to pay homage to a seminal text and to the brilliant gift of Audre Lorde's writing. For it is to Lorde's radical political and artistic legacy that we owe in a significant way the possibility of this book and the possibility of the expanse of the writing included herein.

Well, *Afrekete* is . . . and *Afrekete* ain't.[2] This title also points critically to ever-shifting and not uncomplicated notions of Black lesbian experience and identity promoted both within and without Black lesbian communities. Afrekete is a black Black woman, a primal link to a history and community many of us are accused of forsaking when we "cross" over into the lesbian "nation." For many of us, Afrekete offered a comfortable, reassuring image of ourselves and allowed for imaginings of the lovers who

2. This is borrowed from Ralph Ellison's novel *Invisible Man* and popularized by the late Black gay filmmaker Marlon T. Riggs, whose film *Black Is . . . Black Ain't* opened critical ground in many people's consciousness and both academic and popular discussion of how racial and sexual identity interrogate and problematize each other.

might be out there. She is a perfect creation of the Black lesbian feminist imagination. And yet while we need this myth and others, and at times our lovers, we need them to exist complicated by other Black lesbian lives. *Afrekete* joins the dialogue of other creative and political movements (Afrocentricity; Black nationalism; the progressive Black arts movement; the feminist movement and lesbian feminist movement; Queer Nation, etc., as well as popular culture) which risk essentializing both what Black female and lesbian and gay identity and images should be. Black lesbian writers cannot easily cling to simple notions of racial, gender, and sexual identity and the politics that overarch them. We cannot afford this any more than we can single representations of Black lesbians or a handful of generally recognized texts that portray Black lesbian lives.

AFREKETE is many women. With contradictory selves. And while AFREKETE troubles identity politics—her vision stretches much wider.

So, *Afrekete* is . . . and *Afrekete* ain't.

As editors, it is our intention—with all the limits of this one slim text—to recognize and further promote a tradition of Black lesbian writings. And surely Black lesbians have been central in American cultural production and intellectual debate. Whether or not they and their work can be quickly identified or marked simply as "Black" and "lesbian," their experiences and position bear deeply on their work, and it is out there!

*Afrekete* features twenty writings—fiction, essays, and poetry —selected from over two hundred submissions from women throughout the United States and from Canada, the Caribbean, Australia, and several European countries who learned of the project largely through informal networks. This volume features the work of both new and emerging writers (for quite a few this is their first publication) as well as prominent authors whose contributions appear in a body of writings by Black lesbians that is, with this edition, the first book of its kind. That *Afrekete* is appearing now as a first, after nearly a decade of the so-called publishing boom of Black women's writings, is not lost to us as editors. And while we are also only recently beginning to witness a proliferation in mainstream publishing of lesbian and gay texts, writings by Black lesbians and other lesbians of color have largely been excluded from the collections that have appeared and that have begun to form the "canon" of lesbian and gay writing, although the debate is not yet over.

*Afrekete* embodies diverging aesthetics, experiences, and social and political positions. Miss Afrekete has the red clay dirt of Georgia between her toes; she straps on a dildo; she contemplates the sexual freedom of fags; she battles erasure, so light she could pass; she is Audre Lorde's young poet protégée; she lives on the Lower East Side; she prefers leather to kente; she conjures American dreams; she is an old lady with dreadlocks walking with her Moses staff along the beaches of New England; she has zodiac dreams.

The contributors and these editors identify as lesbian, gay, zamis, dykes, queers, Black, African, African-American, biracial —and often may use these terms and others interchangeably. And while sexuality, or race for that matter, is and is not always at the center of their work, both deeply inform the writer's vision. The work featured is written in a range of styles, a breadth of aesthetics reflecting the birthing and meshing of seemingly disparate artistic sensibilities and traditions: Black and queer, as well as others. It was our intention as editors to present a collection of writing that speaks strongly, both as individual pieces and to each other, as well as work that interrogates assumptions about Black lesbian lives, problematizes or adds complexity to the prevailing dialogue on the politics of race, gender, and sexuality. All of the writers have committed themselves to the work of writing Black lesbians into history and the imagination and challenging the body of African-American, in particular, and American letters as a whole.

It is our hope that *Afrekete* will encourage the publication of more writing that will fill the obvious places of absence in this text and encourage needed critical discussion of the work so that we can somehow move beyond simple discussions of the politics of inclusion and really challenge the artistry. We also hope that it will inspire many more works that recover texts by Black lesbians and document the social histories of our various communities. Most of all, we hope you will find good writing—telling of experiences once familiar and new—in which you will find some significant part of yourself.

*Afrekete* is all that!

*Catherine E. McKinley*
*September 30, 1994*

# *Tar Beach*

Gerri was young and Black and lived in Queens and had a powder-blue Ford that she nicknamed Bluefish. With her carefully waved hair and button-down shirts and grey-flannel slacks, she looked just this side of square, without being square at all, once you got to know her.

By Gerri's invitation and frequently by her wheels, Muriel and I had gone to parties on weekends in Brooklyn and Queens at different women's houses.

One of the women I had met at one of these parties was Kitty.

When I saw Kitty again one night years later in the Swing Rendezvous or the Pony Stable or the Page Three—that tour of second-string gay-girl bars that I had taken to making alone that sad lonely spring of 1957—it was easy to recall the St. Alban's smell of green Queens summer-night and plastic couch-covers and liquor and hair oil and women's bodies at the party where we had first met.

In that brick-faced frame house in Queens, the downstairs pine-paneled recreation room was alive and pulsing with loud music, good food, and beautiful Black women in all different combinations of dress.

There were whip-cord summer suits with starch-shiny shirt collars open at the neck as a concession to the high summer heat, and gabardine slacks with pleated fronts or slim ivy-league styling for the very slender. There were wheat-colored Cowden jeans, the fashion favorite that summer, with knife-edge creases, and even then, one or two back-buckled grey pants over well-chalked buck-skin shoes. There were garrison belts galore, broad black leather belts with shiny thin buckles that originated in army-navy surplus stores, and oxford-styled shirts of the new, iron-free Dacron, with its stiff, see-through crispness. These shirts, short-sleeved and man-tailored, were tucked neatly into belted pants or tight, skinny straight skirts. Only the one or two jersey knit shirts were allowed to fall freely outside.

Bermuda shorts, and their shorter cousins, Jamaicas, were already making their appearance on the dyke-chic scene, the rules of which were every bit as cutthroat as the tyrannies of Seventh Avenue or Paris. These shorts were worn by butch and femme alike, and for this reason were slow to be incorporated into many fashionable gay-girl wardrobes, to keep the signals clear. Clothes often were the most important way of broadcasting one's chosen sexual role.

Here and then throughout the room the flash of brightly

*Afrekete*

colored below-the-knee-full skirts over low-necked tight bodices could be seen, along with tight sheath dresses and the shine of high thin heels next to bucks and sneakers and loafers.

Femmes wore their hair in tightly curled pageboy bobs, or piled high on their heads in sculptured bunches of curls, or in feather cuts framing their faces. That sweetly clean fragrance of beauty-parlor that hung over all Black women's gatherings in the fifties was present here also, adding its identifiable smell of hot comb and hair pomade to the other aromas in the room.

Butches wore their hair cut shorter, in a D.A. shaped to a point in the back, or a short pageboy, or sometimes in a tightly curled poodle that predated the natural afro. But this was a rarity, and I can only remember one other Black woman at that party besides me whose hair was not straightened, and she was an acquaintance of ours from the Lower East Side named Ida.

On a table behind the built-in bar stood opened bottles of gin, bourbon, scotch, soda and other various mixers. The bar itself was covered with little delicacies of all descriptions: chips and dips and little crackers and squares of bread laced with the usual dabs of egg-salad and sardine paste. There was also a platter of delicious fried chicken wings, and a pan of potato-and-egg salad dressed with vinegar. Bowls of olives and pickles surrounded the main dishes, with trays of red crab apples and little sweet onions on toothpicks.

But the centerpiece of the whole table was a huge platter of succulent and thinly sliced roast beef, set into an underpan of cracked ice. Upon the beige platter, each slice of rare meat had been lovingly laid out and individually folded up into a vulval pattern, with a tiny dab of mayonnaise at the crucial apex. The pink-brown folded meat around the pale cream-yellow dot formed suggestive sculptures that made a great hit with all the women present, and Pet, at whose house the party was being given and whose idea the meat sculptures were, smilingly acknowledged the many compliments on her platter with a long-necked graceful nod of her elegant dancer's head.

The room's particular mix of heat-smells and music gives way in my mind to the high-cheeked, dark young woman with the silky voice and appraising eyes (something about her mouth reminded me of Ann, the nurse I'd worked with when I'd first left home).

Perching on the edge of the low bench where I was sitting, Kitty absently wiped specks of lipstick from each corner of her mouth with the downward flick of a delicate forefinger.

"Audre . . . that's a nice name. What's it short for?"

My damp arm hairs bristled in the Ruth Brown music, and the heat. I could not stand anybody messing around with my name, not even nicknames.

"Nothing. It's just Audre. What's Kitty short for?"

"Afrekete," she said, snapping her fingers in time to the rhythm of it and giving a long laugh. "That's me. The Black pussycat." She laughed again. "I like your hairdo. Are you a singer?"

"No." She continued to stare at me with her large direct eyes.

I was suddenly too embarrassed at not knowing what else to say to meet her calmly erotic gaze, so I stood up abruptly and said, in my best Laurel's-terse tone, "Let's dance."

Her face was broad and smooth under too-light make-up, but as we danced a foxtrot she started to sweat, and her skin took on a deep shiny richness. Kitty closed her eyes part way when she danced, and her one gold-rimmed front tooth flashed as she smiled and occasionally caught her lower lip in time to the music.

Her yellow poplin shirt, cut in the style of an Eisenhower jacket, had a zipper that was half open in the summer heat, showing collar bones that stood out like brown wings from her long neck. Garments with zippers were highly prized among the more liberal set of gay-girls, because these could be worn by butch or femme alike on certain occasions, without causing any adverse or troublesome comments. Kitty's narrow, well-pressed khaki skirt was topped by a black belt that matched my own except in its newness, and her natty trimness made me feel almost shabby in my well-worn riding pants.

I thought she was very pretty, and I wished I could dance with as much ease as she did, and as effortlessly. Her hair had been straightened into short feathery curls, and in that room of well-set marcels and D.A.'s and pageboys, it was the closest cut to my own.

Kitty smelled of soap and Jean Naté, and I kept thinking she was bigger than she actually was, because there was a comfortable smell about her that I always associated with large women. I caught another spicy herb-like odor, that I later identified as a combination of coconut oil and Yardley's lavender hair pomade. Her mouth was full, and her lipstick was dark and shiny, a new Max Factor shade called "WARPAINT."

The next dance was a slow fish that suited me fine. I never knew whether to lead or to follow in most other dances, and even the effort to decide which was which was as difficult for me as having to decide all the time the difference between left and right. Somehow that simple distinction had never become automatic for me, and all that deciding usually left me very little energy with which to enjoy the movement and the music.

But "fishing" was different. A forerunner of the later one-step, it was, in reality, your basic slow bump and grind. The low

*Tar Beach*

red lamp and the crowded St. Alban's parlor floor left us just enough room to hold each other frankly, arms around neck and waist, and the slow intimate music moved our bodies much more than our feet.

That had been in St. Alban's, Queens, nearly two years before, when Muriel had seemed to be the certainty in my life. Now in the spring of this new year I had my own apartment all to myself again, but I was mourning. I avoided visiting pairs of friends, or inviting even numbers of people over to my house, because the happiness of couples, or their mere togetherness, hurt me too much in its absence from my own life, whose blankest hole was named Muriel. I had not been back to Queens, nor to any party, since Muriel and I had broken up, and the only people I saw outside of work and school were those friends who lived in the Village and who sought me out or whom I ran into at the bars. Most of them were white.

"Hey, girl, long time no see." Kitty spotted me first. We shook hands. The bar was not crowded, which means it probably was the Page Three, which didn't fill up until after midnight. "Where's your girlfriend?"

I told her that Muriel and I weren't together anymore. "Yeah? That's too bad. You-all were kinda cute together. But that's the way it goes. How long you been in the 'life'?"

I stared at Kitty without answering, trying to think of how to explain to her that for me there was only one life—my own—however I chose to live it. But she seemed to take the word right out of my mouth.

"Not that it matters," she said speculatively, finishing the beer she had carried over to the end of the bar where I was sitting. "We don't have but one, anyway. At least this time around." She took my arm. "Come on, let's dance."

*Afrekete*                                                                6

Kitty was still trim and fast-lined, but with an easier loose-ness about her smile and a lot less make-up. Without its camou-flage, her chocolate skin and deep, sculptured mouth reminded me of a Benin bronze. Her hair was still straightened, but shorter, and her black Bermuda shorts and knee socks matched her aston-ishingly shiny black loafers. A black turtleneck pullover com-pleted her sleek costume. Somehow, this time, my jeans did not feel shabby beside hers, only a variation upon some similar dress. Maybe it was because our belts still matched—broad, black, and brass-buckled.

We moved to the back room and danced to Frankie Lymon's "Goody, Goody" and then to a Belafonte calypso. Dancing with her this time, I felt who I was and where my body was going, and that feeling was more important to me than any lead or follow.

The room felt very warm even though it was only just spring, and Kitty and I smiled at each other as the number ended. We stood waiting for the next record to drop and the next dance to begin. It was a slow Sinatra. Our belt buckles kept getting in the way as we moved in close to the oiled music, and we slid them around to the side of our waists when no one was looking.

For the last few months since Muriel had moved out, my skin had felt cold and hard and essential, like thin frozen leather that was keeping the shape expected. That night on the dance floor of the Page Three as Kitty and I touched our bodies together in dancing, I could feel my carapace soften slowly and then finally melt, until I felt myself covered in a warm, almost forgotten, slip of anticipation, that ebbed and flowed at each contact of our mov-ing bodies.

I could feel something slowly shift in her also, as if a taut string was becoming undone, and finally we didn't start back to the bar at all between dances, but just stood on the floor waiting

*Tar Beach*

for the next record, dancing only with each other. A little after midnight, in a silent and mutual decision, we split the Page together, walking blocks through the West Village to Hudson Street where her car was parked. She had invited me up to her house for a drink.

The sweat beneath my breasts from our dancing was turning cold in the sharpness of the night air as we crossed Sheridan Square. I paused to wave to the steadies through the plate glass windows of Jim Atkin's on the corner of Christopher Street.

In her car, I tried not to think about what I was doing as we rode uptown almost in silence. There was an ache in the well beneath my stomach, spreading out and down between my legs like mercury. The smell of her warm body, mixed with the smell of feathery cologne and lavender pomade, anointed the car. My eyes rested on the sight of her coconut-spicy hands on the steering wheel, and the curve of her lashes as she attended the roadway. They made it easy for me to coast beneath her sporadic bursts of conversation with only an occasional friendly grunt.

"I haven't been downtown to the bars in a while, you know? It's funny. I don't know why I don't go downtown more often. But every once in a while, something tells me to go and I go. I guess it must be different when you live around there all the time." She turned her gold-flecked smile upon me.

Crossing 59th Street, I had an acute moment of panic. Who was this woman? Suppose she really intended only to give me the drink which she had offered me as we left the Page? Suppose I had totally misunderstood the impact of her invitation, and would soon find myself stranded uptown at 3:00 A.M. on a Sunday morning, and did I even have enough change left in my jeans for carfare home? Had I put out enough food for the kittens? Was

Flee coming over with her camera tomorrow morning, and would she feed the cats if I wasn't there? If I wasn't there.

I had had only enough money for one beer that night, so I knew I wasn't high, and reefer was only for special occasions. Part of me felt like a raging lioness, inflamed in desire. Even the words in my head seemed borrowed from a dime-store novel. But that part of me was drunk on the thighed nearness of this exciting unknown dark woman, who calmly moved us through upper Manhattan, with her patent-leather loafers and her camel's-hair swing coat and her easy talk, from time to time her gloved hand touching my denimed leg for emphasis.

Another piece of me felt bumbling, inept, and about four years old. I was the idiot playing at being a lover, who was going to be found out shortly and laughed at for my pretensions, as well as rejected out of hand.

Would it be possible—was it ever possible—for two women to share the fire we felt that night without entrapping or smothering each other? I longed for that as I longed for her body, doubting both, eager for both.

And how was it possible, that I should be dreaming the roll of this woman's sea into and around mine, when only a few short hours ago, and for so many months before, I had been mourning the loss of Muriel, so sure that I would continue being broken-hearted forever? And what then if I had been mistaken?

If the knot in my groin would have gone away, I'd have jumped out of the car door at the very next traffic light. Or so I thought to myself.

We came out of the Park Drive at Seventh Avenue and 110th Street, and as quickly as the light changed on the now deserted avenue, Afrekete turned her broad-lipped beautiful face to me, with no smile at all. Her great lidded luminescent eyes looked directly and startlingly into mine. It was as if she had suddenly become another person, as if the wall of glass formed by my spectacles, and behind which I had become so used to hiding, had suddenly dissolved.

In an uninflected, almost formal voice that perfectly matched and thereby obliterated all my question marks, she asked,

"Can you spend the night?"

And then it occurred to me that perhaps she might have been having the same questions about me that I had been having about her. I was left almost without breath by the combination of her delicacy and her directness—a combination which is still rare and precious.

For beyond the assurance that her question offered me—a declaration that this singing of my flesh, this attraction, was not all within my own head—beyond that assurance was a batch of delicate assumptions built into that simple phrase that reverberated in my poet's brain. It offered us both an out if necessary. If the answer to the question might, by any chance, have been no, then its very syntax allowed for a reason of impossibility rather than of choice—"I can't," rather than "I won't." The demands of another commitment, an early job, a sick cat, etc., could be lived with more easily than an out-and-out rejection.

Even the phrase "spending the night" was less a euphemism for making love than it was an allowable space provided, in which one could move back or forth. If, perhaps, I were to change my mind before the traffic light and decide that no, I wasn't gay, after all, then a simpler companionship was still available.

I steadied myself enough to say, in my very best Lower East Side Casual Voice, "I'd really like to," cursing myself for the banal words, and wondering if she could smell my nervousness and my desperate desire to be suave and debonair, drowning in sheer desire.

We parked half-in and half-out of a bus stop on Manhattan Avenue and 113th Street, in Gennie's old neighborhood.

Something about Kitty made me feel like a rollercoaster, rocketing from idiot to goddess. By the time we had collected her mail from the broken mailbox and then climbed six flights of stairs up to her front door, I felt that there had never been anything else my body intended to do more, than to reach inside her coat and take Afrekete into my arms, fitting her body into the curves of mine tightly, her beige camel's-hair billowing around us both, and her gloved hand still holding the door key.

In the faint light of the hallway, her lips moved like surf upon the water's edge.

It was a one-and-a-half-room kitchenette apartment with tall narrow windows in the narrow, high-ceilinged front room. Across each window, there were built-in shelves at different levels. From these shelves tossed and frothed, hung and leaned and stood, pot after clay pot of green and tousled large- and small-leaved plants of all shapes and conditions.

Later, I came to love the way in which the plants filtered the southern exposure sun through the room. Light hit the opposite wall at a point about six inches above the thirty-gallon fish tank that murmured softly, like a quiet jewel, standing on its wrought-iron legs, glowing and mysterious.

Leisurely and swiftly, translucent rainbowed fish darted back and forth through the lit water, perusing the glass sides of the tank for morsels of food, and swimming in and out of the marvelous world created by colored gravels and stone tunnels and bridges that lined the floor of the tank. Astride one of the bridges, her bent head observing the little fish that swam in and out between her legs, stood a little jointed brown doll, her smooth naked body washed by the bubbles rising up from the air unit located behind her.

Between the green plants and the glowing magical tank of exotic fish lay a room the contents of which I can no longer separate in my mind. Except for a plaid-covered couch that opened up into the double bed which we sent rocking as we loved that night into a bright Sunday morning, dappled with green sunlight from the plants in Afrekete's high windows.

I woke to her house suffused in that light, the sky half-seen through the windows of the top-floor kitchenette apartment, and Afrekete, known, asleep against my side.

Little hairs under her navel lay down before my advancing tongue like the beckoned pages of a well-touched book.

How many times into summer had I turned into that block from Eighth Avenue, the saloon on the corner spilling a smell of sawdust and liquor onto the street, a shifting indeterminate number of young and old Black men taking turns sitting on two upturned milk-crates, playing checkers? I would turn the corner into 113th Street towards the park, my steps quickening and my fingertips tingling to play in her earth.

*And I remember Afrekete, who came out of a dream to me always being hard and real as the fire hairs along the underside of my navel. She brought me live things from the bush, and from her farm set out in cocoyams and cassava*—those magical fruit which Kitty bought in the West Indian markets along Lenox Avenue in the 140s or in the Puerto Rican *bodegas* within the bustling market over on Park Avenue and 116th Street under the Central Railroad structures.

"I got this under the bridge" was a saying from time immemorial, giving an adequate explanation that whatever it was had come from as far back and as close to home—that is to say, was as authentic—as was possible.

We bought red delicious pippins, the size of French cashew apples. There were green plantains, which we half peeled and then planted, fruit-deep, in each other's bodies until the petals of skin lay like tendrils of broad green fire upon the curly darkness between our upspread thighs. *There were ripe red finger bananas, stubby and sweet, with which I parted your lips gently, to insert the peeled fruit into your grape-purple flower.*

*I held you, lay between your brown legs, slowly playing my tongue through your familiar forests, slowly licking and swallowing as the deep undulations and tidal motions of your strong body slowly mashed ripe banana into a beige cream that mixed with the juices of your electric flesh. Our bodies met again, each surface touched with each other's flame, from the tips of our curled toes to our tongues, and locked into our own wild rhythms, we rode each other across the thundering space, dripped like light from the peak of each other's tongue.*

We were each of us both together. Then we were apart, and sweat sheened our bodies like sweet oil.

Sometimes Afrekete sang in a small club further uptown on Sugar Hill. Sometimes she clerked in the Gristede's Market on 97th Street and Amsterdam, and sometimes with no warning at all she appeared at the Pony Stable or Page Three on Saturday night. Once, I came home to Seventh Street late one night to find her sitting on my stoop at 3:00 A.M., with a bottle of beer in her hand and a piece of African cloth wrapped around her head, and we sped uptown through the dawn-empty city with a summer thunder squall crackling above us, and the wet city streets singing beneath the wheels of her little Nash Rambler.

There are certain verities which are always with us, which

*Tar Beach*

we come to depend upon. That the sun moves north in summer, that melted ice contracts, that the curved banana is sweeter. Afrekete taught me roots, new definitions of our women's bodies —definitions for which I had only been in training to learn before.

By the beginning of summer the walls of Afrekete's apartment were always warm to the touch from the heat beating down on the roof, and chance breezes through her windows rustled her plants in the window and brushed over our sweat-smooth bodies, at rest after loving.

We talked sometimes about what it meant to love women, and what relief it was in the eye of the storm, no matter how often we had to bite our tongues and stay silent. Afrekete had a seven-year-old daughter whom she had left with her mama down in Georgia, and we shared a lot of our dreams.

"She's going to be able to love anybody she wants to love," Afrekete said, fiercely, lighting a Lucky Strike. "Same way she's going to be able to work any place she damn well pleases. Her mama's going to see to that."

Once we talked about how Black women had been committed without choice to waging our campaigns in the enemies' strongholds, too much and too often, and how our psychic landscapes had been plundered and wearied by those repeated battles and campaigns.

"And don't I have the scars to prove it," she sighed. "Makes you tough though, babe, if you don't go under. And that's what I like about you; you're like me. We're both going to make it because we're both too tough and crazy not to!" And we held each other and laughed and cried about what we had paid for that toughness, and how hard it was to explain to anyone who didn't already know it that soft and tough had to be one and the same for either to work at all, like our joy and the tears mingling on the one pillow beneath our heads.

And the sun filtered down upon us through the dusty windows, through the mass of green plants that Afrekete tended religiously.

I took a ripe avocado and rolled it between my hands until the skin became a green case for the soft mashed fruit inside, hard pit at the core. *I rose from a kiss in your mouth to nibble a hole in the fruit skin near to the navel stalk, squeezed the pale yellow-green fruit juice in thin ritual lines back and forth over and around your coconut-brown belly.*

*The oil and sweat from our bodies kept the fruit liquid, and I massaged it over your thighs and between your breasts until your brownness shone like a light through the veil of the palest green avocado, a mantle of goddess pear that I slowly licked from your skin.*

Then we would have to get up to gather the pits and fruit skins and bag them to put out later for the garbagemen, because if we left them near the bed for any length of time, they would call out the hordes of cockroaches that always waited on the sidelines within the walls of Harlem tenements, particularly in the smaller older ones under the hill of Morningside Heights.


Afrekete lived not far from Genevieve's grandmother's house.

Sometimes she reminded me of Ella, Gennie's stepmother, who shuffled about with an apron on and a broom outside the room where Gennie and I lay on the studio couch. She would be singing her non-stop tuneless little song over and over and over:

Momma kilt me
Poppa et me

Po' lil' brudder
suck ma bones . . .

And one day Gennie turned her head on my lap to say uneasily, "You know, sometimes I don't know whether Ella's crazy, or stupid, or divine."

And now I think the goddess was speaking through Ella also, but Ella was too beaten down and anesthetized by Phillip's brutality for her to believe in her own mouth, and we, Gennie and I, were too arrogant and childish—not without right or reason, for we were scarcely more than children—to see that our survival might very well lay in listening to the sweeping woman's tuneless song.

I lost my sister, Gennie, to my silence and her pain and despair, to both our angers and to a world's cruelty that destroys its own young in passing—not even as a rebel gesture or sacrifice or hope for another living of the spirit, but out of not noticing or caring about the destruction. I have not been able to blind myself to that cruelty, which according to one popular definition of mental health, makes me mentally unhealthy.


Afrekete's house was the tallest one near the corner, before the high rocks of Morningside Park began on the other side of the avenue, and one night on the Midsummer Eve's Moon we took a blanket up to the roof. She lived on the top floor, and in an unspoken agreement, the roof belonged mostly to those who had to live under its heat. The roof was the chief resort territory of tenement-dwellers, and was known as Tar Beach.

We jammed the roof door shut with our sneakers, and spread our blanket in the lee of the chimney, between its warm brick wall and the high parapet of the building's face. This was before the blaze of sulphur lamps had stripped the streets of New York of trees and shadow, and the incandescence from the lights below faded this far up. From behind the parapet wall we could see the dark shapes of the basalt and granite outcroppings looming over us from the park across the street, outlined, curiously close and suggestive.

We slipped off the cotton shifts we had worn and moved against each other's damp breasts in the shadow of the roof's chimney, making moon, honor, love, while the ghostly vague light drifting upward from the street competed with the silver hard sweetness of the full moon, reflected in the shiny mirrors of our sweat-slippery dark bodies, sacred as the ocean at high tide.

I remember the moon rising against the tilted planes of her upthrust thighs, and my tongue caught the streak of silver reflected in the curly bush of her dappled-dark maiden hair. *I remember the full moon like white pupils in the center of your wide irises.*

*The moons went out, and your eyes grew dark as you rolled over me, and I felt the moon's silver light mix with the wet of your tongue on my eyelids.*

*Afrekete Afrekete ride me to the crossroads where we shall sleep, coated in the woman's power. The sound of our bodies meeting is the prayer of all strangers and sisters, that the discarded evils, abandoned at all crossroads, will not follow us upon our journeys.*

When we came down from the roof later, it was into the sweltering midnight of a west Harlem summer, with canned music in the streets and the disagreeable whines of overtired and overheated children. Nearby, mothers and fathers sat on stoops or milk crates and striped camp chairs, fanning themselves absently

*Tar Beach*

and talking or thinking about work as usual tomorrow and not enough sleep.

It was not onto the pale sands of Wydah, nor the beaches of Winneba or Annamabu, with cocopalms softly applauding and crickets keeping time with the pounding of tar-laden, treacherous, beautiful sea. It was onto 113th Street that we descended after our meeting under the Midsummer Eve's Moon, but the mothers and fathers smiled at us in greeting as we strolled down to Eighth Avenue, hand in hand.

I had not seen Afrekete for a few weeks in July, so I went uptown to her house one evening since she didn't have a phone. The door was locked, and there was no one on the roof when I called up the stairwell.

Another week later, Midge, the bartender at the Pony Stable, gave me a note from Afrekete, saying that she had gotten a gig in Atlanta for September, and was splitting to visit her mama and daughter for a while.

We had come together like elements erupting into an electric storm, exchanging energy, sharing charge, brief and drenching. Then we parted, passed, reformed, reshaping ourselves the better for the exchange.

I never saw Afrekete again, but her print remains upon my life with the resonance and power of an emotional tattoo.

SAPPHIRE

# *American Dreams*

Suspended in a sea of blue-gray slate
I can't move from the waist down
which brings visions & obsessions of & with
quadriplegics & paraplegics,
wondering how they live, smell
why they don't just die.
Some people wonder that about blacks,
why they just don't die.
A light-skinned black woman I know
once uttered in amazement about a black black
    woman
"I wanted to know how did she *live*

being as black as she was!"
I don't quite know how to get free
of the karma I've created
but I can see clearly now
that I have created my life.
My right ankle has mud in it,
I'm in debt.
I need dental work
& I am alone.
Alone if I keep seeing myself
through *Donna Reed* & *Father Knows Best* eyes,
if I don't see the friends,
people who care,
giving as much from their lives as they can.
If you live in the red paper valentine of first grade
    in 1956
then you are alone.
If you live in the world now
of people struggling free
then you are not.

Isolation rises up
like the marble slabs
placed on the front
of cheap concrete high-rises
with apartments that start at 500,000 dollars.
It all seems so stupid
but I understand it now,
why they have homeless people
sleeping in front of these
artificial-penis-looking buildings.

It's so we'll move in,
so such terror will be implanted
in our guts
we'll save our money
& buy a concrete box
to live in & be proud
to call it home.
All anybody really wants
is some security,
a chance to live comfortably
until the next
unavoidable tragedy
unavoidably hits them
& splices open their chests,
& takes the veins from their legs,
& carves up their heart
in the name of surgery
or vicious murder
murder
*murderer*
ha! ha! ha!
*murderer.*
No one,
nothing
can protect you
from the murderer.
Not the police, nuclear weapons, your mother, the
Republicans, mx missiles—
*none* of that
can protect you
from the murderer.

*American Dreams*

Even if you get all the niggers
out the neighborhood
the murderer might be
a white boy like David Berkowitz
baby-faced Jewish boy
who rarely missed a day
of work at the post office.
ha! ha! ha!
*you're never safe!*
Like a crab walking sideways
America hides its belly
under an arsenal of radioactive crust,
creeping along with its
long crustacean eyes,
stupid & blind
sucking debris from
the ocean floor
till there is no more,
while the giant Cancer breasts
get biopsied & amputated
& the crab caves in
under the third world's dreams
& 5 million pounds of concrete.
& the murderer
stabs stabs stabs
at the underbelly &
submicroscopic
viruses
fly out
in
ejaculate

& claim
your life,
while the powers that don't be
join
for a loving circle jerk
& nostalgic reminiscence
of days gone by,
lighting candles for Roy Cohn
& J. Edgar Hoover
as they lay a bouquet of cigarettes
on John Wayne's grave
who is clandestinely slipping
into the wax museum
to suck Michael Jackson's dick
only to find he has had his penis
surgically reconstructed
to look like Diana Ross's face.
& the Trane flies on
like Judy Grahn's wild geese
over a land diseased like cancer
killing flowers by the hour
& a huge hospice
opens up in the sky
& the man quietly tells his wife
as he picks up his rifle,
"I'm going people hunting."
& he steps calmly
into McDonald's & picks off
20 people
& blood pours red
Big Macs fall flat

*American Dreams*

to the floor amid
shrieks & screams
while a plastic clown
smiles down on the house
additives & the destruction of
the rain forests built.
& you smile for a while
feeling ever so American
& in good company
as you eat compulsively.
After all,
the whole country does it.
It's just pasta heaven here
till you get your x-ray
or biopsy back.
Making the world safe
for democracy
& you can't even evade
heart disease
until you're 40,
& it attacks quietly
walking on those big
expensive sneakers
niggers wear
as they shove the pawnshop gun
to your head & say
"GIMME EVERYTHING YOU GOT!"
& for once you are not afraid
cause the nigger has AIDS.
You laugh triumphantly,
finally you've given him

*Afrekete*                                         24

& the world
everything you got!

I was at Clark Center for the Performing Arts
getting ready for my morning ballet class
when this old wrinkled-up white faggot
ran up to me, threw his arms around me & grabbed
     me
in a vise-like grip & screamed:
BE MY BLACK MAMMY SAPPHIRE
BE MY BLACK MAMMY
He held on & wouldn't let go.
Finally I thought to turn
my hand into a claw
& raked straight down his face
with my fingernails.
He let go.
I'll never forget how
hurt & bewildered he looked.
I guess he was just playing.
I was just devastated.
There are no words
for some forms
of devastation
though we constantly
try to describe
what America has done
& continues to do to us.
We try to describe it
without whining
or quitting

or eating french fries
or snorting coke.
It's so hard not
to be an addict in America
when you know numerology
& have x-rayed the inside
of Egyptian mummies 5,000 years old
& robbed the graves of Indians
deliberately blinded children
& infected monkeys & rats
with diseases you keep alive
waiting for the right time
so you can spring 'em
on anyone who might be making progress.

Well, you're miserable now America.
The fact you put a flag
on the moon
doesn't mean you own it.
You can't steal everything
all the time
from everybody.
You can't have the moon, sucker.

A peanut farmer
warned
you could not stay number 1;
number one being an illusion
in a circle, which is
what the world is,
but you still think that

the world is flat
& you can drive out evil
with a pitchfork & pickup truck.

One time when I was a little girl living on an army
    base
I was in the gymnasium & the general walked in.
& the general is like god or the president, if you
    believe.
The young woman who was supervising
the group of children I was with said,
"Stand up everybody! The general's here!"
Everybody stood up except me.
The woman looked at me & hissed,
"Stand up for the general!"
I said, "My father's in the army, not me."
& I remained seated.
& throughout 38 years
of bucking & winging
grinning & crawling
brown nosing & begging
there has been a quiet
10-year-old in me
who has remained seated.
She perhaps is the real American Dream.

JOCELYN MARIA TAYLOR

# *Testimony of a Naked Woman*

Combining responsibility for my body and my desire for political representation has been a continuous learning process. My survival instincts have always surfaced through the more physical side of my self, maneuvering, twisting, and contorting my way through to the other side of whatever problem I was facing.

This sensibility kicked in strongly when I first moved to New York City. I had come out as a lesbian just months before. When the first opportunity presented itself, I left the comfort and security of my native Washington, D.C., a predominantly Black town with close, nurturing community ties, to move to the Queer Capital of the East Coast. I left in hopes of validating and creatively expressing this emerging aspect of my identity—one that was coming out kicking, determined, and increasingly radical.

When I first arrived in New York, I worked several low-paying, time-intensive jobs. I was attending meetings of the AIDS Coalition to Unleash Power (ACT-UP) regularly and had become involved in its media affinity group, DIVA-TV (Damned Interfering Video Activists). We hit the streets with meager equipment in hand, ready to document demonstrations and to protect protesting civilians from dirty dealings by the police. Six months later, I joined House of Color, a multiracial group of video beginners who developed a video project incorporating dialogues about exoticism, marginality, and homophobia. I discovered the link between media activism, representation, and creative expression as a member of that collective. Video was working for me. Cameras weren't too hard to come by; those who had equipment lent it to those who didn't. The thought that I could actually make my own television imagery was appealing.

The more I became involved in the alternative media community, the more I felt resentful that I didn't have the money to spend greater time developing myself as an artist and activist. I could barely support myself. A 9-to-5 job was out of the question. I felt that joining the labor force would consume my time and energy and become a form of enslavement.

The promise of fast cash and more freedom led me into the world of sex work. I started working as a stripper in hustle joints. I bought a dark pageboy wig, some fishnet stockings, a cheap pair of heels, and a tight hairnet. I wore the wig so that my new dreadlocks, which were short yet "radical," didn't show.

I got my first job as a stripper through my roommate at the time, who worked at the Hustle Joint and is now a well-known performance artist. Hanging out with her fueled my exhibitionism, a posture I was increasingly acknowledging. She had a girl-friend, a photographer, who was putting together a series of nude women in public. So, at 8:30 one Saturday morning, the three of us drove up to 42nd Street. My roommate held my coat while her girlfriend took pictures of me standing stark naked in front of the Roxy Theater. The whole thing took about thirty seconds. A couple of guys stood with their mouths agape, unable to believe their eyes. Another man walked by mumbling, "Fuckin' dykes." I guess they weren't used to seeing a naked woman in steel-toe boots getting her picture taken. I pushed back feelings of vulnerability and the voice that served a "racial reminder" on notions and images of Black women as sexual beings. I focused on the belligerence of the act—which I saw as speaking against censures from both within my community and without—and at that moment, I felt liberated.

As far as we knew, my roommate and I were the only lesbians working at the Hustle Joint. Listening to the hetero dancers discuss which men they were attracted to made me ill. It seemed that the straight women had a lot invested in the "Pretty Woman" fairy tale. They were looking for wealthy, benevolent sugar daddies to take them out of their economic misery. Some men *had* come to the bar hoping to meet women. The exchange was always the same: "I'll give you money if you make me feel like I'm in control of my life in a world of chaos." Being detached from the heterosexual-power-fuck relationship between money and sex, I maintained another fantasy. I thought that I would earn enough money to put me on easy street and beat the whole game. Money, in my mind, became the solution to all my problems. Once, a man offered me $300 to have dinner. Of course there was the specter of a larger expectation. Yet, for a lousy three hundred bucks I actually considered spending the evening with him.

I was one of only two Black women who worked at the Hustle Joint. I never really got to know the other Black woman. She was darker complected than I and well tipped as a result of that "exoticism." In the Hustle Joint, "Black girl" is a fetish category just like bearded ladies or tattooed women. We were clearly novelty items. Occasionally, the owner of the bar would tell us to approach some dusty, old white patron who was a regular customer. The owner would say to us, with a gleam in his eye, "He *likes* Black girls." We "Black girls," however, didn't make nearly as much money as the white women who worked there.

We were all, Black, white, and other women, referred to as "girls." We called each other "girls" ("How many girls are working this shift?"). When I walked through the entrance of the Hustle Joint I left my politics at the door. I was most worried about how I was going to pay bills and buy tape for video projects. I was worried about how I was going to *continue* as a radical Black woman if I didn't have the money to survive. I knew that stripping was a means to an end. I knew I wouldn't and couldn't do it forever. Somehow I just found it to be much more palatable than waiting tables or working an office job. Stripping was easier. The Hustle Joint was another world: working there was an exercise in detachment that I performed very successfully. I could slip into my exhibitionist mode, and imagine that I was really in control and, in fact, taking advantage of the situation. I also thought that I was experimenting with an aspect of my erotic self. There was part of me that liked performing, liked having a captive audience who would only watch me.

At this time, I had already started the Clit Club, a lesbian party night for women, but still had big financial struggles. The club started in the summer of 1990, during a dry spell of activities for women in New York City. At the Clit Club, women of all shapes, colors, and sizes were encouraged to stretch their sexual boundaries and to explore lesbian sensuality in the safety of an all-women's space. It was important for those who walked through Clit's door to feel comfortable enough to shed any barriers that might inhibit their desire. It was the first place to unapologetically *emphasize* sexual pleasure for dykes in a club atmosphere. Videos, erotic slides, and dancers were employed to punctuate the club's "sex-positive" vision. The Clit Club was going on strong then and, as I was just beginning my experiment with exhibitionism, erotic power, and representation, I believed that stripping (even though I was stripping for men) was allowing me to discover more of my own sexual agency.

Unfortunately, the money trip obscured the part of me that was seriously questioning whether or not I was trading away my power or perpetuating negative stereotypes; I was too busy trying to sell an overpriced glass of juice. In New York City, hustle bars are restricted from selling sex and booze, but that didn't eliminate the hard sell. The juice was $30 to be exact. We dancers got 20 percent of everything sold. If the customer was really hungry, he was enticed to buy a $300 bottle of nonalcoholic champagne. The $300 also paid for the company of a dancer in a more private area toward the back of the bar. Lots of things happened in those private $300 quarters.

I was reluctant to go that far. Besides, it was really hard to get someone to pay that kind of money. I was almost sure that I wouldn't have to deal with it. I tried to find out what went on behind the curtains. All the answers were incredibly vague: "Well, I dance completely nude for a while, then I give him a little massage." As the question "What do you mean massage?" would begin to form in my throat, my inquiries would be cut off ("Oops, it's showtime, sorry"). I couldn't get a straight answer out of anybody. I packed a few condoms in my purse just in case. I wasn't at ease with the thought of getting fucked, but realistically, I wasn't sure how far I was willing to go with this experiment. I was aware that women received extra tips from the big spenders. My fear was that someone might make me a crazy offer that would be difficult to refuse. I kept thinking, "What if I haven't made enough money to pay bills and rent this month and somebody lays out $1,000 for me to sit on his dick?" I packed a dildo in my purse as well: perhaps I could work it into a situation where I could fuck myself, the customer could watch, and I could still get paid. Eventually, I was able to coax someone into buying the pseudo-champagne, but once he paid for it, I realized that I had made at least $60, and I wasn't willing to negotiate for anything else. I went into the room, did a little dance, moved the toe of my spiked heel in a circular motion on his groin (my special massage technique), sipped some phony champagne, and left. At one point, he tried to stick his finger in my anus. He barely made it in, but my asshole was on fire for the next week. He had put something on the tip of his finger. I was totally freaked out. I was fired shortly afterward. It turned out that I wasn't bringing in my quota of "champagne" buys, and besides, they already had one Black girl there.

In the sex industry, you don't feel, you perform. It's striking to me how removed I was from myself and what I determined was political resolve at the time. I was mildly concerned when objectifying, racist remarks were tossed my way by customers and coworkers. Hell, I was only in it for the money. A bunch of rowdy white college boys came into the bar one day and hooted about getting to stare up into my Black vulva. I showed it to them as long as they were shelling out dollars, but when the money ran out, I walked off the stage. It was the only way for me to assert myself and exercise the little control I had. My favorite thing to do after a day's work was to remove my wig, makeup, and fishnets and don the most butch clothes I could find. Somehow I needed to balance the stripper performance with a shedding ritual (like butching out) to try to ground myself.

On one hand, I was struggling, trying to pull my Black lesbian identity away from the societal fringe. Meanwhile, my concerns about freeing the Black female body and starting the Clit Club were what enabled me to see sex work as a possibility. At the Clit, fierce lesbian women acted out a variety of sexual postures. That was encouraged. I often walked around the bar with next to nothing on. I thought, "Something is so right here. I'm able to be a sexual Black woman in a way that I've never experienced before." I had gained a certain amount of ground in how I was able to celebrate my erotic power. I relied on that power to protect and affirm me while I stripped for men.

I left Washington in 1989 and made frequent trips back to a lesbian community I barely knew. Once, during some casual banter at a lesbo bar, a woman said to me, "You're from New York, aren't you?" I explained that I was born in D.C. and grew up in D.C. I reminded her that she had a sister who used to go to my elementary school ("Oh, you're that Jocelyn Taylor!"). The gap was widening between the hometown and home girl. Close friends became the closest connection I had to Washington. Teresa, my friend and witness forever who helped me to get to New York, came up often to check up on me. I was thrilled when she told me that she would be spending the New York Pride weekend with me. It was my first Pride ever, in fact.

Pride in New York was a lot different than the relatively

*Testimony of a Naked Woman*

smaller scale events at Dupont Circle and P Street Beach in D.C. In New York we were strutting down Fifth Avenue topless. I had accented my breasts with Silence=Death decals. Teresa said she felt rejuvenated by the feel of her chest in the open air yet saddened, too, by the fact that this would never happen at home. The lesbian community in D.C. didn't feel safe enough to experience this during any queer celebration. Even in the "safe spaces" for women, lesbians were unlikely to go bare-breasted in public. Inspired by the visibility and fearlessness of New York dykes, I proposed to Teresa that we do a topless "action" at one of the few women's bars in Washington. We encouraged other D.C. friends to join us in what we thought would be a strong statement toward personal power and self-affirmation.

It was Ladies Night in July 1990, and the women were out in droves. This monthly soiree for lesbians was an anxiously awaited event that attracted predominantly Black women from the city and suburbs. And thirty days was just enough time for the dyke community to heat up enough sexual energy to turn the club into a pressure cooker of desire. Women danced nipple-to-nipple and cheek-to-cheek; the music was happening and the place was packed. Couples were linked in an intimate grind on the outside dance patio. I stopped to watch women's bodies curve into each other and undulate to the DJ's choice of a "slow jam." Folks were touching, grabbing, squeezing, feeling, and feeling "it." I snapped out of voyeur mode when a house tune kicked in and switched into a frenzied dance any exhibitionist would be proud of. "It" began to possess me, and my body became a six-foot-tall erotic nerve ending. The dance floor was writhing. Teresa gave me a nudge to remind me of our mission, and the next thing you know, our shirts were off. Then more shirts came off, but nobody stopped dancing. I could have been on a granola-girl campground shaking my boobs toward the shooting stars; I could have been dancing in front of the mirror at home; I could have been marching down Fifth Avenue. I looked to the sidelines to see a row of Black women snickering, pointing, and jabbing each other in the ribs in disbelief. Hadn't they ever seen tits before? Seeing folks nude in public is surprising, but the reaction of these sisters surprised me. I could tell they were embarrassed, but why did they behave like men watching a girlie show? These women were so uncomfortable they could only impersonate a male "gaze." In their view, our action was not about erotic expression or liberation. It seems they had learned too well that sexualized body parts (like breasts) were to be hidden unless someone was ready to "get down." When some women began to comment on breast sizes, I finally spoke up:

"What's up with you guys?" I asked.

"Why do you have to take your shirts off? Don't you know that's nasty?"

"Well," I said, "it's not about what other people think is decent for me to do. This is about individual freedom."

"Y'all are freaks," she said.

Being called a freak made me stop in my tracks for a moment, so I scrambled for a controlled textbook-like response.

"Freaks? Freaks are individuals"—the term mostly refers to women—"who have no sexual boundaries and who are 'indiscriminate' about their sexual encounters. Women who enjoy many relations are considered freaks, as are sex workers and lesbians. Isn't there something *wrong* with that?" I demanded.

Actually, the real attention-getter was a Black woman in the middle of the dance floor who had already bared her upper torso and was about to remove her blue jeans and panties. When the jeans came off, I felt myself panic. Here I was—bare-breasted—

*Testimony of a Naked Woman*

and suddenly forced to confront the fact that I had prescribed limits as well. I feared for that jeanless woman more than I feared for myself. I could see her curly black pubic hair as she inched the panty line further and further south.

The breast issue has long been at the forefront of the women's movement as an example of what female body parts have been appropriated, tortured, and idealized as measures to control women. Likewise, the vagina has been high stakes in the reproductive rights and abortion battles. However, there's been no organized feminist agenda protecting women's right to public nudity, much less one that specifically protects Black women's right to explore alternative erotic possibilities. Of course there are places where public nudity is not a threat and there is a sense of safety, even if illusory. I was again reminded of my fear and internal contradictions in the face of what I meant as an act of political belligerence.

By this point, the nightclub SWAT team was on the roof shining high-powered flashlights onto the crowd in an effort to locate the perpetrators. Minutes later a security guard approached me and told me to put my shirt back on ("Put your shirt back on or I'll have to escort you out of the bar"). I could only smile, catch my breath, and offer my simple response ("No, thanks anyway"). The guard figured the cards were stacked in her favor so she attempted to call my bluff ("Put your shirt back on or I'll call the cops and have you arrested"). In a perfect world I would have reminded the guard that girls just want to have fun too, and doesn't she remember that on the boys' nights many gentlemen are wearing next to nothing? We would have a laugh, buy each other a beer, and the party would continue. Under the jurisdiction of reality I could only tell her that I wouldn't leave willingly. I laid my bare back on the dance floor and prepared myself for the repercussions ("If you want me out you'll have to carry me out"). As effortlessly as I lay beneath her, she hoisted me over her shoulder and marched toward the exit sign.

Setting me down barely inside the club's doors, the guard continued her reproach. She asked that I put my shirt back on for the sake of my "sisters." Her tone implied that I was not conducting myself in a way that was appropriate for a Black woman. She was embarrassed and ashamed, and obviously disapproved of my insistence that a woman should be permitted to be topless in a lesbian bar if she chooses. Yet, despite my pushy affront, I understood how she felt. My beliefs—the "politically correct" framework which had initially instigated the action—became inconsequential because I was acting out of both self-centeredness and exhibitionism. What my sisters were reacting out of was age-old fear and self-censure in the name of counteracting negative stereotypes of Black women.

Our bodies—our tits, asses, pussies, et al.—have been sewn into an image of the "wild thang"; the different, dark, and mysterious body that is fetishized and exploited. To expose myself in public in front of men (even if they were gay), unfamiliar women, and white folk was to revive a painful image that our female elders taught us to revoke, often to the point of self-abnegation. Though I honestly believe that parents, grandparents, extended family, etc., want to teach us how to "act" in order to survive in a Black-hostile, woman-hating environment, the lessons are often transmitted in the form of policing. We're taught to modify our behavior to an antierotic standard so that we can feel safe in our own bodies. Meanwhile, darker berries provide sweeter juice and I am the "exotic" even with my clothes *on*—still the target of nonconsensual eroticized desire.

I wanted to take my eroticism back, but when the guard

said, "Put your shirt back on for your sisters," I put my shirt on, wiped my face, which was moist with tears, mumbled something like, "I'll be back," and ran out the door. I bumped right into the white owner of the club who shook his finger in my face and said that he wouldn't have called the police if we had asked his permission to remove our clothing. Ask permission? The words still ring in my ears. I told him that I thought I was in a lesbian and gay dance club, a phenomenon that exists only precariously in states where same-sex love is against the law. Lucky for him, Washington, D.C., legislation permits him to operate without fear or retribution. At that time the club had one night a month that was for women only. I wanted to know whose side he was on. Exactly who and what was he defending? Ultimately, he was most concerned with defending his investment and didn't want any publicity that might tarnish his profitable relationship with the queer community or his ability to operate the club. When the cops had left, he surprised me when he decreed that we were "allowed" to take our shirts off inside the bar. Fine. The cops left, women shimmied bare-breasted to the music, and I sat, paused at the bar, with my shirt on.

I felt less than triumphant about that evening. I felt discouraged because it seemed that few understood the political impetus for my actions. Before the guard had removed me, a close friend came up to me and said, "Jocelyn, girl, you are so crazy!" She was half-serious. She said that she would never take off her shirt in public because her breasts are too big. Too big for what? I wanted to ask her how she learned that her breasts were too big. I wanted to change the rules. I wanted to change the meaning of publicly condoned behavior; behavior that is expressed through the human body and therefore is an expression of the human spirit.

I understand that walking down the street topless in the

wrong context is dangerous for my health. I don't want to do it. But I thought that a homo club full of lesbians might be an appropriate spot to explore erotic possibilities. Not! Why couldn't large/medium/small-breasted women be topless in a gay bar? I knew that legislation existed that forbade women to be topless in public (except in places with cabaret licenses, i.e., strip joints), but everyone in the club was already living unprotected from many forms of abuse and discrimination—essentially living outside the law. I was outraged by the contradictions that were operating. I was also deeply troubled that I hadn't resolved the conflict between myself and the group of women who felt uncomfortable with what happened and a Black sister's role in it. I was overcome by a gnawing sense that I was using strategies that didn't translate honestly into the realities of Black women's lives. Of all the women in the club, about 70 percent were Black. Of the thirty or so women who went topless, over twenty were white. My direct action became a reaction rather than an interaction. Direct action as a form of activism is not foreign to the Black community. As a kid, I watched endless newsreels of the Civil Rights and Black Power movements. Although I had attended the March on Washington led by Martin Luther King in 1968 with my mother, I had no other physical memories of the struggle. The newsreels graphically depicted the resilience of Black people and our fervent drive to achieve social equality. That worked for me. That's why I joined ACT-UP, even though it was a predominantly white gay male organization. I was attracted to the group's use of direct action—demonstrations, phone zaps, "die-ins," etc.—which recalled the fervor of that struggle in some way. Eventually, however, race and class divisions undercut coalition building. The AIDS crisis was our focus, some argued, not whether or not signs and placards got translated into Creole or Spanish. Applying what

*Testimony of a Naked Woman*

I learned in ACT-UP about in-your-face activism to the action in the club that night was both admirable and naive. The action caused a mild stir in the lesbian community of D.C., but I didn't talk to anyone there about what happened. I didn't approach any of the women in the bar who were not my friends about what they thought, how they felt, or what they wanted to do next. A little dialogue and a little organizing could have gone a long way in creating a forum where Black women could talk about owning their bodies whether they're in public or private or wherever they may be in the world.

While trying to understand the D.C. action, I had to painfully confront that I am an exhibitionist. As someone who likes to be "out there," I'm always negotiating spaces and actions. I do it partly because I want to be assured that I will get the attention I'm looking for and partly because I want to be sure that I'm safe. Rarely do I perform some outrageous stunt without knowing that I won't get hurt. (Walking down Fifth Avenue topless surrounded by thousands of queers is one example.) The ability to make decisions about my safety and whom I'm performing for is how I place controls on my immediate environment. It's all a mental exercise, though, because some variables can't be accounted for. I never really know how people will respond. I like to pretend that it doesn't matter how people do, because I'm busy trying not to make myself vulnerable enough to care. I often ask myself if I do things just to get attention. I don't know. I think I act out more because I don't want to be forgotten. I want to be seen and remembered. However, the action at the club in D.C. was too close to home. My shield of ambivalence dissolved into uncertainty because I knew a lot of the women there. We had similar experiences, had gone to the same high schools, and had mastered the same task of maneuvering—with varying strategies—in a society that was anti-Black, anti-female, anti-gay, and therefore anti-us.

And then I like the way my body looks. My mother persistently affirmed my Blackness by offering her descriptive personal narrative of learning to love herself as a Black woman. She told me stories of wearing clothespins on her nose to make it look thinner and of special bleaching creams used by her friends to look lighter. Later, when she had gained a stronger sense of self-identity, she, like many Black women in the late sixties and early seventies, wore a large Afro. Then, in the late seventies, she cut her hair very close to her scalp. Hair texture, facial features, and skin color still remain indicators of self-worth for Black women. I was learning that the power to resist and motivate politically can be connected to seeing yourself as beautiful and deserving of love. It took me a long time to get angry about the specific cruelty that women of color are subjected to, but once I figured out that it was *my image* that was oppressed, I set out to use my own body as a political tool to challenge and defy institutionalized self-hatred.

I consider the mere Black female form a source of power and a symbol of resistance. When I think about the worldwide prevalence of the fear of women and the fear of Blackness, and the subsequent frenzy to control these entities, I think about being in a Black female body and how powerful that is. I have fantasies about riding with an army of naked women on horseback down Constitution Avenue in Washington, D.C. The nudity is an important part of the fantasy because it's a strong and fearless image that says we do not believe that our bodies are inferior or ugly, or open to assault of any kind. An army of women is a force that will not lie on its back passively while others eroticize and differentiate. I dream about armies because it's scary to stand up alone and in small numbers. I need a haven where I know that I'm okay and protected. In this war, I will watch your back if you will watch mine.

I took my shirt off that night because I was fed up with the limitations that are imposed on me through my body. My anger leads me to the third truth about myself, which is that I believe in radical politics. Governmental and local authority as it pertains to women, queers, and Black folk has caused me to develop a healthy disrespect for this nation's generic brand of morality thinly masked by the law. Too much legislation has been created by hypocrites and individuals who are more interested in acquiring and wielding power than instigating radical change that serves all people. Living in New York opened my eyes again to activism and taught me important lessons about direct-action strategies. My struggle now was to integrate the truths and contain the contradictions to which I was becoming more fully conscious.


The Clit Club opened two weeks after that experience in Washington. I was anxious to find erotic imagery that reflected Blackness as a desirous entity separate from stereotypical, exoticized expectations. The most difficult task in pulling together the visuals for the club was finding erotic videos of darker women made by lesbians, or made by anyone for that matter. The absence of presentations of Black lesbian desire made me understand very clearly that I was never meant to feel passionate for myself or anyone who looks like me. I set out on a mission to "see" myself even if it was a mirror reflection; even if it was just a picture of me. I participated as the darker sister in photo shoot after photo shoot, hoping to create some parity for a lesbian subculture that is greatly underserved. Many times I was nondiscriminating. Often my exhibitionist-ego side was functioning at full force, but I was determined to get all the attention that I didn't get every time I opened a magazine or turned on the television. I was battling erasure, asserting my sexuality, and getting my kicks all at the same time. No wonder I thought I could handle being a stripper; I was always dealing with racism and misogyny, so what if I did it for money? A few times I discovered a fine line between "being out there" and selling yourself short.

While working on a video about the connections between sexuality and spirituality, a cast member was required to don traditional makeup from some unrecognized East African culture, then scream into the camera. This particular section of the video was about opening your throat in order to tap into your sexual energy. The voice-over instructed viewers to feel free to expose a more "primitive" or "wild" side of themselves. The Black woman chosen to play the part walked off the set. I supported her in her actions, but chose to stay on. I talked to folks on the set about how the suggestion that sexual liberation through the appropriation of East African traditional customs was more than problematic, it was offensive. The implication of a culture and tradition as wild and primitive exposed the producers (a combination of white lesbians, sex workers, and heterosexual women) as racist and Eurocentric. Great pains had been taken to assure the "authenticity" of the makeup (the makeup artist had purchased a book about Sudanese cultures), but there was no effort to clarify any ceremonial, religious, or sexual symbolism behind the image. To this day I'm not sure if the producers understood how disturbing the "African" simulation was. I'm afraid that we were all suffering from the psychological effects of having worked in the sex industry; it's a mentality that allows you to take, borrow, or appropriate anything for the sake of "sexual freedom," "artistic ex-

*Testimony of a Naked Woman*

pression," and of course money. The producers were "sympa-
thetic," and some changes were made. I experienced other
unsatisfactory interactions where I allowed my image to be used
in situations that still cast me as the "exotic" or token other. I gave
up stripping because my illusions of financial gain were rooted in
a pornographic sense of self-denial. Every time I stripped for men
I was stripping myself of emotional response. Yeah, I could get off
on dancing, on just feeling my body move to the music, but I
realize that I was marionetting, performing for an audience from
which I maintained considerable distance. When I thought my
body was being appreciated, it was actually performing for someone else's pleasure. When I thought I was making money, I was
selling part of myself to the nonerotic: trading cold cash for true
emotion and feeling. I don't know how long it took me to realize
that a Black woman is not likely to find her liberation in a Mafia-
owned strip joint.

I approached another crossroads in late 1992. I retired from
stripping after working at it on and off for about two years.
Ironically, I retired from the Clit Club around the same time. The
bar scene had become a tremendous drain on my creative process.
My body became a secondary resource as I began using video
more exclusively as the medium to collect and proliferate images
of me and my sisters. Now my life is all about making videos that
emphatically celebrate Black lesbian sexuality. Bold, sensual,
funny, and powerful, they draw from the lessons of these experiences and provide looks that are beginning to fill the erotic void
that has been present in my heart and the hearts of others for such
a long time. There's so much pain in invisibility. It took me a
while to learn that I don't have to be the one in front of a camera
feeling uncomfortable and thinking that something is better than
nothing. No one does. I've been in New York for such a short

time. Somehow it feels like forever. At every juncture, I learn how I can affect the future without compromise; without altering my political beliefs, my connection to my community or my physical self. The locks I started at the beginning of this journey are below my shoulders now, long and with beautiful specks of gray. Too long to hide under a wig.

HELEN ELAINE LEE

# *Water Call*

Her flesh spoke. Testifying with knotted scars along the hips and knees, angry healing flesh that had faded over time and was joined by the wrinkles and folds of age.

Without, the scars had grown familiar and indistinct. Within, there was the perfect imprint of her desperate choice.

It stayed hidden, mostly, in waking, but survived in that storage space within that holds impressions of our singular griefs: the stamp of a parent's death, the shape of first love, the contours of unspeakable loss.

Sanding the edges of the past in order to move on, Ouida had secreted the sharp memories, mostly, in her private archives, but unannounced, they surfaced, coming to her again and again in her dreams.

There was the gritty scrape of metal against flesh. The smell of blood, and the cold hard distance in his eyes.

There was the cracked plaster of the ceiling where she had focused her pain.

And there was the single grimy lightbulb, swinging from a twisted cord.

Recorded, all, with the memory of the circle that Zella's arms made around her in the backseat of their borrowed car. The depth and width and curve of it visited and woke her in the late afternoon, always in the same way, taking shape in her stomach and then spreading, as if pouring itself into a waiting mold.

After a morning at her sewing machine, joining and ripping out seams and resewing them until they were perfect, she got up to fix her lunch, grasping the edge of the table, and lifted herself with fingers numb and stiff from work, balancing with one hand while she reached with her crutches and tucked them under her arms. She flexed her fingers as she leaned against the kitchen sink, and looked out of the window through African violet leaves. Once she had made her lunch and eaten, she lay down for her afternoon rest, pulling Ruby's unfinished quilt over her legs.

She drifted into sleep and woke, gasping, drawing in her breath and with it the memory, taking in the sharpness, that it be borne. She woke to it, to her panic and her shame, to the memory that lived. To the losing and the getting. To the memory that was the shape of everything she would never be, and everything she was.

----

When her period had been late for a week, Ouida told herself it would come, that she had never really been regular. When a month had passed, she shifted between panic and denial, trapped and without the inkling of a route toward help. When she saw her naked profile in the mirror one morning, she could no longer hide.

Stepping into her panties, she caught a glimpse of herself, and let them drop as she straightened up. She looked from mirror to flesh, and touched slowly, with fingertips first, and then with her whole hand. She returned to her image in the mirror and then backed up and sat down on the edge of the bed.

She sat there for an hour, stunned by the reality that was, somehow, hers. She was hit by a wave of disbelief, even three years after her death, that Ruby was not there, and as she thought of what to do about it, she knew that she needed Zella's help. She waited until they lay in bed that night, their legs entwined, to ask. It was then that she spoke of her other night visitor.

"Zella, you know that luggage with my monogram, that I said my uncle sent me? And the organdy hankies in my top drawer?"

"Un-hunh," Zella responded, half-asleep with her face in Ouida's neck.

"Zella, listen. I have something to say," she declared with quiet urgency as she nudged her arm.

Zella raised up on her elbow and looked Ouida in the eye, a pinpoint of dread dilating in her stomach.

"Well, they didn't . . . they didn't." She looked away, and it seemed that she actually aged in the time it took for her to turn back to Zella's face. "I didn't get them from my uncle at all."

Zella stared at her, unwilling to help her finish what she had to say. She tightened her jaw and braced herself against the coming blow, as Ouida finished. "The white man brought them. The one from Louisville."

Zella was too stunned to absorb anything besides Ouida's last syllable, resounding over and over again in her head, "ville . . . Ville . . . *ville.*" And then she felt the tip of rage as Ouida finished.

"Zella, it's been two months since my last period. I need your help."

Zella looked at her mutely, as the confession came out in a rush, and rose from the bed. And as the numbness faded, the full range of her feelings passed through her. She turned away from Ouida, who sank into her pillows silently. Zella paced the kitchen floor and then sat, facing the window. Hours later, she came to bed.

She stayed, as she knew she would, and reached to turn off the light. They faced opposite directions, their backs not touching. During the night, Zella turned to look at Ouida's sleeping face, emptied of stress but pale and tired, and wondered how she had let herself love so, against the one rule she knew about never getting close to women who love men. She studied the face that she had trusted with an anger that had chilled into something distant and analytical, searching for hints of dishonesty in what now appeared to her to be a mask.

How could the person beside her be so foreign, and yet so known? How did it happen that way? It all seemed a message to Zella of what she could not have. She turned to look at her over and over and asked how Ouida could do this to her. And then, somehow, in an instant, as she studied the face that seemed altogether emptied, she felt that what was happening was happening to them, and accepted the love she felt.

*Afrekete*

When Ouida woke the next morning, Zella was sitting at the table fully dressed, drinking tea. She had stayed. When Ouida saw her there, she felt a surge of panic, but as she came into the kitchen, she saw a cup of tea waiting for her. She sat down, and they looked at each other silently. Zella spoke, "Ouida. What do you want to do?"

Ouida shook her head and said, "Before we talk about it, I have one more thing to tell you. So that it will be clean." She looked straight into Zella's eyes and said, "There was another. There was the barber, Flood."

Zella looked at her, from what seemed like far away, knowing somehow, through her jealousy, that whatever else Ouida had been doing was about something other than love. And so she nodded, and pointed to the cup of tea. As Ouida sat down to drink, Zella set out the choices: the one, crazy, that she felt her way toward in darkness, and the other, reckless, the terror of which was known.


Zella told her later how she had counted up three windows and stood staring for ten minutes. She left, got a block away, and then came back. She stood at the curb looking up, pulling her coat close and wondering how she could climb the stairs, and how she could not.

She had gone first to her aunt Mandy, who ran a boarding-house for young women. She knew not to say the word "abortion," and formed her question carefully.

"Where can a girl who's in trouble get help?"

Her aunt smiled slightly, relieved that the rumors she had heard about Zella were either untrue or had only represented a phase. There was an awkward pause, and then Zella spoke.

"Not *me,* Aunt Mandy. I'm asking for a friend."

Mandy's smile faded, and she lowered her eyes, ashamed, and told her how to find out what to do without really asking.

Zella had memorized the address and had gone there after work. She looked up at the window and finally opened the door, moving toward the third floor with decisive steps. She stood facing the grimy yellow door while she got her instructions in order, and knocked. The door opened as far as its chain would allow to reveal the face of a small black woman with piercing eyes.

"I'm here about the goods. About getting them unloaded. WB sent me."

The woman's eyes moved down from Zella's collar to her feet, and then back up again, taking in her tailored clothes and polished shoes. She stopped at her face and spent a good bit of time there, and when the anguish in the eyes told her that it was love that had brought her there, love and desperation, she decided that it was not a trap.

"The goods are your'n?" she asked roughly.

"No. My friend's."

The door closed for a moment, while she removed the chain, and then she grabbed Zella's arm and pulled her across the threshold.

"Sit down while I tell you what to do."

Zella dwarfed the slim wooden chair and looked around the room. Bits of old rugs were pieced together to cover the floor. The place smelled close and the windows and shades were drawn. The strange, rough woman stood in front of her and shook her finger in her face.

"You go, after dark, tomorrow, at seven at night, to where the Old Stone Road and the street without no name meet, and you make you a right turn. Go to the big elm tree at the next fork in the road, and there will be a black car waitin' for you. Now you tell the man in the car that you come 'bout the cargo, and give him the money in your envelope. He'll take you to the place."

She finished with the most important part. "If you ain't got the money, don't come."

Zella rose and left the room, her eyes meeting the stranger's long enough for her to see something else beneath the harshness of her way. The small, gnarled woman touched her arm before she closed the door, and then, alone again, she muttered to herself, "Lord watch over you, child."

Zella descended the stairwell, the grim green walls marked with fingerprints along the banister, and wallpaper that stood away from the walls at the corners and baseboards. She stopped at the foot of the stairs and touched the wall as she tried to make out the pattern. Faded almost to smudges were traces of spring bouquets.

She went next to withdraw the money from the bank and took the streetcar to the Marquis, where she waited until Ouida finished doing a manicure and pulled her aside. As she explained the plan, Zella couldn't help looking at Ouida's stomach, bound tight with a laced corset. She gently tucked a lock of Ouida's hair back in its chignon and left. The next step was to borrow a car.

They met that evening at Zella's flat and said nothing of the next day. Zella ironed and folded a stack of clothes and tried not to think of the coming day. She tried to bury her anger in order to give Ouida strength. She had never really thought, when she allowed herself to consider it, that she, alone, could have Ouida; she had always been afraid to ask her to define her feelings, afraid of things against which she had no power, things so different from her. She had felt, somewhere inside, that she couldn't have her because Ouida was connected to something else, and at the same

*Water Call*

time she knew that she did, she did have her, and that whatever else there was that Ouida belonged to, the thing that bound the two of them was different, and was strong.

At work the next day Ouida's hands trembled so much that she could barely finish her first manicure. She kept having to excuse herself and go to the tiny makeshift space with a toilet and sink that they made for her in the men's barbershop. She sat on the edge of the utility sink and tried to get calm, but she felt as if she had to keep a careful distance from the center of herself. She felt as if her life had gotten mixed up with someone else's.

She mumbled to herself and returned to her table. Alton kept coming over to ask her if she was all right.

The horror stories she had heard came back to her in snatches as she waited for a customer or held a strange, white, uncallused hand. She thought of the stories she had heard of butcherings in dirty rooms and bleeding from careless hands, and she imagined the profound shame her mother would feel. And she returned to the thing becoming inside of her, not knowing how to think of it, but knowing that it couldn't be.

She remembered the day Vesta's family had moved downstairs, Eula sewing by candlelight when the light bill couldn't be paid, eggs for dinner and run-down shoes. Ouida had just begun to shape her life, and she couldn't give that up. For a man who wasn't willing and whom she didn't want? For all kinds of isn'ts and might-bes. Zella had offered to raise it as her own, had said that they could do it together, but she couldn't even see her way clear to think about that.

She knew that she would have to risk her life to save it. Her hand strayed to rest on the almost concealed roundness of her stomach, and she tried to put aside her fear.

Zella picked her up at five o'clock, and they drove through

an empty landscape caught between winter and spring, bleached of color. Pools of dark watery ice swallowed weather-worn bits of grass, while other patches were still dry from freezing.

Ouida sat clutching her pocketbook, looking straight ahead, until they came to the fork in the road, and she lowered her head. It was dark now, and they got out and went to the window of the other car, and Zella stepped forward and repeated the code words she had been told to say. The man took the envelope that Zella held out, looked inside it, and opened the back door from inside the car. They climbed in, and Zella took Ouida's hand.

They rode in the dark for forty-five minutes, going in circles, Zella thought, and pulled up next to a shack surrounded by pools of mud and gravel. Ouida would never lose the sound of the tires coming to rest on the rocky side of the road.

As they were led inside, a man asked, "Which one?" Zella and Ouida looked at each other and Ouida stepped forward. He pointed to a door and Zella started to follow, but the driver stepped in front of her and said harshly, "Un-unh, lady. You can't go in."

As Ouida walked down a filthy hallway, she heard a scream, and stopped for a moment to look back at the door behind which Zella stood, clutching her handbag, before she moved on.

As she came to the end of the hallway, Ouida looked around for something that reminded her of a doctor's office, and then she realized that this was where she had been headed all along. The man who had met her at the door told her to undress, and handed her a sheet. "Put that over your bottom half," he said, making no move to leave. She stood and stared at him until he left the room, and when he came back, she was standing in front of the table wrapped in the sheet, holding her clothes in front of her. He took the clothes from her and motioned for her to get on the table. He took her feet and put them into loops of rope that hung from the ceiling. And he never washed his hands.

As he parted her and felt inside with his finger, she sucked in her breath and tried to go somewhere else. Then there was cold metal pushing in, and a pain that she would never be able to describe, as he began scraping with the curette. The entire time that he was with her, he chewed on a cigar.

And she focused on the grimy lightbulb that swayed above her, wrapping herself in her cries.

She could hear him messing with a can or bucket, and the sound of metal against metal as he put his instruments in an enameled basin. He took her feet out of the loops of rope and stood over her for a moment and said matter-of-factly, "Some bleeding is normal." He shook his head then, and said as he went through the door, "It's over. You can get up now."

She struggled to get up, as Zella came through the door to help her dress. They had left pieces of cloth on the table, which Zella helped her pin to her underclothes and pull on.

The whole way back to their car, Ouida rested her head on Zella's shoulder and concentrated on getting home. No words were spoken as they got out of the man's car and into their own.

She had soaked through the pieces of cloth they gave her before they had gone fifteen miles, but Ouida told Zella not to worry. "He said there would be blood." But Ouida remembered a night of blood-soaked hands, of blood on the moon, and reeled with fear. Zella stopped the car twice to change the cloths and tried to stay calm.

Ten miles later, Ouida began to whisper, "It's not right, Zella, it's not right," and Zella looked back over the seat and felt a rising panic. She pulled the car over and grabbed at the newspapers on the floor of the backseat, arranging them under and around Ouida to soak up the fevered blood, chanting one of Tennyson's verses they had both been made to memorize in high school.

"'It little profits that an idle king . . .' Say it with me, Ouida, come on now . . . 'By this still hearth, among these barren crags . . .' Zella recited.

Ouida kept up for the first few lines, as Zella tried to start the car over and over, missing her timing with the clutch.

"'I cannot rest from travel, I will drink . . .'"

Ouida whispered, anchoring herself with the long-remembered words. But she heard rushing water in the distance somewhere and, looking for the source, she raised herself up and then slipped further and further down as her head fell back to the seat.

"'. . . alone, on shore, and when . . .'" The water rushing, she knew she heard it, and she turned around, searching in sunken darkness around her, and heard the faint whisper of Zella's voice.

"'. . . have suffered greatly, both with those who loved me and . . .'"

She heard the water, and she could hear Zella. And then she let go.

Zella managed to get the car started, and raced back to the city, going over and over their options. She knew that they could not go back to the shiny black car where the road divided, and that even if they could make it back there, they would never be able to find the shack again. She picked up the verse again, reciting now for herself. "'. . . To rust unburnished, not to shine in use . . .'"

Ouida found herself turning round and round in search of the water that she heard, and then saw the mouth of a tunnel, which she entered, alone, no longer linked to Zella's voice.

She followed the water sounds through the dark tunnel, feeling her way along the sides of the passage with her hands, and came to a little cave, carved from the side, a hole almost, half underground but with an opening above, which seemed to blossom into itself, jeweled green and soft with the moistness of moss and unruly grass, water spilling down over the edges of rocks, once jagged, and now eroded smooth. The earth, wet and heavy, held the blooming place like a secret, and at its opening, Ouida stood.

Zella had almost reached the edge of town, speeding as she continued reciting. " '. . . as though to breathe were life . . .' "

Ouida yearned to sink her fingers into the clay, to touch the tangled roots it hid, to feel it against her and the water raining, beating on her skin.

She stood at the mouth, stunned by its dark and wild beauty. By its secret. And she reached out her hand, to find, between her and the water, a set of iron bars.

She wanted the place, needed it, and thrusting her hands between the bars, she tried to reach it, tried but couldn't reach, but tried, reaching and reaching.


Zella had tried to think of a doctor who would accept her explanation of a miscarriage and take the risk of helping them. The only name she could come up with was Dr. Miles, a family friend. As she drove, she focused on reaching the safety of his house.

When they got there, he told her that he couldn't. Just that he couldn't help, and she had pushed her hand into his closing door and refused to leave until he gave her the name of someone who could. She ran back to the car and drove to the address, her foot shaking so violently above the pedal that she almost couldn't drive, unaware until she got there that he was not a doctor, but a veterinarian.

And he had tried to help. When Zella had knocked at his door, he had answered with a dinner napkin still tucked into his collar. "Yes, may I help you? What's wrong, child? Don't just stand there, tell me what's wrong."

She took him to the car, where Ouida was stretched out on the backseat, surrounded with bloody newspapers, and he stood on the sidewalk looking up and down the street. "Help me get her inside."

Once they were inside, he told her what kind of doctor he was, and Zella just stood there and looked at him with her mouth open.

He gave her some medication and told her to go home, afraid to send her for a doctor. "What I do in this office is one thing, but I cannot allow you to go to a hospital. They will know exactly what you've done." Before they left he asked if they were sisters, and Zella's silence was the only answer she gave.

Ouida woke in a hospital days later, to the sound of a door, shutting? Opening? She wasn't sure. In the quiet of the night, it seemed as if it was the only sound there was.

Reborn in the still blankness, and unsure, Ouida found herself, again and again, waking to the sound of that door.

She returned from the memory shaken, stunned with the past's consumption of the present. The memory would revisit her, a month later . . . a year later . . . in that plateau of the day that has been left unclaimed by tasks. And every time she woke from it, she recognized the smell of rich wet earth.

JACQUELINE WOODSON

# Tuesday, August Third

Boys were coming home crazy as half-dead dogs. Everywhere Wilma turned, someone was talking about somebody they knew who knew somebody who had lost something in Vietnam. The war, people were saying, was just about over. And it was just about time 'cause far as everyone on the block knew, wasn't this many black folks killed since before the . . .

"What's that, Mama?"

"What's what?" Mama was making chicken. The big kitchen crackled and sweated with Crisco. Mama's dark hands were covered with a thin layer of flour and this gave them a strange look—ghostly-like.

"That thing everybody saying so many black folks was killed before . . . ? The emproclamation?"

Now Mama looked off for a moment, then went back to turning the big pieces and stepping back as the grease sizzled up loudly above the pan.

Then she was looking at Wilma—proud but aggravated. "You always in grown folks' business. That's why you think you so grown now. Get out of this kitchen before I send you out airmail!"

Wilma was already on her way when Mama said, "And don't they teach you anything in school? It's what freed the slaves."

"Lincoln's what freed the slaves," Wilma mumbled, low enough so Mama wouldn't know she was talking back. It had been going on like this all summer. Mama looking off, getting sad all of a sudden or angry. Dropping things when she used to be so sure-handed. Ever since the boys had begun coming home and Ray wasn't among them. He'd been gone almost a year now, and more than once, Wilma had heard Mama complaining about how her nerves were tied up in knots. This summer had begun to feel heavy to Wilma—thick like a thunder shower coming. Roy had written saying it wasn't much better over where he was but least there was a couple of trees, and a body could get used to the sounds of bombs going off after a while. *You get used to anything, Lil Bit. Some things get into your blood and stay there.* Wilma hadn't understood what he meant by that last sentence but she had folded the letter neatly, placed it with the stack of letters she kept behind her socks in the very back of her drawer. She read them over and over, alone at night sitting in the bathroom, until Mama got up, knocked on the door and said it was time for her to go to bed. There was a softness to Mama late at night. "C'mon, Will,"

Mama would whisper through the locked bathroom door. "You better get some rest now. Your brother'll be home soon enough."


Wilma had an MIA ID bracelet hanging heavy on her skinny arm. The name on it was Robert Macray. When she got Grans to send off for it, the people sent a picture of Robert Macray's sad-looking parents. They were sitting together on a nice couch covered in plastic, holding a picture of a white boy in uniform. Behind them was a painting of a waterfall cascading down into a pine forest. The picture frame looked to be made out of fake wood like the one Grans had in the living room. Grans had a waterfall too and Wilma figured waterfalls must be going cheap from Brooklyn to Baton Rouge, Louisiana, where the Macrays were. Grans' waterfall picture leaned way forward on the top because no one knew how to make it hang right. Right, Wilma suspected, would be like the Macrays' was hanging—up against the wall, not leaning forward like it was going to fall on somebody's head any minute. Wilma was figuring all white people had nice couches covered in plastic until Grans set her straight.

"Used to work for a white lady," Grans had said when the picture and bracelet arrived. "Had a couch just like that. Didn't have no plastic covers on it. Didn't need none. She ain't allow nobody to sit on it."

"Why somebody buy a couch not made for sitting, Grans? That doesn't make any sense."

"That's they ways."

Outside, Wilma squashed a mosquito against her face and ran to the corner. Across the street a group of Puerto Rican men had gathered around a card table piled high with dominoes. She tried to make out some of their Spanish but they were talking too

*Tuesday, August Third*

fast. What she really wanted was someone she could tell everything to—the way she had once told Roy—even the little things
that people said a teenager wouldn't care about. Roy had listened,
and laughed, throwing his head back until his Afro was dancing.
Mouth full of gleaming teeth, eyes narrowed to slits. Laughed so
hard his stomach shook. *Lil Sis,* he'd said. *As long as I'm alive,
you'll always be someone's favorite.* Wilma swallowed. Missing
someone was like a thirst, like a scratchy dryness in the back of
her throat. Like a brick against her chest. She wanted someone to
sit, be quiet for a few minutes while she whispered the whole
summer to them—right up to this moment with Mama frying
chicken and flying off the handle about nothing. And about the
letter. The one Mama carried everywhere, with the greasy edges
and the fading type saying that Roy would be home before the
month was over. Wilma sighed, sitting down on the curb. Every
time she turned around, someone was cursing Nixon out, calling
him a raggedy crook. But the way she figured it, if Nixon saw to
it that Roy came home in one piece and not like Craig Thomas,
who was walking zigzag down the block and talking out loud to
himself, saying ancient orange and talking about kids running
round screaming 'cause their skin was on fire, then it would mean
that Nixon wasn't a crook after all. Wilma would be ten in just
forty-seven days.

Tennessee was home already but his mama said if he decided
to go back tomorrow, it wouldn't be a day too soon. She said
Tennessee needed another good butt-kicking and maybe then he'd
realize people his age worked for a living and didn't lay up at
home in a nod like they were still someplace they weren't any-
more.

Yesterday, when Mama and Mrs. Dora got to talking about it

in the kitchen, Wilma had been sitting in the living room playing with her bracelet and making believe she was way into *The Price Is Right*. Somebody was going to win a new living room set and a car if they guessed right. Grans was sitting behind Wilma on the couch. Grans didn't much care for Mama and Mrs. Dora together in one place so she had left the kitchen soon as they got started.

"Hope you not watching no stories, Wilma. Be bringing evil spirits into the house."

"It's *Price Is Right*, Grans," Wilma said.

"Hope it ain't no gambling. You know I don't allow no gambling in my house."

"They're not gambling. They just guessing. That lady might win everything."

Grans stared at the TV a minute. "She don't need it. They should give that stuff to a colored lady."

Bob Barker was smiling at a woman who was jumping up and down like she was about to pee on herself. Wilma wasn't really into guessing. She had been guessing the right price for weeks now and nothing new showed up in her house. Her big sister Sherry had said she was a dumb biddy if she thought just guessing the right answers into a TV screen was going to change anything.

"How do I get the stuff, then?" Wilma had asked.

"You got to fly out to California and wait outside showing everybody how excited you can get when Bob calls your name. Only the most excited-looking people get to be on that show."

Sherry was twelve, two years older than Wilma, and you couldn't tell her she didn't know everything.

Wilma had six dollars saved but Sherry said a plane ticket cost a lot more than that and she must be twice as stupid as she was ugly if she was gonna bank on winning enough money to return home.

Wilma sighed and stared blankly at the TV screen. The house was quiet today. The blinds cast thin yellow lines across Grans, who was starting to doze. In the distance, someone was playing *En Mi Viejo San Juan*. Wilma could hear a drunken voice singing along. *Adiós. Adiós Adiós. Borinquen querida*. The sounds made her sad all of a sudden, like nothing she'd ever felt before, like the world was moving away from her, out of reach and she was stuck here, inside, sitting cross-legged on the carpeted floor. Waiting.

In the kitchen, Mama and Mrs. Dora were sitting at the big table drinking Maxwell House instant. Mrs. Dora took four sugars and Mama was always complaining that every time she turned around she was buying sugar again 'cause Mrs. Dora didn't have enough home-training to cut down when she was visiting.

"Maybe you should just hide his shoes somewhere," Mama was saying. "That way, he won't be heading to the park to get high."

"He so gone, he'd walk there barefoot."

Tennessee was strung out bad on horse. When Wilma saw him last week, he was into such a serious nod, she was thinking about asking him to be her science project. But Tennessee was so gone, he didn't even notice her. Up until she was seven, everybody on the block called her Boo. Tennessee had started it. Before he went away, he would sit her on his lap and tell her about a time before she could remember when she was so afraid, she'd scream if someone said Boo. After that, he started calling her Boo, hoping if she heard the word enough, she wouldn't be so afraid. The name stuck for a while until the summer she was seven. For some reason, every time someone called her by her nickname, she'd start crying. Mama had said people should maybe stop calling her that. Saying maybe it reminded Wilma of Tennessee, who had left for the war, the spring before. She had watched Tennessee—all doped up, leaning forward until it seemed like he would bust his head, then jerking himself up again and starting over. Most everything junkies did was in slow motion. This wasn't the Tennessee that had nicknamed her. This boy was too gray and thin. He was like a movie she could watch for hours without getting bored.

"Your boy coming home soon, huh?" Mrs. Dora was saying, slurping her coffee loudly after each sentence.

"I got his room all fixed up for him," Mama said proudly. "Want it to be like he never left. Went down to Woolworth and got a new blanket for his bed. Roy was always one for getting cold."

"I fixed up Cory's room for Tennessee," Mrs. Dora said. "Had Cory sleeping in the room with me but he getting too big for that so I'm thinking about making him sleep on the couch from now on."

"That's why he such a queen," Wilma whispered.

"You talking to yourself, Wilma?" Grans asked, jerking awake.

Wilma shook her head. "I'm singing."

Cory was a year younger than Wilma and already on the fast track to being the block sissy. When Mrs. Dora wasn't around he snuck outside wearing her jewelry and could jump double-dutch better than any girl on the block.

"My two boys . . ." Mrs. Dora sighed and Wilma knew she was in there shaking her head over her cup of sugary half-cold Maxwell House.

It got quiet after that. Wilma flipped to an Underdog cartoon. Sweet Polly Purebred, Underdog's blond doggie-girlfriend, was tied to a train track. A gigantic cat was standing above her, lighting a stick of dynamite. Wilma was about to change the channel again when she realized she had to go to the bathroom. She ran through the kitchen to the tiny bathroom, sliding across the floor in the jelly shoes she and Cory had bought the week before—two pair for six dollars. Wilma's were light blue. Cory had bought pink at first but Mrs. Dora made him turn around and take them back 'cause she wasn't having no son of hers walk the street in pink shoes. Because they had bought them together, Wilma had to walk the ten blocks back to John's Bargain Store to show the salesperson her pair and prove they had really bought them there. That burned her up.

"How come you not out there playing?" Mrs. Dora asked, catching Wilma's arm as she headed back through the kitchen. "No need sitting in that living room with all the sunshine going on outside."

Wilma shrugged, bending down to rub spit into her ashy knees. "Don't want to get too black."

Mrs. Dora nodded, her fresh press and curl glistening on top of her small dark head. "Sun'll turn you into nighttime, you don't watch out. I let Cory out early on if he want but I tell Tennessee he should wait awhile. Cory lucky he got so much red in his blood, don't have to worry none about getting too black."

Mama rubbed Wilma's hair away from her forehead. Ever since she had started letting Wilma do her own hair, her hands were always in it, like she missed it or something. Wilma moved her head out of Mama's reach.

"I told her I didn't want her playing with that Diana any-more," Mama said. "Heard her out there yesterday cursing like she didn't have any sense. Her mother sitting right on the stoop too. Didn't say a word."

"Her mother don't know much English," Wilma said. "And plus, Diana was only cursing somebody back."

"I don't care if she was cursing them back, front or sideways, I don't want you around her . . ."

"But now everybody's hanging with Diana. So what am I supposed to do?"

Mama set her coffee cup down. "Play with Sherry and Ray. That's why you have family."

Wilma rolled her eyes. "Sherry don't want to be with me. And Ray's too little."

"Then be alone," Mama said. "That's how you came into the world and how you'll go out. Or stay inside and read something. That's all you do is hit the streets anyway. Sometimes I don't know if I'm raising kids or wild things."

Mrs. Dora was nodding in agreement. As if she hadn't started the whole thing.


*"Arriba! Abajo! La Yankee va galajo!* Come on, Wil," Diana screamed. She was perched on the base of the lamppost, her fist raised in the air. "Say it with me!"

"Whatchu saying?" Wilma asked, climbing up on the lamppost beside her. She gave a quick look back toward her house, figuring she was far away from Mama's chicken-frying eyes.

*"Arriba!"* Diana screamed. *"Abajo! La Yankee va galajo!"*

*"Arriba!"* Wilma repeated, raising her fist in the air. *"Abajo!"*

"Up! Down!" Diana bellowed. "Yankees go to hell!"

"I have to say it in Spanish, Diana! Mama might hear."

Diana nodded. "It sounds better in Spanish anyway."

Wilma figured she'd have to give Mama another day of being mad about Diana's cursing. After a while, she usually forgot about it until the next curse word was overheard—then it started all over again.

"Why we want the Yankees to go to hell?" she asked.

"The Mets is better," Diana said, jumping down and hoisting her pants up over her butt. "Who did your hair?"

"Grans straightened it but I braided it myself."

"I'ma get mines cut!"

Wilma blinked. "You better grow some hair, girl, before you talk about cutting it off!"

"When you cut it, it grows more faster."

They headed down the block, stopping to pick up Popsicle sticks.

"Tell your mother if you could spend the night. My mother's making *arroz con gandules.*" She sang the words *arroz con gandules,* knowing it was Wilma's favorite dish.

"She's gonna say no." Wilma picked up a stick with a chunk of chocolate on the edge and flung it into the street. "She's been acting all evil. Maybe when Roy gets back, she'll get in a good mood again."

"Roy's gonna be crazy like Craig," Diana said, fanning her five Popsicle sticks like a deck of cards.

"No he's not."

"Everybody who went over there is all fucked up," Diana said. "Roy ain't gonna be different."

At the corner, Wilma's big brother Tyson and a group of his friends were playing spinning tops. Wilma watched Tyson draw his arm back and fling his top against the ones already spinning in the circle. It cracked against a green top and the boys howled.

"Roy's gonna be just like he was. You watch."

"Hah!"

"Fuck you, Diana!"

"Fuck you back."

When it seemed like the world had gone completely crazy, Roy showed up at the kitchen door, grinning like he'd only been gone ten minutes. Wilma heard all the commotion and came slamming in from the backyard where she had been sitting under the porch, counting, for maybe the hundredth time, the days till her birthday.

Wilma screamed when she saw Roy, trying to push past the others. Ray, Tyson and Sherry were crowded around her big brother, making it hard to reach him. Wilma shoved them out of the way to get her arms around Roy's neck.

"Little Bit," Roy laughed, his dark eyebrows shooting together between his eyes. "You all arms and legs now, ain't cha!"

"I'ma be taller than Sherry," Wilma said. "In four days, I'ma be ten too."

Roy grinned. Behind him, Grans stood with her hands on his shoulder. Mama was at the other end of the table nodding at Roy's every word.

"Roy," Wilma said, still out of breath. "Sherry been bothering me and Tyson been calling me names like Bone Jones with a Monkey face! Cory's a big sissy. He want to—"

"Child," Grans cut in. "Roy don't want to hear that. After all he been through. I'm sure all he wants is some good food and some peaceful sleeping. Doncha, Roy?"

Roy nodded, grabbing Wilma around the waist and giving her a solid hug. "We got time," he whispered. "You gonna tell me all about it."

*Tuesday, August Third*

Wilma pressed her face against his, even though she knew Sherry and Tyson would be making fun of her about it later, talking about how she's too old to be acting like a baby. Calling her Boo. "You gonna tell us about what it was like over there, Roy? You got any gook ears in your bag?" she asked.

Silence, so cold it crept up the back of Wilma's neck, fell over the kitchen. She thought maybe she felt Roy shiver, pulled away from his cheek. "I didn't get to see your face, Roy," she said. "Didn't get a good look at you."

A shadow was racing across Roy's brown face.

"Where you get that junk about gooks from?" Mama scolding.

Roy was looking down at his hands, shaking his head like there was something wrong with them.

"You all take your brother's stuff upstairs," Mama said. Wilma picked up the smallest bag and followed the other three.

"You always got to mess something up, Wilma," Tyson grumbled, trying to sound all grown.

Wilma didn't know what he was talking about. Behind her, Sherry dug her nails into Wilma's arm until Wilma jerked it away and turned to smack her. But then she thought better of it. She'd save it for Roy. Roy was home. Roy was gonna look out for her. He'd kick everybody's behind.


Then the world snaps and crackles and pops.


When Wilma walks into the bedroom, she sees first Roy's shoes, placed together at the foot of his bed with the socks balled up inside. The shoes are black leather with brand-new laces and a slick shine. The socks are Sunday socks, thin and black.

Her neck hurts because it's hard to keep her head down at such an angle for so long. But Wilma can't look up. And up. And up to the place where the rest of Roy is swinging back and forth slow as clothes blowing on the line in spring. Roy up there with the rest of his clothes still on but those shoes on the floor. Roy always took real good care of his shoes, and if Mama didn't bury him in them then maybe they'd be Ray's one day and Ray wouldn't be smart enough to keep them shined. Wilma couldn't look up because Roy had only been home three days and she can't go back to this house like it was before—the sadness choking her, and Mama's moods swinging like . . .

Everybody waiting for Roy. Downstairs waiting for Roy. *Go see what's taking your brother so long* and Wilma running up the stairs, taking them two at a time in patent-leather T-straps. No, Mama. He's not ready yet . . . This house, back to its silence and sadness.

Wilma sneaks a look past the place where the shoes are waiting and can see right past Roy out the window. If she had stopped talking and looked, maybe she would have seen that place in Roy's eyes that went way deep and far back to where nothing was. Like sadness. Like missing someone deep and hard. That place behind the soft brown where a war was still going on and he was just home, a body without real eyes because the eyes that had seen so much happening needed to stay over there where they were or else bring all of that stuff home. And now Roy was following those eyes, swinging, trying to catch that deep place. Roy, on that rope that must have been left over from when Mama put a new clothesline out the window, was finding that place, going there on his own time. Going home.

She turns ten on a Tuesday and doesn't want a party. And in the shock of it all, the family forgets. Eleven follows quickly and by the time she is twelve, the days move too quickly to count. Mama gives her a gold name chain. Tyson gives her a Black Barbie doll. Lil Ray makes her a card and puts two quarters inside. Sherry says, "I didn't know what to get you so anything of mine you want, you can have."

The family moves in silent circles around her and the air grows thick with their remembering. They wonder who she will turn into, who they are all going to become. But she could tell them now, now that she is older and has a language for the sadness. If any of them asks, she would tell them that it isn't about what you find or what you see that flicks the light off behind your eyes. It's about what you choose to remember. And what you make yourself forget.

And Mrs. Dora comes in, uses Mama's sugar and cream in her coffee, says, "Tsk, tsk, tsk . . . Woman, what you gonna do with that one?" And Mama looks over at the child, shakes her head. Says, "She's gonna come to one day," but the doubt echoes, bounces off the linoleum, settles against the grease-stained walls.

And there's a hollow child walking through this world. And there's an angry child cursing. Across the street, an eleven-year-old drag queen ducks the blows of the spinning-top boys. There's a child in a nod disappearing. And one who's disappeared.

And Wilma asks "What's that, Mama?"

"What's what?" And the sound of the *what* singes the

kitchen walls. And all the black folks gather round the kitchen table, round the TV screen, around their cups of Maxwell House, waiting, waiting . . .

And another day passes this way.

ALEXIS DE VEAUX

# Dear Aunt Nanadine

Dear Aunt Nanadine,

As much as I love to write, I've never written you a letter. And "What do we need with letters?" you say. "We live in the same city, a bridge and a subway apart." Well, yesterday I took from the back of my closet that red three-piece walking suit you gave me. "Too fat to wear it now," you said, pushing it in a Macy's bag. "Take it."

So this letter is to say I used to admire you in that red suit; how it colored your light handsome beauty. And made you look so rich, so pockets full of freedom and loose change. Red, you instructed me, was a color *I* should *never ever* wear. I was absolutely "too dark." "Whose little black child are you?" you'd tease. "Who knows who you belong to?" Did you know then that your teasing mirrored my own apprehension? *Who did I belong to?* Who does a dark-skinned child belong to in a family where lighter skin is predominant, in a society where dark can't mean anything positive? It's not supposed to. Who do you belong to and who do you trust?

Should I have not trusted you then when I was eight years old? Not listened when you advised me at ten that not only reds but certain bright pinks, yellows, blues and oranges were also off limits to me? And to other girls my color, like Cheryl Lynn Bruce, who grew up on the South Side of Chicago (grew up to become an actress). Cheryl was ten, and dark, and recalls: "I remember going to my grandmother's house one day (she taught piano). I put on a red outfit—red coat, red dress, red shoes, red everything. I was fascinated with the color red. And off I went to my grandmother's house. Well, my grandmother gasped when she saw me, and called my mother, and sent me back home. My mother opened the door, grabbed me inside and said, "Take off all that red. You are too dark to wear all that red." I hadn't understood there was a construct that decided what colors a dark girl could wear. I was ten at the time. Red is such a vibrant color. It calls attention, and it was calling attention to my skin. After the red incident, I felt there was a search to find a color I could wear that would not draw attention to my color. Mother dressed me in navy blue a lot because it was a neutral color. I became very conscious of how colors affected my skin.

Quite frankly, Aunt Nanadine, I was a little surprised when you gave me the suit. On the train, I wondered if you still thought I was "too dark." Was I lighter to you now? More acceptable? Had your feelings changed after some twenty years? At home, I stuck the suit in the closet of my writing room. I never wore it. It waited among my piles of complete and incomplete ideas, filed away, an unfinished draft of an old story. One day I would get back to it. But I could not sincerely thank you. And the next month, rummaging through some old notebooks, I came across this fragment of story: *I am a little girl. I am in the third grade. I come home from school. I run all the way today. My favorite dress— the navy one with tiny white polka dots—is torn at the sleeve and neck, with buttons missing and Lord, it's so dirty. There are dried tears on my face. My hair stands all over my head. I am pissed-as-shit. I know my mother is going to kill me. I bust through the apartment door.*

*"Girl, what happened to you?" she say.*

*"Had a fight."*

*"Fight 'bout what?"*

*"Livia and them keep calling me Blackie—"*

*"I send you outta here to go to school and learn something. Not to fight, miss."*

*"She started it. Callin' me Blackie and Lil Black Sambo."*

*"Well the next damn time she do, you tell her YOUR MOTHER say sticks 'n' stones might break your bones, but words will never harm you. Hear me?"*

*BULLSHIT, BLACKIE AIN'T MY NAME, I want to say. It hurts. It's painful. It's embarrassing, Momma. Livia is dark as me. Why everything Black got to be evil, everything dark got to be ugly? I say nothing. I learn the bravado of strike back. Incorporate the language of segregation: "inkspot," "your Momma come from Blackest Africa," "tar baby tar baby," "Black nigga." I say it in (great) anger to others on the block. This is a skill. It is a way to hurt another deeply. We all practice it. In 1956, nobody wants to be a "Blackie" or a "darkie" or no other kind of African nothing. Africa to (most of) us*

*Dear Aunt Nanadine*

*is Tarzan 'n' Jane: uncivilized life on the "Dark Continent," half-naked cannibals on TV. Africa was something to be ashamed of. The closer we are to that which symbolizes it, the greater our potential for shame.*

Reading and rereading the story, I wondered if anyone, any Black person, ever dared to call you Blackie, Aunt Nanadine, you with your elegant, light skin. And what would you have done to them if they had? What would you have done if *your* grandmother anointed elbows and knees religiously every Sunday with Pond's Vanishing Creme, to keep away the ashiness of "dark"?

I am not ungrateful for all the things you did teach me about my color: how to use Nadinola bleaching cream as a foundation under makeup; to buy my stockings in a shade of off-black; how to assimilate and integrate to survive; to *fade in* as much as possible (however ridiculous, at times); to "act my age and not my color." All the ways you penetrated the interior of my feelings, where you and I lived, I believed then, in a separation of shades; where our different colors wedged between us like a yoke. Separated and politically bound us to the psychological and psychic brutality that was American slavery. *That still binds us to generations of self-hatred,* a hatred of our darkness. Hatred for the overwhelming, monumental, lynching pain attached to it.

"Color has made extremely deep scars in Black people," says Sandra Ross, a good friend. (You might have seen some of her work, Aunt Nanadine. She's a freelance lighting designer in theaters around the city.) "It has affected what we do with our lives, what we *think* we can do or accomplish. It has shaped our self-esteem and sense of personal and group power. In my family, color wasn't mentioned. We talked about Black and white, but we didn't talk about light and dark." The neighbors did, though indirectly: "She's pretty for a Black child, smart for a Black child," they would say.

Is it just circumstantial that we are blood kin, women, products of America, descendants of heroines and slaves, that we have shared family crises and skeletons, but never talked intimately or honestly about skin tones and color? That I have never said to you: I like my color. I want to be even darker, blacker, still.

"I'm glad I'm as dark as I am because there is a certain point beyond which I can't compromise, beyond which I can't assimilate," Cheryl Lynn said to me over the phone. "I like to wear a lot of colors and bells and stuff to remind me that *I am different. I am an African.* And all the stares I get on the street and in the subway, even from my own people, are a healthy sign because we all need to be reminded that Black *is* beautiful, inherently beautiful, and we can enhance that beauty or twist it into something grotesque when we hide it."

When we deny it. When I am wrong *just because I am darker than you.* When my color *and* my sex are considered heavy deficits in the outside world. When, like Sandra, I cannot see myself as attractive for a long time, because I am, society says, repugnant and exotic: with my large breasts, my period, my pussy. "Just a dark, nappy girl." And as such, I must never call attention to myself. Never want it.

And never deserve it; because a dark girl was also unfeminine, unworthy, ignorant. *Neither ambition nor achievement was expected of me.* I could be propositioned by Black men, old enough to be my uncle. Rubbed against by a strange man in the subway on the way to school. I could be trespassed against in any number or variation of social ways, simply because, after all, I was only a Black girl. What a sad thing it was to learn that *a dark girl*

*Dear Aunt Nanadine*

*meant an ugly girl.* That my people had no standard for judging colored beauty. That within our race we judged ourselves by outside criteria. That there was no beauty underneath the nappy, unruly hair I was taught to fry and radically alter; no grace to my African buttocks squeezed into panty girdles at fifteen. Could I ask my mother if she thought I was beautiful? Could I demand to know if colored people had the *right* to be beautiful? If all the Sojourner Truth in me, all the Harriet Tubman, the Ida B. Wells-Barnett, all the Hatshepsut Queen of Egypt, all the dark, handsome history of my smell, talk, dreams, would not, indeed, one day rot inside the choking rope of

> *if you light you all right*
> *if you brown stick around*
> *if you Black git back*

Can you see how your red suit in my closet would make me see red? That to open the closet door daily was to open a Pandora's box of racism between us? Because we are in the closet too. A color closet we cannot get out of. It is too personal, too much a knife in a never healing wound. There is nowhere inside my color, inside your color, to be objective. No way to fade in. No way not to be dark. *And what color is dark? Who is dark? Compared to what, compared to whom? Is a dark woman in a darker skinned family light or dark? Is a light woman in a high light/mulatto family dark? Will we end the racism or shall we perpetuate it?*

"What do you think?" I say to Cheryl Lynn, taking notes. She replies: "I've seen so many ranges of color since I became conscious of my own color that sometimes it seems pointless to make any distinctions between dark and dark. I've seen navy-blue people and dusty-gray ones and some a sandy, translucent black.

Is an eggplant person darker than a maroon person? What does it mean, beyond that?" Some of us are darker than others but, Aunt Nanadine, we are all dark peoples.

That's what the sixties taught me. In the red, black, green artifacts of my African heritage, I could *learn to love* the dark me that was the Civil Rights movement here in America. The dark me that was the independence movement in Africa. That was an outside shade of brown. When I went on those marches and stood on those demonstration lines and chanted against our oppression, *I felt Black.* And the natural Black was beautiful to express. And it was as beautiful to express my anger as it was to express my natural, nappy hair; to express my skin by painting it. I celebrated every ritual that celebrated my darkness: Kwanzaa, nose piercing, braids, nationalism. I wanted American saturated with the henna on my lips. I wanted color: I wore reds and yellows and greens in provocative African combinations. *I wanted the freedom to be dark;* I could not get dark enough. In the summer, I disappeared on the beaches for days at a time. "Stay out the sun," you warned me. "It's just making you dark and oversensitive." "There's nothing wrong with being dark," I defended myself. Remember?

I remember *believing,* in the sixties. Many others do too. Like Carole Byard: "When we chanted 'Black is beautiful,' we were very assertive because we were *involved* in turning history around," she reminisced. "But some of the young people are not as aggressive as we were at their age. For many of them, it seems as if the sixties never happened. They are culturally embarrassed. There seems to be more of a willingness to merge, and not to assert cultural identity, particularly if it relates to Africa. Maybe they feel less threatened [than we did] by involvement with white cultural things."

I remember believing I wanted to judge myself from then on

*Dear Aunt Nanadine*

against *my own* darkness. And the darkness of my history. The sixties gave me a solid foundation, a bridewealth of "Africanity." Taught me to carry cultural beauty in my hair, my clothes, the words in my mouth. Taught me that while there was a "cultural Blackness" (artifacts), there is a "genetic dark," an *inside dark,* I must learn to love. *Learn to love the dark and trust it* because there are schools, clinics, governments, families, freedom, art to build between us.

But the sixties were only a beginning. And while it released some of our racial tension, it did not free us from our own color prejudices. When our slogans and anger no longer served us, when government and social backlash tested our spirit in the seventies, and Black was defined by Madison Avenue instead, some of us forgot that *our struggle did not begin in the sixties* and would not end there. Some of us mistook the invisibility of our darkness as the end of it.

Maybe that's not the stance to take at all, Carole disagrees, "Maybe the way we went about it is just no longer necessary. Maybe that's the difference between this decade and the last ones. Maybe we who were active in the sixties are like generals from another war. Maybe it's a *different* war, with different equipment for fighting it. Maybe it's not all gone, just different."

Different, but the same. Whether in Brooklyn, Baton Rouge, or Baltimore. Whether in Africa, the Caribbean, or America; at the core of our struggle lies an ugly pattern of color consciousness between family, strangers, friends. Lies deceptively, and hides, beneath our global view, like a pain. Or a journal entry:

*After dinner, Margo and I lay on her bed. Her quilt is a weave of cloth from the Ibo of Nigeria. We talk about her master's thesis topic: "The Impulse to Love in the Narratives of African American Slave Women." We smoked a good joint. Margo is a light-skinned Black woman. Her 'fro is big, but not kinky. Margo has African facial features. She's attractive. I am much darker. I have a short kinky 'fro. I have African facial features. I'm attractive. I was born in Harlem. Margo was born in Mississippi. She attends a prestigious Ivy League school. We live in Boston. Margo is very, very intelligent. Her mind is mercurial. When Margo smokes reefer she is aggressive. She sees how tall she is, how tall I am not. Wrestles me on the bed: "Let's play," she says. Punches me: "Let's fight." "No," I say. "Stop." When Margo's nose gets clobbered she cries, turns red. "You Black bitch," she spits. "I didn't mean to call you that," she says later. "Forget it," I say. Margo is my friend. We were lovers once. I quit her after that.*

Aunt Nanadine, it is the impulse to love that does not quit. To love my history sex skin. Not in spite of it but because of it. *To love myself.* As Carole says, "We must deal with the internal aspects of 'Black is beautiful.' Work on a stronger sense of self to make the whole group stronger by caring about our family histories, our health, our spirit, what kind of people we are. Our self-love. *If I love myself then I have to love you too.*"

And I have to love the visibility of mass protests that created the sixties, transformed lives forever, Africanized me. And still love it now, as it regroups underground; as today's fashions and the current national politics turn back the clock—turn our 'fros to Geri Curls and our cornrows to "extensions." "We have to evolve to a point of caring about contributing to the whole," Carole is quick to encourage. "It's a personal thing. Something each one of us has to do. In the sixties there was a lot of emphasis on mass health, mass healing, but now we have to strengthen the individual parts. We have to remember that the whole is equal to the sum of the parts."

Remember that in these ugly times, there *is* something to fall back on. Remember that it is the impulse to love that comes

*Dear Aunt Nanadine*

between the silence between aunt and niece. Comes in this letter saying I love you. Comes, as I write, struggling to internalize beauty, because *color is still a critical issue between our people.* We still discriminate against our own. The darker ones against the lighter ones. The light ones against the dark. Little kids on the street today still call each other Blackie as a way to hurt each other deeply. And yet we cannot afford that "luxury." Or any other "luxury" of segregation that diminishes our numbers. We cannot afford to believe that we have been defeated; that "Black is beautiful" is dead. That dark is ugly. I am not dead and I am not defeated. I am beautiful. Black is in my heart, blood, work; in the eyes of my dreads, in the amber/cowrie of my tongue.

So Aunt Nanadine, I have taken the red suit out of my closet. I am going to the cleaners with it. Then to the mailbox to drop this letter. Please get in touch with me. I'd like to know how you feel about all this. Perhaps I can come see you soon. Next week I will give a talk on "Writing as Activist Art." I will wear our red suit. Thank you for giving it to me. I have always loved it.

> Take care.
> Moving forward to freedom: Your niece,
> Alexis
> Brooklyn, 1982

MICHELLE PARKERSON

# Odds and Ends

## (A New Amazon Fable)

The babylonmobile sputters, coughing phosphorescent dust and war debris. Rear lasers blown. Furlough over. Loz Wayward is pissed. She savors her lost freedom, drifting mid-terrain.

Near a checkered skyline, the fortress blinks. First red then sungold to green, beaconing like a lighthouse, pornographic, through smog and early fallout. It flares digital patchwork across her almond face.

But Loz lingers in Sephra's afterglow: pussy fresh on her hazel lips. Such love keeps her dancing or killing, when all else fails.

Lieutenant Loz Wayward is a reluctant warrior, worn with

carnage, with three-day-pass romance. She activates her emergency reserve. She is late and there will be questions.

"Wayward, what delay you?"

"Yes, Advisor . . . well, uh, my rover malfunctioned at about 1300 hours."

". . . and where you get *dese* munitions, Wayward? Answers, please!"

Commander Bey had not built her career on social graces or cutting slack. Her militia was her pride. She snatched a chartreuse grenade jutting flamboyantly from Loz's pocket. BON VOYAGE, it read, DIDN'T HAVE NO CHICKEN. LOVE SEPHRA.

Loz stood ill at ease in the Commander's tent—a recycled Winnebago. She braced herself.

"I was in the 7th Sectron, Advisor," Loz stuttered, "where Squeek's Bar-B-Que and Miss Edna's Curl Palace usta be . . ."

Nervous, Loz shifted her sturdy Black legs beneath her Zimbabwe daydress. Through clenched chipped teeth the Commander barked.

"Wayward, you got no people in Sectron 7. And today of all days! De Eldress been askin' for you. So what I s'pose to tell her? You lollygaggin' round Jupiter? Go report, Sister Wayward!"

". . . yes, Commander."

"And Wayward, resume revolutionary decorum. Pull de stars from your eyes, girl—"

The Commander returned to charts and strategies. On the Mylar of trenchtown pumps, Loz turned. She was a dark beauty despite regiment. She was too lonely to tell. Two eclipses till the next feel of civilian clothes. Three thousand light-years from Sephra . . .

In the adjacent galaxy of Mu, the Urban Underground prepares. Training chants of new guerrillas swell, then fall. Some ten years before, the race wars of Earth escalated to cosmic insurrection. Colored peoples everywhere had had enough and had taken up arms.

It had become a season of death. After a millennium of strife between the dark majority and a ruling few, hatreds festered at the turn of the century. Global turf wars erupted over technology. Gender pogroms were waged over the ultimate power of female reproduction, while the color line remained the color line.

In such times, anarchy was the only order. The scales of justice struggled violently to right themselves. In the midst of cataclysm, Black generations came of age. This growing tribe of have-nots fought on throughout the universe.

Mu was no exception . . .

Inside her bunker, camouflaged as Mt. Nebo storefront church, Sephra scribbles in a tattered diary. Her fingers are long, exacting. She writes:

> *Life has its contradictions. Like me and Loz: how we be in love in war. But this is 2086 and everyone must do their part.*
> *Still no word from my older brothers, Rastus and Malcolm. Lil Bit been fine though since she moved to Sectron 4. She likes men and the war is slower there. Even sent a picture of her new baby. Soul Papa's ten months old now. But I been worried for my sister. The Rosicrucians are opening her mail, torturing her husband. I owe them some death.*

Carefully, Sephra wraps her secrets in kinte tucked in ragged fatigues. She is a Demolitions Expert and part-time architect for the Underground. A sunshade Rastress.

Sephra is last in a notorious line of lye throwers and lovely renegades. Her gracious hands know firing mechanisms and how to womanize. Hands with a natural curiosity for thunder.

*Odds and Ends*

Beginning with the M16s, Sephra works. The Underground raids Exxon tomorrow. Repairs keep her blues busy. In Sephra's dreams, white clones rust in their own bloodshed. She wants an end to the slaughter. She wants those responsible erased.

Will there ever be enough lifetimes? When will there be kisses for Loz, her compassionate loveblade? A purple stain of woman.

Sephra allowed herself a memory: how, hours before, in an isolated corner of her workspace, she and Loz unraveled from a cocoon of rough-hewn sheets and fierce lovemaking.

"Baby," Sephra whispered, "you said one kiss."

"I lied," Loz purred. "And I love you."

Checking her chronograph, Sephra calculated lost time.

"Loz, get up. That was two hours ago. Armageddon's waiting."

"And it can wait a little longer," Loz mumbled. Tenderly, she ran her fingers through Sephra's dreadlocks, then rose stubbornly from her pallet. Sephra lay across the bed, studying the line and curve of her lover's nakedness. Loz dressed hastily in her discarded jumpsuit and combat bustier.

"God, I'm weak for a woman in uniform," Sephra sighed. "When you coming back this way?"

"Mid-solstice, maybe. Brigade rotation's due soon . . ." Loz resolutely strapped on her weapon.

Sephra frowned. "Love across enemy lines."

"Do we have a choice?" Loz challenged.

That unflinching reality sobered their fragile bliss. Sephra sensed a quiet aura of authority and resolve stealing over her lover as Loz faced her return to the Front. Sephra held her young woman close.

"The moment I first saw you at the Intergalactic Tribunal, the upstart young envoy from Earth, I knew we had chemistry."

"So then, why did I end up making the first move?" Loz teased.

"Earthen," Sephra said knowingly, "you are so backward when it comes to desire. Don't you realize restraint is everything?"

Sephra presented Loz with a grease-stained shoebox.

"Here. A love note," Sephra smiled. "Read it on your way back to the base."

Eager as a child, Loz grabbed and opened the box, pulling from it a hand-painted grenade. Lovingly, she attached it to her flak jacket.

"Lots of lovers came before you, Loz," continued Sephra. "But it's the first time in a long time I can count on love." Sephra gently pulled Loz into a deep kiss. Their tongues danced languidly over each other. Impulsive Loz placed her dog tags around Sephra's slender neck.

"Sephra, marry me! I mean, if not right now, tomorrow."

"If we're given it," Sephra reminded them both.


Suddenly, the memory vanished.

Suddenly, Kai appears at the door, a block patrol guard no more than sixteen. He is hysterical.

"Sephra!" he screams. "They broke through!"

Blood flames from his mouth. Bullets slice him. Down the hall, she hears trampling.

wellwhaddyaknow/they've/gotta/Black/bitch/making those

damn bombs      no/wonder/we can't/win/this/war

Head by head, clones barricade her dwelling: hell-bent, col-orless, in need of overhaul.

how/long/sinceyoubeen/fucked/jemimmait's/Miller/Time

Sephra reaches quietly into henna locks. Pulls from her for-est a One Megaton Grenade. Unpins it.

Loz Wayward sensed some strange wrong. She entered the Eldress's makeshift quarters slowly. Under solar touch, black vinyl lay scattered. It shined: Ben Webster . . . Miriam Makeba . . . The Shirelles . . . Leontyne Price . . . Bootsy . . . Last week's offensive on the U.S. Archives yielded a rich take. The Eldress emerged proudly from the rubble.

"Not bad, eh, Sister Wayward? Come in. I've badgered the Commander long enough."

"Must say you're looking empowered as ever, Motherforce. You called for me?"

In all the time Loz had known the woman, the Eldress retained her handsome, brown illumination. She was terrorism in a knit suit and holster. Loz's first serious crush. It was said in another age she'd been Bessie Smith.

"Lieutenant, your bravery on the Front is well known to us. I speak for all the Pyramid in congratulating you on your recent conquerings. You done good, baby!"

Loz listened, ran calluses through her challenge of naps. The Eldress strolled toward the message decoder.

"Loz, I've watched you sprout breasts as an orphan of this war," she began cautiously. "Groomed you for battle myself. Losses have been so heavy. It seems endless. Wayward, the clones have forced our hand. The Megatomic Bomb was exploded just before your arrival . . . These some plutonium-drinkin' motherjumpers we dealin' with. They're immune!"

From her desk, the gentle Eldress handed Loz a scrap of paper. Radiation seared the writing.

I A CHILD OF DREAD
BORN OF VEILED FACE AND MASTER NUMBER
A SABLE EYE FULL OF LOZ AND ARMAGEDDON
GOT LOVELOCKS IN MY HAIR
AN OUTLOOK ON THE FUTURE
ONE LOVE.
    SEPHRA

"But she was just in my arms . . ." Loz said, unbelieving.

"You're all that's left," the Eldress replied.

Loz Wayward crumbled. Tears napalmed her steel composure. Into the decoder, the Eldress inserted a hieroglyph. It neatly monitored:

PLEASE BE ADVISED . . .
MU SECTRON DESTROYED . . .
ALL LIFE FORMS DESTROYED . . .

PLEASE BE ADVISED . . .
THERE ARE CLONE SURVIVORS . . . REPEAT . . .
CLONE SURVIVORS . . .

Already, the evacuation alert was sounding.

The Eldress gathered young Wayward, rocked her rage, her mourning.

"You know, baby," she whispered, "Black folks has always figured how to make do and make love despite the odds and ends. How can we ignore destiny?"

The message decoder fades to black.

*Odds and Ends*

MALKIA CYRIL

# What Has Yet to Be Sung

*In Tribute to Audre Lorde*
*January 18, 1992*

Backing to breaking down
I always come to why, to
the unfair, painful
part of life
which runs through everything
like children's crayons
or mud streaked
into the secret rooms of my house.

It gets easier and easier to sit
and watch the sun set

forgetting how it rose
how the glow lifts
black children's faces toward
tomorrow and another chance
waiting with everything that I am
to know the world
and fill it up with one mighty word
one poem to rage catastrophic
on my enemies
one powerful poem to fly past silence
and bleed will into children trapped
by public schools and private traumas.

Forgetting in between spaces
that deny opposition I invite chaos;
the only direction for me is out.
Audre, I am learning not to sacrifice
belief, not to murder hope.
Still sometimes I wake in the middle
of the night screaming dark alleys
and an ex-lover's body desecrated
and buried in time for papers
to catch the story.

That is not
the whole of life,
whole—I can't explain is where
she took me, is where you bring me
to become the poetry of our mothers,
the survival of our fathers
to love beginnings

*Afrekete*

taking trips back to loving hands
into the sit back, yes on track
stand up way Audre had of obliterating
silence so that even while midtown maniacs
with billy clubs are smearing
our future with blood
we know we are still the plenty of our love
the height of promise.

I have known a woman who was a movement
in my life,
like welcome back to love;
we become the women
whose tongues have been stabbed
and sing anyway,
the women who learn from
teargas and tears how to make
a bomb cry, the soul rise
to meet the earth
crushed under buses
splintered onto sidewalks
we learn death is not the end of life
that language and change
are the beginning
I want to be a beginning
for me
for you.

*What Has Yet to Be Sung*

CAROLIVIA HERRON

# The Old Lady

*For Cheryl Abbott/Once Eagles and Oceans Fell Upward*
*to the Moon*

The Old Lady, the old black lady with the Moses staff and the African hair walks north from the center of Gloucester, across the footbridge to Good Harbor, over the cliff to Long Beach toward Rockport, then back around the summer cabins by the marshes, stops at Amelia's for spaghetti, buys a pistachio ice cream cone at the Dairy Queen then walks back down Thatcher Road. Every day the old lady, the old black lady, walks by the sea.

   In the winter, when Amelia's and the Dairy Queen are closed, she takes an apple out of her side bag when she comes to the triangle road by the two shops. In the winter, she carries a thermos of Russian Caravan tea in her bag and she stands in front of the Dairy Queen sipping scalding tea in the cold. The heat of the tea is always a surprise. When there's snow, she doesn't walk over the cliff, she doesn't take the back walk between the frozen marshes and the closed summer cabins. When there's a storm of snow swirling and she can't see the sea as she leans northward, the old black lady walks back clinging with one hand to the banister of the seawall in front of Long Beach, striking the ice with her Moses staff in her right hand and her African hair muffled down under a wool hat with wide woolen ties attached. She comes walking every day by the sea in Gloucester.

## GOOD HARBOR

Once the old lady was young and leaned over Myrna for a kiss, the kiss that explained what they meant, what everybody meant really when they said love will take you, passion will come, this was that kiss to make true the love lies, to clear the confusion from all they said about how love feels, how you just want to make love sometimes when you kiss a man they said. All those years of reading her father's *Playboy,* getting ready for a kiss, but those manboy kisses were no good, they were spit, she was cheated, lied to, had, took, until the day she and Myrna leaned into each other and kissed. "So this is what that young girl in high school meant," she said, "what she meant when she whispered to us at the back of the high school armory that it feels so good to her that she doesn't even wear underpants when she goes out with a boy, I always thought she was making it up," said the old lady when she was young as she held Myrna in her arms and rollicked on the bed there in the dorm, hiding, wondering, amazed she was when she was not an old lady and she held her first love in her arms. This is their favorite beach it seems, Good Harbor Beach, look at these crazy white folks half-naked, out catching skin cancer, mad dogs and white folks go out in the noonday sun without hats and umbrellas without clothes. Sandy and clean this beach is, the brush has grown back since the storms last year, there's the beckoning curve toward the north, the northward houses by summer light, sublime in the light, dancing, swinging in the light like the swingers of birches before the eyes of the old lady, the old black lady who defiantly chunks down her large lavender visor over her eyes, and her thick African hair bundles up black cotton over the top of the visor, the old black lady who has had no visitor for year upon year and will never have a visitor again, but who never eats directly out of her own serving dish in case someone should come. She is always ready for company, she is ready to place the dishes on the jigsaw puzzle she glued together for a serving pad, she is ready to dish out fried corn and beans at the dining room table and her private spoon has never violated the communal dish.

She could have lived with Myrna but Myrna was breaking her own heart over being a pervert, perverted she called herself and the old lady when they were young, perverts, and she couldn't change and she couldn't leave. The old lady when she was young could have urged Myrna to stay but who wants a lover crying pervert at you? The old lady could not bear it, so she left Myrna. She could have stayed a long time but she left Myrna who wasn't strong enough to leave on her own, couldn't set herself free, didn't want to be a lesbian and when the old lady was young she would not listen forever to Myrna loving and not wanting to love, "So I left," said the old lady, "it seemed like forever to grow old then," said the old black lady, who walks with her Moses staff and her African hair every day by the sea.

*The Old Lady*

## SALT ISLAND

Once when the old lady was young she met Diane the librarian in Santa Fe, New Mexico, met Diane every day for lunch on the grass near the Federal Building. And every morning when she prepared to meet Diane she packed something odd and new to eat so that she wouldn't eat up half of Diane's lunch but it never worked. Diane always had strange good foods with unheard-of flavors from Asia, saffron ginger extracts and she couldn't ignore Diane's food no matter what she thought of to bring. Diane always laughed every day and leaned over on the desert lawn to make an extra set of chopsticks out of the dry salt twigs, an extra set and when she was young, the old lady used them she used them to eat up half of Diane's lunch on a platter of waxed paper, every day, with Diane laughing and showing her the strange corners and hiding spaces of the Japanese lunch box. Diane, a good good friend to keep, the last the old lady heard was that Diane had moved to the eastern desert of California, salt land and spice. The old lady stands at Good Harbor Beach and looks over at empty Salt Island. "I went to see Diane in Berkeley and we watched the moon above Crescent Beach on that other ocean but I never went to the eastern desert of California, never." Salt Island where the fishermen used to stop on their way in, barren beauty, land cast away there, castaway, "I cast away here."

She taught me *I Ching* and she took me once to see a Buddha high up on a hill, what place was that? I can't remember, no salt there, it was water, all water and high mountains, and my arms trying to reach around the wide trees, the water crashing around the huts and shelters of some people who moved there, who had headed for the hills indeed, but for what? I can't remember.

I could have stayed there, I'm sure of it, forever, Diane had been showing me around I was weary with traveling and I could have stayed there and lived, gotten used to the mountains and the fresh good food it was a community, a community of fervent calm, Buddhists they must have been, a haven, a retreat, calm they were over the things of this world and Diane and I stood, how cool and deep green it was. She meditated in front of the Buddha but I just wanted to sleep, said the old lady, the old black lady who far from making peace with the things of this world still runs out to buy things fast whenever her check comes, fast, before she looks at her budget, so that she can have something she really wants before she looks at what she needs. She runs out to buy things even though she has almost enough money now, doesn't really have to do that any more to get extras, but she runs out anyway and buys things so fast, a new jigsaw puzzle or a plant, "A holdover from poverty," said the old lady, the old black lady who walks every day by the sea in Gloucester.

## CLIFF ROAD

The cliff is hard walking up and the brush thick in the corners of the rocks but at the top, after the road narrows and takes you back to the earlier time, roads making their way to someplace different, and down and up to the second cliff, get to see the rough sea battering hit splash, rough on the rocks below with tortured plants, twisted yet just a little way out so calm, it's because the ocean hits deep here, the sea hits deep on the cliffs, no

*The Old Lady*

sauntering up to the sandy shore but batterdash hard and the mansions with wind-burned patios hesitating above, nervous watching of their compact with the sea. Please don't take us back yet, the houses whisper to the sea, not yet, give us a little while longer of wide windows to board up when winter comes, widow's walks for the stamp of seagulls. Yet just a little way out, just a little, so pale blue calm, a storm is unimaginable this moment, there are no underlying rocks just there to stir it up only deep water. Yes, please please, the people houses whisper to the ocean, let us keep a little longer this land before you take it again, again.

The old lady has to rest after the cliff walk, rest until she's ready to walk on, soon autumn winter, soon already the tipped air leaning toward the horizontal ice rain of winter but it's worth it, it is so much worth it to the old lady to pull her body heavily uphill for the vision of sea changes. Florence would never let her rest enough, whenever she went hiking with Florence, where was it? maybe it was New York State or maybe it was in Virginia tramping with heavy boots and water bottles beside a river she went hiking with Florence who knew so much better how to hike how to get back home, how to take care. I could never rest enough, said the old lady panting still at the height of Naomi Drive rubbing on insect repellent that was probably poison, "I could never rest," said the old black lady sitting on a rock above the sea.

The river had turned around them, the old lady young and Florence. The river they walked beside swirled and she couldn't keep her heart from delight for the sunlight through the green leaves on the right with the river on the left, yes, that same old sunlight through those old green leaves that she tries to get used to but can't, what is it about layered filtered green light that unnerves the heart and collapses delight into laughter? The old lady sits upon the rocks and looks down upon the brushland green knotting the cliff, it is not the green of light through trees, no, here a rougher green at the top of Cliff Road, the circle of Naomi Drive and the wind-wracked seascape grumbling low today. The old lady, the old black lady leans with the rock, her Moses staff beside her and her African hair gleaming silver and black under the low bowed sun, her visor is toward the northeast, an aura around her head.

Finally after many years the old lady has bought pink flowers in white pots just like all the rest, well not just like, the pink is wilder, a red-violet pink and the white pots are stone and not plastic, even so, pink flowers in white pots just the same and not the same as her neighbors, this is her gesture of peace, they aren't so ugly, pink flowers, one can get used to them after a time, just like after a while even white folks don't look so ugly, and they got the nerve to call other people red, they're the ones red out there burning up, yep, mad dogs and white folks she looks at them on the sundecks below her, "They need to go find some color from somewhere, but if you squinch your eyes to blur them up a bit and put your mind in neutral they don't look so ugly."


LONG BEACH


Down from the cliff circling by the motel to Long Beach down, the old lady walks between the small houses that jostle each other for a view of the sea. The mussels squish between the rocks, black shells bubbling back at the come-higher water.

When it's high tide by midday at the full moon season nobody can walk here at the southern rocky curve of sandy Long

*The Old Lady*

Beach where the solid blue square house watches the yearly covering and uncovering by season of the shipwreck bones. The ship they say foundered a hundred years ago. The ribs won't come out for the summer houses in their belly curve toward the open sea, in their leaning huddle upon the seawall. The hull of the shipwreck returns from beneath the sand only for the winter people hulk and ship bone dead. Dead, where now hot dogs and ice cream roam through the hands of the children. Beside this ancient accident, beside the nurturing place of the great accident-engendering sea, where at least once some protoplasm and protein and stuff got together accidentally, and here we are, the accident, well why not? One myth is as good as another.

The old lady, the old black lady is an interruption on Long Beach in front of the bright red yellow of summer children and their people. What are the people doing? The people love. The people are trying to love each other with their calls and screams, with their letting the little one hold the fishing pole when the swimming is over for the day and the high boots come out with baskets and fishhooks and dusk children.

The old black lady is mysterious, she walks by summer afternoon and by dusk with her Moses staff and her nappy hair and plenty of clothes, the old lady the old black lady sea struts the sand and stops near the far end of the cabins to look out at Milke Island. Stands on Long Beach to see Milke Island where the scientists did experiments on some kind of life there. Elizabeth sent love letters from Italy.

Here the backward shore is most hidden. Here the rock outcroppings chuck the horizon just barely under the chin at either end of the cove, here the sea points farthest. Not even a tree on Milke Island, it's got some kind of special ecology and sometimes the scientists go to look at the queer stuff that lives there, it's an uncanny meager almost desert, it's a silvering, tarring, amber thick sticky puddle like syrup on a table, it rises just barely from the sea, "Elizabeth kept sending letters from Italy or Israel or Greece and I wanted so much to answer those letters why couldn't I answer them? Why?" said the old lady looking out to sea, the old black lady who walks every day by the sea with her Moses staff and her African hair.

Have you ever stood a moment and watched how the light flickers in the water of a shower how many shades of clear there are how many blue hints in sparkling falling water in a shower when the oblique light from the skylight slants down and you stop in the warmth of clear, clear bright water falling, falling around my head, yes, is it not beautiful?

The old lady, the old black lady stands in the face of Milke Island wishing she had answered Elizabeth's letters, one came from Venice with a marvelous glass bird "There is a world I've never seen," Milke Island is awful in a storm barely above the surface of the water, an accident maker with rocks for shipwreck and crevices for protoplasm. The old lady, the old black lady walks and walks and walks by the sea in Gloucester. How many colors of light in the falling water as the ocean waves fall from the center of the earth toward the moon falling.


THATCHER ISLAND


The mind stutters the mind blanks blinks. The old lady walks to the end of Long Beach and crosses the summer bridge to Eagles Rocks, her Moses staff thumps the wood as she turns her head toward Thatcher Island which has two houses for the keeping of lights.

*The Old Lady*

Soon they will come and take the bridge down, end of season and the old lady, the old black lady will wear her high yellow boots to wade across the shallow green stream to the last wild roses and brush. Dirt paths lead between the bushes to enclaves of rock and rushing water. On the other side there is Pebble Beach where the houses stop and swimmers don't go. Only some fishermen at times on the harsh large pebbles without sand, round rough on the foot, a steep bowl sometimes filled entirely with seawater, racing to the top, the very top leaving no place to stand.

But from Eagles Rocks the old lady, the old black lady turns still turns her high head turns her African hair, looks over and down the rushing dangerous water cupping in rough stone jagged hollows. Wild. A temptation swirls there upward beckoning jump, jump. Jump for the joy of it, jump for the death of it, the betraying irresponsible sea calls. Play with me. Come play. Thea spoke the truth and I could not bear it I got up and walked away and did not return not for anything, phone calls, letters, cards, messages through friends nothing never again. No I won't play with you any more.

How is it she knew when I didn't know? Stirred up a forgotten maelstrom in me, I couldn't escape the memory but I escaped Thea, who told me the truth.

Some people who live right here in Gloucester think that the white lighthouse never shines. They know that the red lighthouse shines but they have never seen the white light in the near lighthouse, yet if you stand on the rocks across from the solid blue house at low tide you can see a pale white light shining. I've sometimes seen it from the seawall but never is there anyone near who has seen it with me, said the old lady, the old black lady leaning on her Moses staff as she looks from Eagles Rocks toward Thatcher Island.

*Afrekete*

There are places on Eagles Rocks, yes where you can hide yourself from the view of houses, you can snuggle crouch down and get used to the raging water racing, you can settle down and live yes, an eagle, an aerie, to us an eagle is high and far, but to an eagle an eagle is close and huddled down warm in the high places, you could hunker down on the rocks and stay.

Life and pain is stirred from the innocent waters, sponge, seaweed by accident but when the water calls jump, jump, do not listen to the water, do not jump, don't jump. Think of the warmth of pancakes and your mother trying to explain to you when you were a little girl, that white folks are trying to insult you when they say you like pancakes, and you answered, But I do! You didn't understand. Don't jump don't because there is still popcorn left to be eaten. What accident of love imagined pop-corn? And there are root beer floats still in the world. "No one in the world can contemplate suicide in the face of a root beer float. No one," said the old lady, the old black lady who doesn't need root beer floats any more, but once there was a lunatic time, once, yes, eagles and oceans fell, they fell upward to the moon.

TWINLIGHT

The old lady walks, rounds the curve from the crashing sea to the summer-calmed far end of Eagles Rocks where both light-houses, the lighthouse who keeps the white light, and the light-house who keeps the red light, are full in her eyes beyond the wild summer roses. From here there are people in view again, by swim and by sail. Here fishermen hang to the end of the earth smiling, framed by the roses, thornbrush torn, roses and fish and the red lighthouse blinks out safe, all is safe by clear day.

*The Old Lady*

But on blue mist days when clouds fall down ripped upon the sea, then the red lighthouse becomes a lavender foghorn beaming crying Care, take Care, once Thatcher was a living man, Thatcher was a living man with a living ship until his ship met this island. Away, if you are lost in a fog, away, stay away from me and take care.

Upon this mild island and this homing sea my rocks are without mercy, it was three hundred years ago we took Thatcher out of the world. Rachel lives in the Rocky Mountains, so much sky and almost enough air. Rachel of mountains, or have you moved to the Oregon coast? Do you still debate your departures from the Sangre de Cristo Mountains? Where are you now? I thought I would return to your mountain desertland far from oceans, your land that was once an ocean, yes, once a shallow ocean where the Rio Grande now slides from Ski Basin to the Gulf. Brush desert now and you a light firelight glow by piñon and juniper upon the mountain.

I said I would return to you and the mountains at the end. I said I would come with one book and one pen and one pad of paper. I said I would come to write something or think something or make something. I said I would return to you and the mountains. At the end of what? My life? How shall I recognize the end and know when to come when there's still enough time to finish? to finish what? Rachel. The old lady, the old black lady who walks every day by the sea in Gloucester, turns from the ocean toward the west.

Have you ever had a chill that you knew would last forever? You come in from your seawalk thinking the winter blowing is no worse than usual, but as the meager heat of your house grabs weakly at you, you know that you are going to die before you get warm. Or walking up a mountain where the air has gone to the other side of the moon, and there is nothing for you to breathe, and you die. But trembling, panting you stumble upon the belief that there is heat in the world, there is still oxygen, you have to believe first. Then slowly, trembling panting, the core of your body takes a leap of faith toward the struggling electric blanket, your lungs take a step toward imagining the idea of air. You live.

It isn't so much the heat as it is the light I need to get warm, "I turn on the light," said the old lady, who stands at the end of summer at the end of day upon Eagles Rocks with her Moses staff and her African hair under the lavender light.

I said I would come back if only for a bowl of chili, if only for rellenos at Tertulias, if only for the smell of real piñon and not the incense, I said. I said I would figure out what I have to do and come there before I do it. I said. But I stayed here. I live here. This is my home. Whatever it is I had to do is done. Here. By the sea in Gloucester. The sun that is leaving me now is hot above you there, Rachel, if you are still upon your mountain.

Do you remember the ice cream cones in the plaza? Just after I remembered my great trouble. I came to Santa Fe from Albuquerque by Greyhound. I needed to see the sand paintings at Wheelwright's but the museum had given them back to the Navajo. I had wanted to see humped B'ganaskiddy again bringing food under the hand of Hosteen Klah.

I came in a wheelchair and found Many Moons and Doug Coffin who carved glass upon the moon, upon the ice rock of the moon, vision of possibility. I left with an idea and found my home here by the sea, upon this North Atlantic, in Gloucester, I left your Santa Fe, the Royal City of Art, and came home.

Can you see it, Rachel? Look from here at the wide water and the meandering sail bending around Gloucester Harbor toward Plymouth. This is where I live. The body relaxes into

*The Old Lady*

warmth after fronting an ocean chill. "The vision is worth the chill," said the old lady, gesturing with her Moses staff from east westward under the high spinning arch, the lavender sunset cartwheel above her African hair.

## WHALE WATCH OF THE SEVEN SEAS

Small crevices of dimpled bright water, small pockets of smeared rumpling lightfolds leap from the water, fly down the sides of the waves. The crevices of light rise in rows and patterns into herrings skirting the highways of dashing water.

The old black lady once sailed on the Seven Seas Whale Watch boat, and saw Cora and Isthmus, two humpback whales. Cora came spiraling up beneath a smudge of green churning, spiraling up a water tower within water with the fish leaping up through the air away from the open mouth clamping shut to a grin. The old lady saw it from the deck of the Seven Seas, until then she had not believed she would see a whale. There may be whales for everybody else, she said, but there can't be any whales for me somebody has to make up the ten percent who sail seeking but do not find the whale.

Isthmus wheeled in circles beyond the bow of the boat, stunning the water and entrapping his food. Isthmus with a splotch of white and a flourish to his tail, performed once while the old lady sailed north of twinlight. There was a woman beside her and her children who pointed out the Gloucester places as they went, The Retreat, they said, that's The Retreat, and there is East Harbor where we live.

Returning, the sea escorted the boat with dolphins, sleek black joy pods rising with white splash following fins high by

*Afrekete*                                                                                   *114*

flashing water, Hi! Bye! playful dolphins scalloping the air sea, teasing, clustering about the boat to sport and laugh, bringing the boat in, openers of the way, dolphins surrounded and passed the ship and came back and passed and escorted again leaping. Dolphins sleep fast, eat fast and well in order to play twenty-two hours a day or twenty-three!

The old lady turns north and around to leave Eagles Rocks. Bright summer roses from here north beyond Rockport, beyond the Seven Seas Cora Isthmus, she was so cold when she got back home after that whale watch, she had not realized that she was so cold.

Farther and farther the boats go, I have not gone far and yet it is far enough from where I grew up in the city. And it's no accident that I'm here. "The sea and the sky and the land and the sun may be accidents, but these eyes that see them are not accidents," said the old black lady who has a God but has no heaven. The old black lady walks and walks and walks by the sea.

SWAMP

The old lady walks down from Eagles Rocks, crosses again the footbridge toward Long Beach and turns slightly away from the ocean, to the swamp behind the irregular rows of summer cabins. A wide warm marsh water stream is on her right, delicate small gardens on the land side, dirt roads carving dusty semicircles surrounding the hidden beach beyond the cabins beyond the seawall, on the left.

It is the end of the season, cars and pets stalk the sidelines. The Club House. Crackling brown wood and water stain on the screen porches. The tennis court is old, ancient, and many of the

*The Old Lady*

small cabins were built a century ago. This back road follows inland this wide large shallow stream flowing out from Gloucester among marshes, a lurid green, with pond slime and algae. The old lady follows the stream beside vines, the undergrowth is woven with deep old flowers along the sides, binding the land to the water under the trees.

Forgotten hint of southern lands here. Here the harrowing of ocean sounds by crickets and frogs. Here the mosquitoes and dragonflies rise in high summer, here the ducks hiding, here the estuary nursery, and boats turned over under the brush. Here honeysuckle and willow, and a path leading across water lilies toward the houses on the Rockport side.

The old lady stumps along, the old black lady with her Moses staff in her hand and a rugged grip on the staff, her body wants to give up right here in this close heavy swamp place, this thick New Orleans memory—tropic and thick air come also to Gloucester, Massachusetts. The buzzing cricketing life counterpoints the ocean, the ocean fading back now on her left, beyond the frontage houses.

Once the old lady young went swimming in the ocean off Senegal, once she went swimming with Maureen in the African Atlantic. This is the hardest moment of the walk for the old lady. It is the hardest moment when she cannot see the ocean, when she is farthest from home, and her body aches.

She doesn't come this way by winter and yet by spring summer, she comes. Why? The warp of space, to see worlds living side by side, the world of the northern ocean beside the world of the southern marsh, to know something different, as if the marsh were a globe within the orbit of the sea, or the sea within the marsh. As if she, the old lady with her African hair and her Moses staff could just so easily as that, just so easily, take a slight turning to the right instead of the left, and find herself in another place entirely. Only in spring or summer. The marsh freezes by winter, the snowdrifts are high, there are no crickets.

Who holds the ice pick? Always at this point of her walk someone jabs the ice pick into her hips, harder on the right than the left, jabs until the black knuckles of the old black lady turn ash white gripping her Moses staff. Her head, her African hair offset in a shadowy circle, her eyes cast unseeing upon the ground. There's no place to rest on this back walk, and no ocean to steal this scene from the ache of the body. There is pain.

I wanted Maureen so much, the bend of her head, her slender turning, I lay beside her and wanted but did not touch. I lay for a night restraining passion. I did not speak. I did not touch. In the morning we went swimming in the Atlantic which was almost enough to cool my desire. African Ocean. Soft speaking woman. The spasm of bursitis has passed. The old lady, with the Moses staff and the African hair lifts her head and walks to the end of the dirt road, striding by purple flowering marsh reeds. Her walk is strong.

I didn't know it was still possible to remember wanting her, to hold another human love in my arms, it isn't possible. I would have touched her breasts and kissed her shoulder and back and played with her hair. We talked that night. Afterwards I could not fall asleep. I wanted to touch her. Desire. I didn't know I could still remember. Once when I was young I went to New Orleans for Mardi Gras and visited a nudist colony, and I ran free and black on the grass running. Maybe I'm as crazy as white folks, I was naked except for a pair of white socks and thick blue sneakers to protect my feet as I ran and played. "I did that," said the old lady, "but at least I had some color!" said the old black lady with the African hair and the Moses staff who always forgets

*The Old Lady*

that she always remembers as she walks every day by the sea in Gloucester.

## LEAF

At the end of the dirt road, there is another road swerving out to the right beneath trees. The old lady has never taken that road. It invites, but if she goes that way, she'll miss her last close glance at the sea before walking home. Long Beach. Every day she walks, every day she debates the other walk, every day the other walk invites her, every day she turns instead back to say good-bye to the sea one more time before going on to Amelia's.

Croaking. A toad leaps over a rock. Sandy. Sprinkling sand as it hides. Seagull. The old lady walks the paved footpath between the houses, turning her back on the covered archway leading away, back beyond the swamp.

If she should go that way. What if she should go that way? Mayetta touched her hand and there was a leaf in a window in a southern house a brown leaf and a song Mayetta kept singing. Not even once has the old lady taken the wide sweeping backward path that follows the swamp. The lilac bushes there are larger than trees, higher. And in the spring the purple white lavender flowers cascade, cascade from the roofs and balconies, cascade from the limbs of trees, from the cars from the reeds, the lilac scent is overwhelming then. Then the old lady just stands and breathes. Breathes the sweetness. She has never lifted her hand to take a lilac from those bushes.

The softest touch. Why did I never? why did the leaf stay in my mind? a shuddering touch, brown leaf on the screen touch. There was no reason for the leaf to be there. Leaf, leaving. She has seen both ends of it. The path. The mind stutters. The mind blanks, blinks. The path is heavy with overgrown trees. The old black lady doesn't take that other path every day as she walks by the sea.

It is the mid season. The season between the lilacs and the horizontal ice rain of winter. When the ice rain comes that is the day when she ceases to come this way until spring. That is when she comes back by the seawall, back with her Moses staff in her right hand and her African hair muffled down under the wool hat.

There is the last view of Long Beach sand castles and the twin lighthouses on Thatcher Island. Wildfire. One cannot make love to wildfire. Mayetta the wild. I was strong enough for you but I chose not to go that way, to be with you. No, not that way. The old lady, the old black lady walks away from the sea.


AMELIA'S


The old black lady steps down from the seawall of Long Beach, and walks down Rockport Road to Amelia's for spaghetti. Beach balls, sand shovels and more red yellow skipping in the way children, cars, noise. Park five dollars a day not fifteen like at Good Harbor. Filled parking lots. Tan sunny day, going to Amelia's to eat, going to the Dairy Queen for ice cream. Ice cream after spaghetti. Going.

The old lady, the old black lady walked through around with the crowd, down past Long Beach Motel, past the beach houses, past the Voyage House, the Portuguese house, the parking lots. Gravel and sand and the line at Amelia's stretches out to the road. Red bunting and pink balloons on the columns. But they're fast here. The food comes quickly. Greek salad. Seafood salad. Tossed salad. Clams crabs shrimp lobster combo plates sea fingers sea thumbs sea thighs french fried onion rings, and plenty of ketchup, always plenty of ketchup here. Do you need a fork and a spoon to go with you? are you going to eat on the beach are you going to eat at home. If you're going to eat on the beach? we can give you everything here. We can keep it warm, we can make it cold. I'm sorry the prices on tonic have gone up again, plus the deposit. No rest rooms. No telephones. Posters of old movies. *Casablanca*. Have you ever seen *Casablanca*? That's a good old movie. The usual today? Yes. And no cheese. Right? You're the one without the cheese. We're going to have the chicken special again tomorrow. You want to come by and try that? Mind it? We don't mind it at all. We don't need to rest now, we can rest in the winter when nobody's here. Good and we'll bring it to you at the table right over there. She gets the usual. It's OK. You don't have to wait in line.

The old lady, the old black lady looks at the clustering families, napkins, grease, the old lady sits twirling spaghetti and listening, listening to life love. The teenagers gather outside, linger lounge saunter next door to the Dairy Queen. Echoing. The old lady, the eyes of the old black lady brighten. Spaghetti doesn't have to have cheese to be good. And pistachio ice cream doesn't have to be green to be good. Standing in line jostled friendly by the teenagers waiting for ice cream. Brighten. The old lady smiles. Late afternoon toward evening. The old lady, the old black lady switches her Moses staff to her left hand so that she can hold her pistachio ice cream cone on the right. The old lady walks away from the triangle of shops down Thatcher Road, away from Long Beach, beyond the parking lots for Good Harbor, to Bass Road, home. Every day the old lady, the old black lady, with her African

hair and her Moses staff walks back home from the sea in
Gloucester.


THATCHER ROAD

The black lady walked by sunset linger from Amelia's down
Thatcher Road. The sea traces along beyond the fields and parking lots of Good Harbor Beach. The old lady does not see the
ocean. It is her own thought driving her home, now her own
thought and nothing else. Driven. Herself. She is her own ocean
now. Gaze that vision. Joyce taught me how to make tea when I
went away to Eastern Baptist College. I lived on the first floor and
she on the fourth, the top, and she had a tea set on old packing
cases of thin rounded wood, like hatboxes made from that same
thin wood as toy airplanes from the five-and-ten, when I was
young. I didn't know until then that tea didn't always come in
bags. Tea and *Demian* she left by my door that weekend when I
was on restrictions and couldn't leave my room. She left it there
and knocked and ran off to the farmer's market to help her uncle
sell eggs. Mennonite she was and is still somewhere. Those old
days. How often I thought and still think, standing by an open
door, and I walk toward the door breathing the brisk wonderful
air from beyond, still, still I can breathe that air so fresh. Joyce
had a way of getting to answers, she played Messiaen's *Quartet for
the End of Time* for me. I couldn't be the same after that, it
changed everything, Joyce, standing at the door of artistic passion,
mysterious, arousing in me a longing to do something, make
something, I flowed out so clean and pure. How I wish I were
with her now. Or she with me. I would like to talk to her. A tree
by a river of waters in Pennsylvania. She was. Is Joyce. She sent

*The Old Lady*

me a card once since I moved here. Long ago. And the card still had the fresh air scent of her leaning out from the fourth floor and me on the first singing up. The wall angled away right there, so we could see each other aslant. The others complained about us. Laughing too much. She was a tree by a river of waters. We danced under the rain. Under the night. And years she worked with John in the Caribbean during the war. Vietnam. An orphanage where the little boy had epilepsy and screamed so in the night.

Driving. The tree of avocados. Mangoes. I need to rest. Look at the sunset. How the light alters. It's as if I thought then she would take me somewhere. Somewhere to a world. I wanted to get there. Oh Joyce, so many visions. Rain forests and lakes we paced with our conversation. The sudden horrors of other sometimes, we spoke of it. The strangeness of other human souls. And grief. And having just enough strength. Folk festivals and farmer's markets. And did we get anything done? I thought we had, but I don't know, I don't. How I wish I could see you again. I was happy.

Passage out and full sail perhaps. There's a place right here in Gloucester called The Retreat but I've never been inside. I've seen it from the Seven Seas Whale Watch boat. I wonder what it's like there. Have I lost all my friends? Where are you? The old lady, the old black lady with her African hair and her Moses staff, the old black lady who walks every day by the sea in Gloucester, walks to the end of Thatcher Road, and across Bass Avenue on the Good Harbor side, and comes home.

It is as I left it. Tall thin house attached to a row on one side, standing on a hill of sand. The sun has gone and in its leaving it has tossed this color away. Seagulls clapping light. What can I do? Sometimes I get so cold. Natalie. Hair so dark and eyes upon me. I don't know how to get there where you are. I am forgotten. A pot of tea. And this strange puzzle I have as a pad on my table. A puzzle called the library, but a library where no one ever read. Too many candles and fragile flowers in the way of the books. You'd knock the lamp oil right on the books if you ever tried to reach for them, read them. Who made it? What was the idea? A library without reading. Who thought of such a puzzle? Is it someone who never read at all, who thinks readers do such things to books? Or is it someone who only thinks she loves books? Here. Now I'll rest.

Russian Caravan tea is best for reading. The rich red-brown color loves books. No one. Your face Natalie, you the prize, but I didn't know how. Love. No one. But peace, yes. I've lost everyone. I looked into your eyes and loved the best I knew how, Natalie. But I didn't know how. No one. Whose eyes? What book? You are a gem on a precious chain, twirling, I see you, Natalie, where have you found the deep metal carvings, and the luminous setting of your patterned precious stones? I see you. I see.

Falling, falling upward toward the moon, accident-maker. No retreats. This is where I live, where I stay, by the sea in Gloucester. It is comfortable here with the tea and the evening. I'm used to regretting you now, it's a part of my peace now to wish I had loved you. Colors falling upward from the year, light

*The Old Lady*

clapping wings. I love you Natalie, I love you now, I love you as I love the sea and as I love the great maker of the great accident. "I do love," said the old lady, the old black lady sitting with her cup of tea by dusk, quiet by darkening light spiraling above her head, "Or at least I want . . . , at least I try . . . , at least I walk toward love in the way that I can," said the old lady, the old black lady, who walks every day by the sea in Gloucester with her African hair and her Moses staff; the old lady, the old black lady, for whom even now the winter comes on that brings no spring.

JEWELLE GOMEZ

# *Wink of an Eye*

Saturdays were Father's Day for me during my teen years. Living separately, with only assigned weekends in which to play father/daughter, Duke and I made the shape of our relationship through tasks and conversation. I loved the sound of clinking change, cascades of silver—quarters, nickels, and dimes—my father's tips from the Regent, the corner bar where he worked as bartender. I lined them up neatly on his glass-topped desk where he'd count them out and then grandly sweep a share off into my hand. He made a jolly ritual of this payment for my dusting his record collection. We discussed jazz and blues singers and his eclectic selection of books and magazines. These talks were as much a part of my education as any of the courses I took at school. Just as importantly, they taught me who my father was—a man of immense curiosity and charm, erudition and wit.

His sensuality was apparent in the easy way he wore his elegance, and the soft roll of his eyes; in the subtlety of his social observations and the belly-laugh timbre of his jokes. But he could be with women and not have to prove he was a "man." He had no difficulty looking any of us in the eye. I listen for him when I try to create male characters in my fiction and look for him in all my friends—male and female.

I'm not certain if it's simply my getting older or that the times are changing. As the years pass, it becomes harder to find Duke in male friends. Each year the Black men I know express more bitterness, less hope. There are many valid reasons, of course. Much is made of manhood, and the subtle and blatant ways that Black men are told they will never be good enough are stunning. I see it every day. Although I've worked in administrative jobs for the past fifteen years, it still continues to provoke a visceral pain inside me when I see disdain directed toward Black men delivering packages. No matter the age or state of dress, they are invisible to white people. This is certainly a question of class as well as race, but the "manness" of Black men seems only recognizable to whites as a threat in this culture.

Working for an advertising company for many years, I developed a friendly familiarity with the regular messengers who were Black. When a white coworker heard one messenger inviting me to a musical event in which he was performing, she acted as if I'd been conversing with my typewriter table: not shocked, but confused; unable to imagine that this Black messenger was also a man, that he had a life with aspirations and connections to something other than his bicycle and her packages. She also seemed incredulous that I, who'd been lifted up from what she seemed to perceive as the mire of Blackness and blessed with a career, might feel connected to this messenger.

Today, more and more, that common bond between me and Black men seems stretched thin. It is balanced less on personal interactions, like the wry wink the messenger returned to give me behind my coworker's back, and more on vaguely remembered historical events. The sixties were a time when we had official titles—Brother and Sister—as if to negate all the other names slave owners had given us: mammy, uncle, Beulah, Remus. When I talk with heterosexual Black men we speak of The Movement as if it were a shared adolescence that makes us siblings for life. But, like any vision of the past, it's never exactly the same in everyone's memory. And my assessment of the disadvantages of being a woman within the context of the Civil Rights and Black Power movements is certainly different from that of my brothers. None of them seem to remember Stokely Carmichael's heartily greeted pronouncement that "the only position for women in the Movement is prone." That's not a sentiment any revolutionary can endorse. Feminism has not taken away my pleasure at the hope that period signified for me. It does require me, however, to insist that both political consciousness and action be more comprehensive this time. In the nineties I demand that my brothers look past rhetoric and see me.

With our past in deep shadow, being continually reinterpreted by revolutionaries turned stockbrokers, it is increasingly more difficult to find the shared contemporary experiences or opinions that might help me as a Black woman work with Black men to shape a bright future. There were always several groupings of Black men with whom I was never able to make serious connection. In college there were the strivers, those who I suspected would drop "the community" as soon as the right job came along. I could recognize them by the elaborate efforts they made to keep their dashikis well pressed. Growing up in a tenement, living on welfare with my great-grandmother, I wanted crisp pleats and the right job as much as anyone, yet I thought their attitude reeked of escape rather than social consciousness.

Recently, I heard a brother talking about finding a parking garage for his BMW as if that were a political triumph. He'd proudly maneuvered the baroque racism of corporate real estate in New York City, and I felt as if the beautiful sweat on the face of Fannie Lou Hamer had been rendered invisible. I knew he and I had taken different paths that were unlikely to meet. And on an East Coast campus I was visiting to do a reading, deliver a lecture, and meet with some of the writing students, the Famous Black Male Writer in Residence didn't bother to show up. One of his female students told me not to take it personally, he never came to the readings that women writers did.

When I heard, in the fall of 1991, that Spike Lee had begun his much publicized course on Black film at Harvard by initially neglecting to include a single film by a Black woman, I wasn't even surprised. In this case, as in others, I felt as if an artificial construction—economics, academia—had rendered me superfluous to the Black male ego. I knew Duke would have been sorely disappointed in Spike, though. Just as he had been with Black men who feel duty bound on public streets to comment on women's body parts. Or those who call Black women "out of their names," as we used to say. Or those who must trash other ethnic groups to feel like men. There's a level of solipsism pervading Black male culture in the U.S. that Duke would never tolerate and that I still find myself surprised to see.

Some of my heterosexual Black male friends seem to have

escaped, or at least curbed, the curse of culture and chromosomes. Clayton, a writer, has known me since I was in college, when he was struggling with his own career. Over the years he's offered the most consistent, uncondescending encouragement for my writing, acting as an editor of my early clumsy efforts, while he wrote for the *New York Times.* He never appeared threatened by my attempts to catch up with him. Another good friend, Morgan, stuck by me in the deep emotional clinches that men aren't generally trained for: when my great-grandmother died, when I was out of work in New York City, when I couldn't figure out what to do next. He was managing a New York acting career, not the most lucrative undertaking for Black men in this country. But he offered himself and his family support system while I thrashed about trying not to drown.

In the mid-1970s I think Clayton and Morgan, unlike many of my other straight Black friends, saw my coming out as a lesbian as a new aspect of me—perhaps a surprising revelation, but not an invasion by an alien being. They weren't afraid to like me even if our relationship wasn't about sex. These brothers took their title seriously. Their friendship kept my eyes open for the Black gay brothers I knew had to be out there somewhere.

In the glitter-ball disco world of the seventies, it was difficult to connect with them through the light shows and quadraphonic sound systems. But, as with Clayton and Morgan, it was because of intense personal aspirations—theater and writing—that I first caught the subtle gay winks of Black men, thrown past unsuspecting heterosexuals, letting me know there was a community. The first time I remember trying to make social contacts as a lesbian it was with Black gay men, actors who worked with me on a variety of productions in Black theater. I would casually mention the name of a gay club, like The Garage, and we'd glance at each other to check the response. Then, as with the wink from the messenger, we'd confirm our unity.

Until the mid-1980s the public worlds of lesbians and gay men remained relatively separate. Except for the annual Pride marches held around the country, we shared few cultural events, clubs, or political activities. But for Black lesbians and gay men the world was not as easily divided. The history of oppression remained in our consciousness, even for some who were too young to really remember The Movement. And since we often were not accepted fully into the white gay world, we frequently socialized with each other. We hung together in the corner at the cast parties and invited each other over for holiday dinners knowing the food would taste just like home.

When I went to the first national gay march on Washington in 1978, I had to be at the bus leaving Greenwich Village at 5:00 A.M. I slept on Rodney's couch, around the corner from the meeting place. We'd come out to each other years before when he was acting in a play I stage-managed. I was fascinated by his midwestern Blackness and the way he paid attention when people talked to him, just like my father. I think he found my Bostonian manners and the rough ways of the theater a funny combination. We sat up talking most of the night, mainly about our lover relationships and what it was like to be Black and gay in the New York theater world. It was a world of contradictions, where gay men and lesbians were fanatically closeted and heterosexuals were vying to see who could be the most iconoclastic and arty. When I left Rodney's house before dawn we hugged and kissed good-bye, and I remembered how much I'd missed Black men since I'd stopped sleeping with them.

In reflecting on my friendships with Black men in general

and Black gay men specifically, what is always at issue for me, whether conscious or not, is how they view Black women. That, of course, is an excellent indicator of how a man thinks of himself. And my great-grandmother always told me, "Never keep company with a man who doesn't think much of himself." That the male-female sexual tension is largely eliminated between gay men and lesbians allows, it seems to me, an opportunity for both to really see and think about each other, rather than reacting in socially prescribed ways. With straight friends like Morgan and Clayton, and later with gay friends like Rodney, I'm drawn to their ability to actually see me, not just see a woman as an object. They perceive my professionalism, intellect, and passion. And in turn they share their own attributes with me, rather than trying to use them to dominate me.

And then there's the unexpected pleasure of being able to view the object created by this culture—woman—alongside a man. It has been liberating to see another friend, Dan, let go of the strictures put on maleness and indulge in femaleness. We go through Black magazines and scream at the brown-skin cartoon fashion figures because we know how far both of us are from that fake ideal—me with my size-sixteen figure and graying hair; him with hair everywhere. Dan dresses up in the very things that made me feel inadequate, the things I broke free of: heels, sequins, makeup. In doing so he has helped to create a space where we both can step back and see ourselves as separate from society's constructs of gender. From our perspective, the idealized glossy photographs as well as the other misleading clues about who women and men should be are more easily dismissed.

Because neither of us would give up our Blackness, even if it were possible, both of us can paint and primp, don the masks, and laugh at whatever society imagines we both are. We share the wink behind the backs of both the straight and the Black worlds. It's a special bond forged for me only with Black gay men—a bond not broken in history by a slaver's lash, or today by the disapproving sounds of air sucked through teeth.

For many years I've been going to concerts by the Lavender Light Black and People of All Color Gospel Choir. It's a lesbian and gay group that renders the songs of the gospel tradition in the most vibrant and moving ways I've experienced in a long time. What I see when I sit in the audience watching the Black men I know—Charles, Lidell, others—is an abiding respect for our tradition and our survival. They sway in robes I'd recognize anywhere. Yet there is that extra movement, giving just a bit more to the spirit. And that extra beat signifies an insistence that the tradition can be carried on by all of us, not just heterosexuals or Black closeted choir queens. Charles and Lidell prefer to commune with their people and their God out in the open.

Although the sexual tension may not be there between us, what is allowed to flourish is the sensuality. When I'm with Black men, we revel in the feel of being brothers and sisters. We talk that talk and walk that walk together. There is a sensuous texture of Black life: the music, the use of words, the sensory pleasures of food, of dance. We appreciate these things with each other. The commonality of our past and the linking of our future make the bond sensual and passionate, even when it's not sexual.

Several years ago I spent an afternoon riding the train up from Washington, D.C., with poet Essex Hemphill. We both were surprised at the unexpected opportunity to talk for a couple of hours without interruption. When the train pulled out, the conversation started with "Girrrrrl . . ." in that drawn-out way we can say, and rolled through the writing of Audre Lorde, Cheryl Clarke, and James Baldwin, the U.S. economy, the treachery of politicians, Luther Vandross, disco, white people in general, and a few specific ones we knew, and broken hearts. We touched these things that have deep meaning for us in an unguarded way, using the familiar gestures and music of our fathers, mothers, and grandmothers. It was a synergy not so different from my intimate conversations with my best friend, Gwen, when we were in high school. And it felt much like those exhilarating moments when my father and I talked about books and music. Essex and I revealed ourselves to each other as writers, as a man and a woman, as brother and sister. We took each other in unreservedly. And we had barely begun before the train pulled into the station and we kissed good-bye.

And now AIDS. The first Black friend I heard had died from HIV-related illness was Robert, an actor. He'd done a lot of television—*Kojak* and other series—and some small parts in films. But onstage he was a tall bundle of American and African energy, large eyes, dark, slightly wavy hair cut close, and mocha skin.

In a play by Adrienne Kennedy *(A Movie Star Has to Star in Black and White)* at the Public Theater (New York), his character was on a hospital gurney during the entire performance. Even in that position he commanded the stage—an able partner to Gloria Foster, herself no small force on the boards. When Clayton called to tell me Bob was dead, it was so early in the epidemic we didn't even know that AIDS was what we'd come to call it. It seemed like an isolated, terrifying disaster. He'd been luminescent, an embodiment of the brilliant talent we each hoped we ourselves possessed.

Since then the grim roll call has grown too long. And again we must draw together as Black people. Until recently, men of color were barred from participating in the testing programs which utilized experimental medications. And although women

*Wink of an Eye*

of color are the fastest growing group in the U.S. contracting the AIDS virus, many of the symptoms that women specifically exhibit are just beginning to be accepted as indicators of AIDS. Thousands have already been left without adequate health care. So that in the horror of disease, just as in the horrors of war and poverty, African-Americans as well as other people of color are unprovided for.

I was a speaker at the Gay Pride rally in Central Park when the New York City section of the AIDS quilt was dedicated, and I walked the carefully laid-out rows where quilt workers had strategically placed the needed boxes of tissues. The beautifully crafted quilt panels went on for what seemed like acres, and my brothers were there—the photos, the kente cloth, the snap queen accessories embroidered in red, black, and green. And it seemed too cruel to try and squeeze our wondrous survival of the Middle Passage, slavery, Jim Crow, and benign neglect into such small squares of fabric.

I think it's fitting that a womanly art, quilting, has come to embody a memorial instigated largely by gay men. When we try to discern what gay culture is, it is often found in the combination of things that highlight an irony or a difficult truth. When I watch the few popular media depictions of Black lesbians or gay men, I'm disappointed with the flat acceptance of surface elements —campy mannerisms, colorful clothes, attitude—all of which fall quite short of that difficult truth.

When I look at TV's *In Living Color,* I may chuckle once or twice, but for the most part the Black gay characters, Blaine and Antoine, completely miss the irony of the new vision being created. The writers seem easily satisfied with their ability to startle viewers by showing Black men who lisp, in funny outfits, rather than drawing a real picture of a Black drag queen, a truly outrageous and complex figure in our society. And never would the writers or the stars admit they might like (if they ever took the chance) these two characters they've created. Their casual contempt shows through. When my friend Dan makes over to look like Patti LaBelle, he's acknowledging layers of cultural references that only begin with the feathers. He's postulating many relationships to the ideas of maleness, femaleness, and Blackness. He is a Black man, and it is not an easy laugh.

When I see the AIDS Memorial Quilt, I perceive those layers of cultural reference, where they've come from, and how they are expanded when used in this new way. The Quilt is the reviewing of traditional crafts, imbuing them with more poignant meaning. And the relationship between Black lesbians and gay men is also a similar re-viewing of an old relationship. It is sisters and brothers raised on many of the same foods—some nourishing, some not—reconnecting with different spices in the pot.

Such a new dish is not always easy to prepare. Often the bitter aftertaste of our pasts, as well as heterosexual expectations, are too heavy. Even Black men can think they're John Wayne. And a few of us mistakenly imagine we're Miss Scarlett, or even more problematic, Every Man's Mother. In some cases Black gay men and lesbians have chosen to find no common ground and reject exploration of that which history has provided us. U.S. culture encourages that separation. Men huddled together in front of televised football or wrapping themselves in the pursuit of the perfect dance floor are each a different side of the same attempt to exclude women from male life. And lesbians, certainly more than our straight sisters, often find it easier to reject the rejector than to continue to knock on a closed door. More than once I've found myself ready to walk away from Black gay men who cling stubbornly to male arrogance and gleefully condescend to women.

*Wink of an Eye*

Where the connection seems most easily forged is in activities that provide first an opening and then a context for our caring. My reputation as an out lesbian writer and activist puts me in a fortunate position: Black gay men who know my work will assume the connection and the safety in our relationship.

Between me and other writers, such as Essex Hemphill or Assoto Saint or Colin Robinson, the writing provides a path to each other. Our passion for the use of words as a way to save our lives became an important frame of reference for trust and communication. We form a tenuous yet definite community. The great sadness is that with the AIDS epidemic, too often loss is that reference point.

Recently I rode with four Black men from New York to Philadelphia to attend a memorial service. On the trip we joked about how Black people name children, agonized over what we were writing or working on, caught each other up on gossip. It could have been almost any family trip.

The Black minister leading the service at the church felt compelled (in the face of over a hundred gay people swelling his congregation) to emphasize God's forgiveness of our "sins." On the way home, each of us commented on the minister's lapses. But we really were more interested in talking about our lost brother and all the family things that the minister clearly felt we had no right to. We laughed a lot on that drive back, as Black people frequently do when faced with the unfaceable.

I was in college when my father was dying of cancer. Duke never lost his sense of humor or sense of humanity in his hospital bed. He told me with a mischievous twinkle that his nurse, Walter, was the best in the hospital. The two of them kept up a stream of flirtatious patter right to the end. And my father never acted like that made either of them less a man. All that mattered was that he could still make connections with other people and light up a room with his wit.

Twenty years later, riding home from the memorial service with my friends, I could see the same light. Duke may never have been able to envision such a ride or such company for me, but had he been there, he would have laughed the loudest. And I wonder if his wit, like theirs, was one way to withstand life's harshness. Cocooned in the smooth ride of the rental car, the sweet sound of their voices, the ribald laughter, the scent of aftershave lotion, I again heard the sensuous music of Billie Holiday and John Coltrane I'd learned to love while tending to my father's records. These Black gay men were comforting and familiar, like the expansive clink of my father's pocket change.

JAMIKA AJALON

# *Kaleidoscope*

Dearest Lana,

Time collects itself around empty vessels. This is what I've
come to know—that time can mildew if reflected upon too ada-
mantly. The more we reflect on the past, the more it becomes
obscure. Manipulated by our viewpoints, time remembers what
we make up, although we do not. What is really remembered,
unchanged, are the moments in time when we are fully aware of
life, whether they are the result of unbearable pain, a strong smell,
a song, or high ecstasy.

Memory is time in concentrated moments. And within any
one moment my existence is timeless. Can't say I live by the clock,

and all that hickory-dickory tick-tock shit. A watch is not something I want right now; I'm not interested in trapping time. But you, Lana, taught me to watch my moments.

My first lesson was in London. I was there trying to make my way back to the States. I came with a one-way ticket and very little cash, which quickly dwindled. My visa was up soon and jobs were hard to come by, especially because I was not legal. After months of playing my bongos, doing performance poetry in the tubes and doing odd jobs, I had only made enough money to survive. I was stuck. I don't remember exactly how we met, you and I, or how I ended up in your room that day (though you have an uncanny way of getting me into new positions before I know I am there). It was summertime. It was the first of many days we would spend wedged into the windowsill, our dangling legs catching a breeze now and then. You asked me then if I ever watched time pass.

Sometimes you look out the window and concentrate on something subtly moving through space. Perhaps a leaf. You watch from one moment to the next, using it as a measure. You traced a line along my jaw. "For example," you said, "concentrate on the way my finger is moving down . . ." Your fingers stroked my lips. I put my hand on your face and was pleasantly shocked at the contrast.

My darkredbrown hand against your cheek, like the toasted core of an almond under the afternoon sun that baked both of our skins. Our eyes locked and I was there with you, suddenly without fear. My insecurities made me feel like a rogue. At that moment, the second before our first kiss, when I held your face in my hand, I realized neither one of us cared about much of anything really except the passion in our souls and enjoying the way our complicated rhythms complemented each other. The grace with which we danced made my mind cells melt molten, and we did glide into this grind. I hardly knew it was happening—this dangerous dance of darker and lighter, this class clash mamba. I was uncomfortable in a house that only lots of money could afford. This discomfort seemed to mock our connection, which happened so gracefully in spite of our seemingly opposite positions in life.

This grace is why I have finally allowed myself to write to you. I'm not trying to rehash the past but trying to locate some of the places that left us terrorized to the touch of each other.

This terror is probably what brought on all these strange psychic travels that began after I found this stone. Yeah, it's nothing but a rock, but the places it took me mirrored the fears that eventually had us at each other's throats.

About a month after we met in London, you came to the U.S. to go to school. I was ecstatic. Back in the States, the fears I held at bay (perhaps that we both hid) now rose to the surface. We skillfully danced around them for a long time . . . It got to a point where I truly began to wonder why I bothered. We kept having these arguments that seemed meaningless but unavoidable, which is why I found myself having a tantrum one night in my apartment.

"Why am I so fucking fucked up over you?" I screamed up at the ceiling, in my Lower East Side studio. The stone in my hand held me in check. Its smoothness was strangely comforting. I found that stone in the park right outside your apartment, Lana. After that argument we had.

Hmm, that fight. It was all triggered by that bloody going-away party those people from the Black Poets Co-op gave me in Brooklyn. I'd spent years in and out of this cooperative as a performance artist, needing a space to share and have my work nurtured in some measure. I was often criticized for coming from the "school of angry Black woman" artists or for being too white-influenced (especially the work that was clearly homosexual). I was increasingly nervous as we made our way to the party. I knew we wouldn't pass their "Blackability" test. I grasped your hand as we climbed the steps to the door. Looking down at our intermingling fingers, "Jungle Fever" screamed in my head. *"Fuck you, Spike Lee,"* I thought, "we're both *Blaaack.*" So what was I so nervous about? These people were my supposed peers, yet it seemed as if I were only marginally accepted. I felt you squeeze my hand, Lana, sensing my nervousness. I held on tight.

We opened the door and entered, both of us knowing that we would somehow disrupt some safe illusion of Blackness disguised in appropriated African Nationalist identities. These people were middle and upper class (in their values, if not economically), straight, conservative really, reeking with illusory pride. Their hairstyles reflected these "new" Afrocentric ideals—from hair extensions adorned with cowrie beads, to short Afros, to dreads. Every nuance, sound, gesture, posture, was dictated by the perceived correct way to be Black. Medallions of Africa swung around many a neck. All that rigid uniformity gave me a headache. I felt as if I were walking into some secret society. A strip of kente providing access through the first gate.

We stuck out in our semi-grunge wear that people related with the East Village, our haircuts mocking theirs. I was painfully aware that the shaved parts of my head in some people's eyes disqualified the dreadlocks up front. Your nearly bald head was also a shock; what happened to your womanly crowning glory?

I was aware, though no one acknowledged outright that we were dykes, that most people thought you were the femme. I knew that in some ways my naked dreadlocks and dark skin reflected the dominant notion of masculinity. Or perhaps it was just coincidence that almost immediately I found my niche rapping with a bunch of men around the drums, while you stood across the room with the sisters.

Okay, I did feel a bit of a boost being partially accepted into the men's circle. I liked the power the "butch" role gave me. It turned me on a little even though at the same time it was a bit nauseating to realize that it was *expected* here that I was the butch.

We laughed about this in the bathroom later. Remember? We snuck away to catch our breath and be affectionate in a way we did not wish to test on this particular public.

"So," you said, forcing me against the wall in the bathroom, "you looked like you were in some pretty intense conversations with your men friends."

I laughed and said, "You didn't seem to have a problem with the girls . . . were you scamming on them when I wasn't looking?"

"Maybe I was," you said, pressing in tighter, "and what would you do if I was, seein' how you are the big bad butch?"

I laughed then, catching the sarcasm in your voice and understanding your true meaning. This was always a game to us, these butch/femme roles, but to most of the people around us one of us had to be the man.

"It's funny how clueless these people are," I said.

"Uhuh," you said, unbuttoning my shirt.

"You know," I said, in a breathy sigh, as I felt your hand massaging my breast, "you could have come over and joined the conversation."

"Well, I wasn't asked and you know us womenfolk—we don't have anything intelligent to say," you teased, now kissing my breast. Your tongue circled my nipple. Then you stopped and looked up at me. "I'm more African than any of these mutherfuckahs. Half these assholes goin' on about all of this African shit wouldn't know African unless it had a label on it."

I laughed. It was true. Your father is Ghanaian. What confuses people is the fact that your mother is white, and you are the mix. Your nose, lips, and kinky hair identify you as your father's child, but your light skin almost wipes all that out to an untrained eye.

"All we talked about was lipstick shades," you continued, "and then we started talking about lingerie and . . . ."

"What color *is* your underwear?" I interrupted, running my hand up your thigh.

"Wouldn't you like to know?" you said, moving my hand away.

Then there was a knock on the door. We looked at each other and laughed in unison. *"Buuuusted!"*

"You go ahead," you said, sitting on the toilet.

Outside the door stood Mr. Wanna-be-Eldridge himself.

"Um, Lana is still in there," I said as gracefully as I could, trying to get past him. I always ended up in arguments with this guy. He was a real Mr. Black Power, a farce of a militant, who condemned everything outside the "nation," yet his contradictions screamed. Quiet as it's kept, his girlfriend was white.

"Your girlfriend is a hot number," he said, elbowing me. "Is she all the way gay?"

"Listen, let's not go there," I said.

"Go where, sistaah?" He smiled. "I like 'em darker myself." Yeah, right.

Then you came out of the bathroom. You had a strange look on your face, but I ignored it. I was anxious to move away from this brother before I cracked his nuts. I asked you if you wanted to go out for some fresh air.

It wasn't until later, back at your apartment, that you started into me.

". . . all I'm saying is that they give you props because you can play and look the part of an insider," you said. "A brother had the nerve to come up to me and ask if I was in fact Black!"

At this point I was still so worked over the Eldridge brother. At one point at the party he told me I talked and behaved just like those "Village freaks." I suppose he was talking about the crusty artist with the wild haircut and multiple piercings. He was telling me this as a "brother," concerned about his "African sister" who was about to take this European journey . . . I think he was more concerned that neither one of us was in any way interested in his endangered Black dick. As far as I could see, you had it easy; that same Eldridge that questioned your color would be the one that would try and get inside your underwear, no matter what color *they* happened to be. He would never confront you as he did me. His hard-on would forgive your "deviant" lifestyle.

"Why are you constantly on that tip," I spat back. "Half those so-called peers of mine are always giving me the Oreo treatment."

You were standing your back to me in front of the fireplace.

"What I can't understand, Latto, is why you didn't say anything to that moron when he talked shit about my not being some dark and lovely."

"*Fuck*, Lana, what did you want me to say!?" I was exasperated. A log broke in the fire, forcing a flame to suddenly shoot higher. You were unmoved. I decided to move you. I decided to hit low. "He was probably reacting to your highsiddity . . ." I

*Kaleidoscope*

realized then that in some ways, to me, you *were* a spoiled, rich, wanna-be-ghetto, who had no idea what it was like to really struggle as a black Black person.

You did a diva twirl. I braced myself. Here we go, I thought.

*"What the fuck are you talking about,"* you screamed. You were running your hand over your almost nonexistent nappy hair. "Shit, they labeled me immediately as your dizzy girlfriend, and if I try to act like I have a brain, I'm suddenly a *snob?*"

I knew I was skating on thin ice.

"Well, a lot of us don't get weeklies from our faaaaathers."

"If you think money is who I am . . ." you started.

*"No,* shit . . . no, it's just that you have never had to worry about certain things and your complexion does give you a certain . . ."

"Certain what? *Privilege?* Is that what you have to say, Latto? Because if that is what you have to say, then this time we've spent 'getting to know each other' is all *crap!*"

"Why is it that you have to cop such an attitude whenever we get on these subjects?" I shouted. Wasn't this part of getting to know each other?

"I'm more upset than it seems to matter to you," you said, your face in mine now. You were so angry, and this turned me on, but I also knew I needed some space before this argument went too far and got too deep.

"Listen," I said, grabbing my coat, "I'm tired, and I'm starting to talk out of my ass." I kissed you on the cheek. Besides, I knew the best strategy was to leave in the middle of a fight. I knew you hated that. You slammed the door after me.

I walked down that same road, through Tompkins Square—the same park I crossed so many times on the way back to my own crib. That is where I found this friggin' stone. It's through this stone—and I know you think I'm crazy—but the journeys this stone has taken me on have twisted my world a bit. With the stone I could do something akin to time traveling. It was as if I would enter other worlds and parallel realities through shifting light and color. You see, I understand some things now that I didn't before. Out of my utmost respect and love for you, Lana, I am sending you my journal entries from this time in my life. Please don't think I'm crazy. Maybe after you read this we can come to someplace where we can work this out . . .

*Lana put the letter aside. That girl had balls to write to her out of the blue like this, and then send her fucking journal!!! It bothered Lana, this assumption that she had the time and desire to read all this. She absentmindedly picked up a photo booth picture of the two of them. It was an awful picture really, the lighting not meant to pick up the subtleties in shades. Latto looked much darker than she actually was and Lana looked . . . well, she almost looked white.*

*Fact of the matter was, the eye of that photo booth camera and the eyes of most people were, quite often, the same. How often she'd rebelled against this, how often she rebuffed questions regarding her race with one cutting glare. Sometimes she longed to have some of Latto's color to save her from the constant battle for "legitimacy" with her "own" people. The sad irony, which Latto was helping her to recognize, was that a person's Blackness did not automatically make you "family" to all Black people. Hmmm, Lana thought to herself, though she felt Latto had handled some things too impulsively, in her overreactionary way, she was now understanding what some of this "race rot" was about. So she decided to write her back.*

*Just received your letter, Latto, & the journal. I haven't opened the latter just yet—but I wanted to drop you a note to let you know how excited and apprehensive I was to get it. Why the fuck did you take so long to write me? It's been over a month. We never did resolve anything before you split on me. You asked me why I always had to "cop an attitude" whenever we start talking about this "privileged light skin" bullshit. Well, the reason is that I never felt you really took the time to understand my position. Now I've been forced to sort it out for myself, with myself, and it's hard. Anyway, do you think you can just run in and out of my life like this? Yes, I am bitter.*

*Since you went back to London, a certain mad mood has possessed me as I've been forced to take a closer look at myself. The onion has begun to peel itself. I've had to come to terms with my white side, thanks to my very British mother, who I always resented for not really understanding my Blackness. You know I came to school in the States, to a school with "diversity," hoping I would stumble across the information and nurturing my mother could not give me back home. I've been doing research, you see, on Blacks in America—trying to find some connection, but there is so much that doesn't fit. My language, though English, is so different than American English as you know. So, often simple ideas are lost in translation—hmmm somehow I feel I've gotten lost in translation myself, as I feel extremely rootless. To top it off, I'm pissed that I have to deal with this "tragic mulatto" mess. It's all bullshit really. I'm sure you know what I mean in some ways . . .*

*I say some ways, Latto, because I still think you believe that the world revolves around you. You certainly have heart sending me your fucking journal. It takes a lot of guts to trust me with your journal. I'll read it first then burn it (smile). I'll send this note to you directly . . . Will write more to you later.*

*Love as always,*
*Lana.*

———

March something or other 1994

After Lana and I got into it I left her flat and boogied on down the road to the melody of some sort of aching blues. Something made me stop in the middle of that friggin' dirty park, and that's when this stone caught my eye. I picked it up, and it seemed to fit perfectly in the palm of my hand. I laughed. I wished I'd come up with that pet rock fad.

Shit, I'm brooding over the state that Lana and I are in. I can't let things go on this way. Especially since I'll be leaving for London soon. I want her to come with me. I need to get the fuck out of this diseased place. Things are too muddled here in this rotten apple, and I hate this gotta-do-do-do-fill-my-datebook-and-be-professional-rat-race city. I need a different space to look at some things. It's funny. Time seems to confine me these days . . . and in all the time I spend trying to find time, I seem to lose it. I can't see where I'm going, barely can make out where I've been. It's as if some demon is constantly on my tail trying to rob me of my memory. I need some space to reflect. I hope Lana understands.

Anyway, I'd been doing enough good old lesbian melodrama processing so I decided to vegetate in front of the boob tube. Fuck relationships any fucking way. I pulled myself up and went into the front room.

I remember putting the stone on the set. I remember clicking on the set and the first thing that came blaring out was some irritating talk-show host, Opie, Hopie, or some such hag going on about some multicultural X generation bullshit. I clicked the channel but she wouldn't leave, so I settled back on the couch.

I must have been sleepy. Some static-like force or wave flew through me. I opened my eyes . . . and I am one of the guest panelists on Mz Thing's talk show.

". . . now, Latto here is caught between two worrrrrrrlds, ladies and gentlemen," she preached. "She says that she has some of the same problems as her sisters of lighter complexion because she is often seen as an Oooooreeeeo! Why do you think that is, Latto?"

My voice—I couldn't find it. I whispered "I am dreamin'," but I knew somewhere deep down in my gut that I wasn't.

"Excuse me, what's that?" the hag babbled on. I looked around at the audience and locked eyes with Lana. Before I could say anything to her, the Eldridge brother from the party stood up.

"What I want to know, Latto, is since you recogniiiiiiize that you have, should I say, been polluted by the white neighborhood you grew up in, why is it that you live with the Village freaks instead of with your brothahs and sistahs?"

I look at Lana again, and then just as quick as that I'm back at that party again and Lana is giving me that same "save me" look. The brother is there standing in front of me, waiting for an answer.

I left the brother and went over to Lana . . . and just as it had happened earlier that evening, we went to get a bit of fresh air. We went outside and sat on the porch. I lit a spliff.

"Thanks," Lana says, taking a drag. I put my arm around her and waited for her to talk to me.

"I'm gonna miss you."

"I won't be gone for long—you can always come with or meet me."

Lana took a long drag and then exhaled, saying, "You know I can't do that, babee. I have school. But hey"—Lana shrugged her shoulders—"you know I want to be with you."

I took a pull off the joint Lana now held to my lips and

scooted in closer to her. "I understand you, babydoll," I said, smiling my mischievous smile.

"Oh yeah," she played along with me. "What is it that you understand about me?"

"I understand this," I said as I kissed her sweet lips. Her sweet . . . sweet. Well, anyway. After a bit of necking and schmecking, Lana suggested we go home. Yeah? I remember nodding my head yes.

Then boom—I'm on the friggin' talk show again, staring at Lana, only she is mouthing to me, "You don't understand me," and boom—I fall back into my own friggin' couch in my own friggin' living room. I took that stone off the TV set, chalked it off to just that—being stoned—and put it in a box on my altar.


March 31, 1994

. . . damn, it's as if I'm waking out of some long acid trip. After the first stone adventure—as I've come to call these inexplicable trips I've been on—I looked up Lana and tried to explain to her what was going on. We were of similar mind-sets. Both needing some TLC. Okay, we were both extremely horny, and it was accentuated by that fact that I would be leaving in a couple of days. We commenced to loving each other. Doing the nasty. It was *all* that.

Her bedroom floor was covered with shoes (she had a bad shoe day—getting ready for the party the night before). Shoes, shoes, shoes—platforms, low-heeled sexy shoes. She was up against the wall peeling her clothing off. I watched in boyish awe. Woulda lost all ability to stand if it hadn't been for my sturdy black engineering boots. She dared me to come over, challenging me to finish the job. Her panties were still on, inviting. Grace helped me move toward her without stumbling. I hesitated a moment, kneeling before her. My tongue did a slow drag from under her rib cage to her belly button. I teased, pulling at the elastic of her panties with my teeth. My dick was on hard, my tongue begging to taste. Her legs kept me locked against her as I pressed her into the wall. The grind that ensued sang in swank rhythms. She had me. It seemed to rain a bit in her room . . . warm and gradually hot sprinkles drenching us both in ebb and flow/in liquid penetrations/streams—then waterfalls. I wanted to take her there and feel her shake . . . watch her catch hot raindrops in her mouth.

Bright rays of sun blasted me into the next morning. I noticed I'd put my pet rock on top of Lana's copy of that book by Nella Larson, *Quicksand and Passing*. I was beginning to wonder what was up with her. There was something she was trying to say to me that she was not saying. Wait, I just confused *myself* with that last mess. Anyway, I'd read the book earlier and was curious to see how far into it she'd gotten. I reached over to remove the stone when I felt some strange buzzing in my ear and the rush that I'd felt before meshing with the boob tube the other night. Then I heard a very sad sigh. I shifted around in the bed to give her a cuddle, but it wasn't Lana that I saw lying there.

Instead there was this extremely light-complexioned woman, her flowing green dress sprawled out on the bed, almost making her appear a precocious little girl. Her eyes were wide, as if she expected some response from me. Then she shifted her lids, looking down. She drew some invisible design on the bed with her long, slender fingers.

"Oh come on, you can't be so angry with me to deny me,

Irene," she said in an odd, flirtatious manner. "Perhaps you are still caught up in your dreaming. I'm sorry for waking you."

"Wait! You must have the wrong bedroom," I said, turning to look on the nightstand where the book should have been, "because I'm not Irene and La—" I stopped in midsentence. I heard myself whisper *"Quicksand and Passing,"* but the book was not there. I looked over at the woman, whose hair was a curly mane around her face. I was gradually awakening to some vague memory that I was angry with this woman. "Clare?" I asked.

"I know you're upset with my putting you in the position I did with my husband," she said, getting up and walking over to the mirror, adjusting her petticoat. I flashed to what must have been "earlier," her husband, making some joke about niggers. His pale face relaxed into a smile. He didn't know that we ('cause there were other passables in the room with us) were those niggers he was going on about. His stiff stance gave off the air that he could not, would not, be challenged. He took his privilege for granted. Only Clare laughed out loud, shattering the deadly tense silence her husband seemed to be unaware he caused. I remember feeling this huge rush of anger, but nothing would come out of my mouth. I became an accomplice to my own degradation. I could only glare at Clare, who now challenged my glare in the mirror, then turned around and looked at me with huge pleading eyes.

"Come on. Be a friend. I need to come here and be around my people. My husband is such a bore . . . so very bland . . ."

So now what? She'd chosen white, I had chosen Black, and now she was trying to get her Black back from me. Well, I was not having it! I'd spent so much time coming to terms with myself, my race, my place in "the community." Her very insistence threatened my safety. The incident with her husband earlier only served as a bitter reminder that I was no Blacker than she.

At that point I jumped out of bed about to explode with a tirade of angry accusations, I wanted to kick her out, this reflection of who I tried to forget, but there I was looking at myself in the mirror and Lana's reflection was behind me waking in the bed.

There was some residue of anger that I aimed in Lana's direction in response to her stirring. Why did she constantly give me grief about these Black people not accepting her when I was going through the same thing? Didn't she understand what I was going through, what I was dealing with, knowing that I could never really expect acceptance from many Blacks myself? I can't live up to their standards of what it meant to be Black. I dress "funny," talk "funny," I am a dyke. Even though I am quite obviously Black, this was not "Black" behavior. Even though I could easily act . . . the . . . part . . . *That was it!!* I realized some link. That what Lana had been trying to say to me was that I could pass for "Black." I could assume an acceptance that she did not so easily attain, though she was also Black.

"Babeeee, what are you doing up?" Lana squirmed a bit, cuddling the pillow next to her. "Come back to bed now . . ."

"Lana," I said, crawling next to her. "Why are you attracted to me?"

" 'Cause you're a stroooong Black woman," Lana said playfully, wrapping her arms around my back. "Why do you ask?"

"Just curious," I said.

"What about me attracts you?" Lana came back, kissing my neck.

"Perhaps there's a part of you that I can't reconcile within myself . . . it's part of me that I want but I can't allow myself to have." I was staring off to some distant place.

"Whoooa, honey, it's still too early to be so deep," Lana said, stretching and yawning. "Besides, there is not a part of me that you can't have." She wrapped her legs around me. "I'm all here for you."

I smiled and kissed her. But I had to know. "But what is it that you like about me? Is it the blackness of my skin that's appealing to you?"

Lana grudgingly sat up, to have this conversation she didn't really want to have. This was our last day together. We should have been spending this time loving each other.

"Well, to a certain extent it is, but—" Lana began. This was all I needed to hear to validate my suspicions, to ignite this anger that I still couldn't quite pinpoint.

"I can't believe I've been so blind," I said, getting out of bed and grabbing my jeans off the floor.

"Babee what is *wrong* with you?" Lana asked, confused.

"And you're blind too." The more I thought, the more accusatory I became. I was completely dressed. "I have something you don't have, lots of melanin. You love my skin. You have no idea who I am!"

"Don't you even try and fucking leave on that fucking bull-shit note, Latto." Lana had pushed the covers back and was out of bed now. "I'm tired of you just leaving when the shit gets hot! And why is all this anger directed at me? I know why. Because it's all about you and your I'm-so-black-and-oppressed ass . . . ." Lana's face was red. "You're not even *loooking* at who you're talking to!" She grabbed my shoulder and turned me around to face her. "Look at me! Look me in my dark brown eyes and tell me *I don't know who you are!*"

*Kaleidoscope*

She, in her naked stance, screamed Africa to me. Like one of those Black women whose sway and hand on hip, just so, puts anyone who dare cross them in their place. Something left a bitter taste on my tongue. I shrugged her hand off my shoulder and turned around to head for the door.

"Don't even try to pull that color thing on me, Latto," Lana said in an even, direct tone. "Especially considering the fact that most of the women you've dated have either been white or light like me."

Oooops, there it was. I spun around ready to lash back, but couldn't because I knew she was right.

"Yeah, well, maybe I'm a masochist," I spat.

"What is wrong with you?" Lana said, demanding an answer.

"What is wrong with you, Lana?" I counterattacked. "There is obviously something below the surface that is bothering you," I said, walking over to the nightstand and picking up the book. "What's up with this?"

"What, I can't read a fucking book?" Lana said, snatching it away from me. She threw it against the wall. "Your problem is your ego is so big that you can't get beyond your fucking self. Me-me-me. Well, the world doesn't center around you and I'm tired of you expecting my world to center around you. In fact, it's a damn good thing you are leaving . . ."

All this sounded too much like a breakup to me, and that's not what I wanted. I felt I needed her in my life, but I couldn't come to terms with the why of it all.

"Babee, I want to know what's goin' on with you, but you won't tell me," I said, feeling a little guilty.

"You haven't been listening, Latto." Lana sounded as if she

was about to give up. "Look, just go. I'll pick you up for the airport tomorrow. This talk is useless and I'm tired." Lana fell back on the bed.

No, I thought, I can't leave like this. I slid into bed next to Lana and lay my head on her chest. After a moment she began to play in my hair. No, she didn't really want me to go.

"Lana . . ." I started.

"Ssssh," she interrupted me. "Just listen for a second." She took a deep breath. "You're right, I do have a lot of shit going on concerning a lot of shit that I can't really understand right now. And uh, honey, I think I've been too involved in *your* life, your world, and not my own. That's what I mean when I say it might be better if we separate for a while."

Something inside me begged me to run. To leave this woman and tell her not to bother to come pick me up. Something stronger, feeling safe cuddled up with her, forced me to stay. I curled up into a ball and closed my eyes.

This thought hit me like a sledgehammer: Though I had often wondered if I was somehow a passport to Lana's "Blackness," now I had to wonder if she was my passport to some sort of "otherness," some freedom from racial prescription.


April 1994

Take off in a plane. Your chest is heavy and your head is light. There's nothing like it, especially because my chest is heavy to begin with. "A Love Supreme" whispers to me through my headphones, inviting me to sweet Lana memories. We fucked to all kinda 'Trane and Miles . . . now miles and miles drifting between us . . . it's still all so close to me. As I defy gravity crossing the Atlantic, I hear Africans screaming beneath the ocean's roll. Do you know that their voices still echo into the wind?

I've begun to believe the mosh that I must be doing a Bessie Head and like Elizabeth in *A Question of Power,* crackin' up. Even Lana is peeved. I think she thinks I'm avoiding her, but that couldn't be further from the truth. It's as if I'm on a quest and I can't stop until I've completed some metamorphosis. But yeah, if I were Lana, I would want to send me to the nuthouse too, especially after the hours before I was to leave for the airport.

I'd tried to explain to a friend earlier today that I was on a journey, and I knew, sooner or later, I would have to go back to Europe. This day was the day. My final good-bye. Yet time still eluded me, and though this connection with Lana is deep, I'm wondering if it's worth this struggle. I need music, but I've already packed all my shit up except for these old broken headphones and this crazy stone.

April 15

I sat on my favorite stool, by my windowsill, stone in one hand, my headphones on. Only the headphones weren't plugged into anything on this plane, you see. The stone had inspired some high lullaby and I was diggin' on some old blues. The bluuuz was thick—so thick I could see 'em. I mean I could actually see the notes floatin' in front of me. Whole notes, half notes, quarter notes in a fucking procession of colors. Then the music jumped frenetic, and the notes began to spin around and collide. Soon it was one blur of cracked and shifting designs. I was trapped inside some kind of virtual kaleidoscope. I was trapped inside my mind.

The familiar electric wave did swoosh through my body. I began melding into the music, the colors blinding me. The colors combining and mixing, until it was all white light. At this point I realized I was staring at a lightbulb. One of hundreds of lightbulbs which hung from wires on a low cracking ceiling. I was in somebody's basement. The hissing sound, the sound at the end of a record, made me turn my head and see a Black man sitting— head in hands—over an old phonograph.

He looked up and smiled at me. "Oh, it's you at last. I've been expecting you." A certain hopefulness in his eyes broke the dank atmosphere. There was a smell similar to a stagnant swamp. I took a closer look at the man sitting beside me. Slowly I began to recognize this space, and him.

This basement. These lights. That phonograph with the seductive blues . . . it was the Invisible Man.

"H-h-how did I get here?" I stammered.

"All those who realize their invisibility end up here, underground, at some point," he said. I started to open my mouth to tell him I knew exactly what he meant when he put his hand over it.

"Sssh," he said. Beads of sweat dripped black from his forehead. "Just pay attention. I'm gonna take you on a little journey through a couple of my memories, and then, if you aren't too queasy, you'll get to meet a couple of my friends." A cynical smile spread across his face. He locked eyes with me, and immediately I fell into a trance.

It was through his dark eyes that I became a shadow inside his body. There was that buzzing in my ears and I felt myself spiral into some warm darkness with images flashing around me. Snapshots of what I guessed to be him in some southern setting walking, following some rail tracks . . . of what I guessed to be his family, waving him good-bye . . . then I saw his face—terrorized, sweat dripping. He was blindfolded and bleeding. Then I felt a fist pounding my/his face in.

In the next beat there was a voice—a distinguished-sounding Black man saying something about whites being able to lie so well that it becomes the truth. Then boom, another pounding fist, and loud cheering voices. Then boom—we were sitting in a small musty office across the desk from a very small stout Black man.

". . . but Mr. Bledsoe . . ." I felt Invisible Man's mouth move.

Mr. Bledsoe interrupted him. "You're a nervy little fighter, son, and the race needs good disillusioned fighters!" And bam I heard a door close and we were swirling and diving into that warm darkness again. "Disillusioned fighters" echoed like carnival around us.

In the next moments everything was silent except for the clip-clap of our boots on wet pavement, we were walking up to an apartment building.

"That's enough of that for a while," he said. "I'm afraid that I have almost made you late." Before I could question him he hurried me up the stairs and through the doors of this very small studio apartment. I turned just in time to see the door close. He was gone.

From the kitchen two shadows, a man and a woman, were having a heated discussion. They were both smoking, a bottle of Scotch placed between two partially full glasses. I walked toward them. They seemed not to notice me. Once I was close enough, I recognized both of them from the backs of book jackets. It was Lorraine Hansberry and James Baldwin, shootin' the shit over some Scotch and fags—I shit you not!

*Afrekete*                                                                                                  *160*

"This cultural multi-sculptural mash is all about makin' po-tatoes," Jimmy said, smashing his cigarette into the ashtray. "And I'm not into trying to make some liberal or open-minded Cauca-sian understand me. I'm trying to battle this demon that wants to leave me in fragmented, well-defined pieces. I ain't with that melting pot shit, 'cause I'm that pot, and my Black Latino brother over there at Harvard is that pot, and that high-yellah sistah— always-just-got-her-head-did chick—we called Niecy is that pot. We are a nation of mutts, and America is too cold to be anybody's melting pot. Ain't that right, sistah?" Jimmy directed his question in my direction, including me in the conversation.

Then Lorraine piped in, "Categorized and homogenized. Shit, I'm goin' back under the veil. It's too cold out here for my ashy-black ass!" I laughed so hard at that I nearly fell on *my* ass. Lorraine pulled up a stool for me.

Yep, I tripped with Baldwin and Lorraine, all kinds of criti-cal vibes shooting around. Attempting to get over the pain of being pegged spade, or mulatto, or spic, or Tonto, the Lone Ranger's sidekick. We laughed as we talked about the forgotten episode never broadcast on aboveground TV, when Tonto left his tomahawk in the gringo's back to the tune of "keno sabe," "keno sabe."

. . . and then, tipsy after much libation, I began singin' Frank Sinatra with a little bass, "just have to be meeeeeee!" Boomdadaboomshit boom, give me room, I'm gonna zoomzoom-zooma zoom. Jimmy and Lor joined me in my dance, zoom zooom zzzooom, I gotta be meeee! Tossin' back a bottle of Scotch . . . a pack of Lucky Strikes were now stubs in the ash-tray. Then laughter went just over the edge to tears, and we cried and cried. We were havin' the same vision . . .

You see, Jimmy and Lor had this special kinda boob tube.

The channels didn't pick up regular stations. No, this was more like a crystal ball. You change the channel and you might be watching something that happened in 1846. Click it again and it might be the year 3046 when . . . a person of color, locked in a white room in a graying straitjacket, is moaning, "My mothers-mothersmothersmothersmother mother's mother was a slave." You see, we got to peek into this future, and time seemed to have dragged an eraser across some history—some memory. That type of history might make the natives restless, you see. Amerikkka had finally succeeded in making everyone believe that we were, and always would be, one big happy fucking family. "Can't we all just get along" was the new national anthem.

So yeah, this poor imprisoned colored individual was diagnosed insane because everyone in the thirty-first century knows there were no slaves. There never had been, and there never would be . . . There is no record of it.


Memory.
Just fade out and press delete.


We wept and held each other and that is how Lana found me.


She kissed my lids to wake me.


"What's wrong, baby?" she asked. I shrugged my shoulders. How could I explain? I finally understood that what she and I had been dealing with was bigger than both of us. This whole fucking society is invested in keeping us in boxes and making sure we are afraid to venture outside of these cages. Whenever someone finds the courage to reach outside these cages there is inevitably conflict and fear. Fear of the unknown. Fear of alienation. Fear of being entirely alone in the world.

Lana and I rebelled against these boxes and tried to ignore the source of *our* conflict. We could no longer ignore it or merely place the blame on one another. This light skin/dark skin drama had everything to do with how we saw *ourselves*. We had to stop looking outside ourselves for that love that diminished all the "race rot" crap and the insecurities born out of it. Neither one of us had made it to that point, though the nurturing we gave each other was a step in the right direction. I also knew that nothing I could say would make any of this easier. I asked her when the next space shuttle was due to leave. Her reply was, "Whenever you are."

"I don't want to leave you," I said, staring into Lana's eyes.

"Then why are you?" Lana challenged.

"I have to," I said, trying to convince myself. "I think you are right about the space thing."

Lana moved away from me, pulled her car keys from her bag, and sighed under her breath, "Run girl run."

"Lana, that's not fair," I said, stepping up to her.

"Latto," Lana asked, her body now a stone in my arms, "what is fair?"

I could say nothing so I kissed her, and what we needed from each other boiled over as the fuel level rose to full and then ignited itself.

———

*Kaleidoscope*

April some shit

Here in U fucking K coolin' at a friend's flat, trying to grasp some memory, the moment, and the illusion of time. I realize that all my peoples and our peoples' memories and history are fading with the Afro. How many Black people you know can tell you what a revolution is? I know what Lana and I have is a piece of it.

That's why we, she and I, we gotta go scandalous and boogie this terror out of our bones.

JACKIE GOLDSBY

# Queen for 307 Days:

## Looking B[l]ack at Vanessa Williams and the Sex Wars

Watching the spectacle of star-spangled white women compete for the ideological honor of being decreed Miss America was a ritual that frustrated me, my mother, and my two sisters every September. Nevertheless, we tuned the telly to NBC annually only to be disappointed annually—nary a Nubian princess strolled down the ramp of righteousness bikinied or gowned, much less crowned.

It is, then, a small, peculiar consolation to me that in 1983, before she died, my mother got to see a black woman win the Miss America pageant. Small, because the scarring prospects of radiation therapy all but confirmed my mother's worst projections of her dark-skinned self-image. (Who would want to behold and declare *beautiful* the sutured spot where her left breast once appeared, where the skin of her torso and right nipple were toughened from rads bombarding her chest?) Peculiar, because when my mother witnessed Vanessa Williams's victory, she got to see a black body, a black woman's body—her body—venerated as beautiful and *feminine,* qualities she feared she was losing and which I, her uncloseted dyke daughter, worried I didn't possess as I prepared to go to a black gay bar for the first time that same night.

Actually, my outing had been in the works for a couple of weeks. Hoping to find a scene not overrun by the sorority-pledging Karmann Ghia-driving dykes who were our peers on campus, a school friend suggested that we check out queer nightlife off the beaten (white) track. Fate shook the dice so that our date fell on pageant night. Neither of my sisters was at home to watch the show with my mother, thwarting my plan to slip out of the house unnoticed, unchecked by my mother's silent dissent. I shuddered to think of the long, quiet stare that would've told me everything my mother knew I knew she wanted to say at the sight of me with another woman. It was one thing to be out to my family as gay; it would be another challenge to be seen *being* gay. Scared to leave but unwilling to stay home that night, I showered and dressed for the evening, conflicted over the stand I was about to take. Time was of the essence. Eleven o'clock couldn't come soon enough. I also feared it wouldn't come at all.

I stalled my dread by fixating on the tube and the sizzling sistah from Syracuse University, Miss New York, who was *working* the pageant. Homegirl expertly fielded the banal interview questions, tossing back answers with a quick wit that scored with the audience. During the swimsuit competition girlfriend strutted her stuff like she had no concern for her straightened hair at the imaginary water's doo-defying edge. And then Miss Thing sang some silly show tune like tomorrow was *not* another day. If snapping was as outrageous then as it is now, my fingers would've been blistered. My mother smiled incessantly. I anxiously eyed the clock, wondering if I had time to change my Benetton sweater and L. L. Bean button-down shirt for . . . what? At that moment, I longed to be a beauty queen—confident, radiant, beyond reproach; anything but a nervous, bookwormish college senior who wouldn't be given a second glance by the *serious* sisters I wanted to meet at the bar.

Those last minutes converged: Sue said she'd pick me up at eleven; only ten minutes remained between the last commercial break and the always-boring Saturday night newscast. Those last minutes intensified: the crowd of fifty-two (including the beauties of the colonized commonwealths of Puerto Rico and the Virgin Islands) had been narrowed down to the final quintet, the four runners-up and the one queen. Those last minutes remain precious to me: three white girls smiled graciously as they were named second to fourth almost-wons. My mother edged forward on the couch. I found myself alongside her. Vanessa Williams and Suzette Charles, two black women, were vying for the title. *There was no way we could lose.* My mother held her breath and pulled me close. I checked the clock, hoping Sue would be late. When Suzette Charles's name was called first, my mother hugged me, beaming. "Finally," she half whispered. "Finally." The doorbell rang.

## II.

On weekdays, the Maya Aztec was a Mexican restaurant that catered to white-collar types laboring under fluorescent lights in downtown Oakland. The menu changed on Saturday nights, Sue told me as she killed the ignition, when the space served as the hot spot for the city's black queers.

Waiting in the foyer to pay the cover fee, I could see beyond the crushed red velvet curtains to the TV perched above the bar. Glasses clinked and toasts were shouted over the flickering din of an anchor's voice announcing that Vanessa had made history. The dance mix soared around the room. In between the end of the pageant telecast and my arrival at the bar, in between my mother and Sue, Vanessa's victory aligned my worlds into Aquarian orbit. As Gary Collins serenaded Vanessa during her stroll down victory lane, my mother wept, gave me a kiss, and sent me out of the house with the quietly advised wish that I'd "have a good time with your friend." The black queers at the Maya Aztec were buoyed so high that when the club closed at two o'clock the party moved out and over to East Oakland, where the energy rode itself as far and long as it dared to go.

I even drummed up the nerve to ask an absolutely stunning woman to dance. And I wondered (as I tried not to stare too hard and long at her) whether, on that early autumn night-turned-morning, all of black America, homo- and heterosexual, was reveling in the knowledge that the nationalists hard-lined during our second *fin de siècle* after Malcolm and Martin were killed and before Watts/Chicago/Detroit burned: black *is* beautiful. Now America knew, I thought, as I spun around and faced my partner. *Yes, yes, yes. Wave your hands in the air like you just don't care.* Deal with it, Atlantic City: black is, as Nina Simone declared, the color of my true love's hair, and colored my love was that night. Vanessa Williams's triumph freed me to find every black woman in the house simply FINE.

## III.

July 20, 1984. Bob Guccione sits in his gilt gold faux-royal throne, wired for sound across the continent via the CBS, NBC, and ABC morning news. Leisurely situated, he aggressively defends *Penthouse*'s "journalistic duty" to publish photographs of Williams that would reveal our cultural icon to be less than virginally proper and morally irreproachable. With a sense of timing nothing short of suspicious, photographer Tom Chiapel has emerged with a set of incriminating pictures taken when Williams worked as his studio assistant in 1982. With two months to go before her reign ends, Chiapel sells the sexually explicit images to Guccione, who, on this date, announces his decision to feature them in the September 1984 issue of *Penthouse*. The American public deserves to know about Williams's past, Guccione insists. Pressing his obligation before the media, he waxes ethical: "She [Williams] committed a fraud on the pageant. . . . If she had not accepted the title then someone who was so much more deserving —who had nothing to hide—might have been Miss America in her place."[1] Feeling principled, Guccione rests his case and his back into the plush cushion of his chair.

*Why did Vanessa do such a thing? Didn't she know that, whatever it was, it would come back at her?*

July 23, 1984. The camera lights beam unbearably bright heat. Shutters snap furiously. Microphones cluster like a thorny bouquet in front of her. Williams fends off the volley of questions by insisting on reading her prepared statement: "It is apparent to me now that because of all that has happened during the past week, it would be difficult to make appearances as Miss America."[2]

With these words, Vanessa Williams relinquished the crown and inscribed a large, peculiar place for herself in the history of the pageant. No sooner was she memorialized as the first black woman to earn the Miss America title than she was unceremoniously deposed, having been caught in various sexual acts with a white woman. How "bad" were the *Penthouse* photos? Bad enough to make Williams renounce the title and hand over the tiara to Suzette Charles. Bad enough to sell out the issue of the magazine in which the photos appeared. Bad enough to drive Williams out of public life and into near seclusion for years.

IV.

Recalling this event now, what fascinates me is the seeming ease with which it has been forgotten. Black folks have turned on the force field of memory—which is to say, we've opted not to remember that it happened and instead elected to disregard that the episode bears something worth coming to terms with. *Leave the girl be. It wasn't her fault that white folks turned on her and put her down. Let her get on with her life and move past that ugly thing.*

Lesbians ignored the incident then and, by our continued silence about it now, perpetuate the "we-care-but-we-don't-know-how-to-explain-race" approach so annoyingly common to (white) feminist politics and scholarship. *We, as white women, cannot possibly talk about this issue because we, as white women, cannot fathom how black people, especially black women, must have felt about such a pernicious occurrence of racism.*

But Vanessa Williams's fall from social grace wasn't just about racism. In retrospect, lesbian feminism's absent response to the incident seems particularly disingenuous because, by July 1984, dyke activists and theorists were engaged in—indeed, we were embattled by—the very issues raised by Williams's ascent to, and abdication of, the Miss America crown. The buildup of Williams's public persona as Redeemer Queen and her subsequent demolition as Fallen Dyke encompassed some of the major themes contested in the "sex wars" debates of the 1980s: Just what constitutes sex work and what is its cultural value? Where does the line fall demarcating pornography from erotica? How does a viewer's gaze enable or circumscribe the subjectivity of the object (s)he beholds?

Lesbians kept mum about the incident, but our silence was heard at the time. In what remains the most perceptive analysis of the scandal, Barbara Ehrenreich and Jane O'Reilly astutely observed that Williams's downfall occurred during the same week as Geraldine Ferraro's nomination as Vice President on the Democratic ticket. The electoral prospects of the Mondale-Ferraro pairing triggered a cultural panic over the threat of women's political power. This fear, Ehrenreich and O'Reilly explained, provoked a backlash of misogyny that expressed and justified itself in the persecution of a symbolic homosexual—Vanessa Williams, who had been "documented" in lesbian sex acts.

Writing in the right-of-center *New Republic,* they criticized sex progressives for avoiding this important coincidence. "Given the sexual anxieties aroused by the Democratic convention," Ehrenreich and O'Reilly wrote, "no one has come forth from the sexology profession, from the lesbian community, or from what is known to insiders as the 'pro-sex' wing of the women's movement to offer an exegesis of the photographs themselves."[3]

Perhaps Ehrenreich and O'Reilly were wrong. Perhaps lesbians *did* talk about the photographs among ourselves. Maybe we bought a copy of that September *Penthouse,* and maybe we looked at the pictures alone, with friends, or with lovers. Maybe we liked what we saw, and maybe we talked about why the pictures made us feel that way. Or maybe the photographs angered us. Embittered us. Embarrassed us. Frightened us. Confused us. And maybe we talked about why the pictures made us feel that way. Who among us felt these (and certainly other) ways? To ask Who knows? is my point: no record exists detailing whatever monologues or discussions took place, because lesbians were unwilling to defend or defame the episode publicly. To ask Why not? is the point of this essay.

Why was it that the black woman became the pariah? Starting with Vanessa Williams's shifting claims to the Miss America title, I want to read b(l)ack into the era of the sex wars, in order to interrogate the premises on which we assumed then and continue to assume now that "whiteness" figures the normative center of political and theoretical discussions about sexuality and identity. My questions don't depend on coercing racism out of this moment (that comes to the top, like flotsam) as much as they are concerned with locating *race* in a historical context in order to understand the effective silence which greeted and so defined Williams's fall, to consider why public discourse about colored sexuality remains conventional in its outlook on and response to boundary-shattering incidents such as this. Reviving the episode, then, I don't seek to demean Williams any more than she already has been demeaned. Nor do I intend to suggest that Williams is anything other than what she is: straight. It's not her person that interests me, but the institutional representation of her as a cultural persona, a sexualized type. In fact, the photographs of her matter more, and what they actually show means less than how meaning came to be ascribed to them.

The publication of Vanessa Williams's split images as the beauty-cum-porn queen marked a crucial moment wherein lesbian feminists could—and should—have theorized about the historic workings of *race* in relation to sexuality because it, and not racism, explains most critically why Williams met the infamous end she did. On that basis, by reading retrospectively, by looking b(l)ack into the event, I want to complicate some of the paradigms we currently claim define contemporary lesbian sexual culture. Or, put another way, I want to ask: where and how do (mis)representations of black lesbian sexuality occur and so continue to inform racial antagonisms underlying lesbian feminism, even in the queer, lipstick, baby-boomin' nineties?

## V.

Williams's story begins with the issue of *legal* misrepresentation. From her point of view, she agreed to pose for the pictures under what turned out to be false assumptions. Williams believed Tom Chiapel's assurance that nude stills were common fare in models' portfolios and that the graphic scenes he wanted to compose of her would be discreetly shot—a screen was to have made Williams's face unrecognizable. Not only did the resulting proofs reveal Williams's face, it turned out that she had signed a loosely worded contract that authorized Chiapel to use the photographs for "promotional purposes." Once Williams won the pageant, Chiapel cashed in on the "slip" and the clause. After *Playboy* graciously bowed out of the bidding contest, *Penthouse* stepped forward in the queue, as publisher Bob Guccione secured the rights to copy Williams's image to the tune of $5 million in projected newsstand sales. The decision, for Guccione, was "a simple business choice; whether I get Vanessa into a rift with the pageant people versus the desirability of these photographs in the eyes of my readers. Of course I went with my readers."[4]

By doing so, Guccione also touched off arguments about the nature of "desirability" itself. By purchasing and printing the photographs of Williams's "modeling session," Guccione not only engineered a monetary coup for his magazine, he also leveled a body blow against the concept of the pageant itself: the photos framed the Miss America contest as simply another for(u)m for sex work. *Penthouse*'s publication of the images implicated the pageant in its cultural practice of making a commodity out of sex. Pageant chairman Albert Marks, Jr., may have decried the photographs as being unfit to show to his wife,[5] but presenting Williams for his readers' consumption as a centerfold treat, Guccione dealt back the pageant's card of respectability, for the pageant, no less than *Penthouse,* exploited Williams as an object of appeal. Indeed, Williams's status as the feminine-elect established common ground for these seemingly opposed venues of "womanhood," as the chaste queen and the salacious poser became one and the same thing.

Seemingly siding with the feminist critique of beauty pageants, *Penthouse* also positioned itself in line with what would ostensibly be the "sex radical" response to the crisis. Publishing the photographs championed anticensorship politics and affirmed the legitimacy of the social display of sexuality. However, linking these perspectives only served to isolate their weakest points, which made them seem discontinuous, and so, illogical. For *Penthouse* didn't merely print the photographs; the images' resonance mattered as much as, if not more than, their literal appearance on the magazine page. *How* they came to appear when they did— *how* the images functioned to confuse their own place in time, as history—constructed a meaning for the images for which feminist theory couldn't account. Simultaneously conjoining with and upending the critiques of beauty pageants and censorship politics (in other words, by fucking with them), *Penthouse* dissed them both.

On one side, Williams's election knotted arguments decrying the exploitative nature of the pageant. The crowning of a black woman deflected charges that the competition endorsed the sexist objectification of women; Williams's victory confirmed America's liberal promise of do-it-yourself political improvement. How could anyone complain that the contest's outcome was anything but "progress"? Didn't the nation have another racial "first" to add to the mythic melting pot of American achievement? Wasn't this a fulfillment of the Civil Rights dream state of affairs—a black woman representing the ideal of American femininity? *Didn't my mother cry at the thought of this affirmation? Didn't I see black women differently that night?*

Failing to condemn the racially specific iconography of "womanhood" promoted not only by the pageant but by the culture at large, antipageant feminists were hard-pressed to say anything about Williams's coronation one way or another. Once the scandal reared into view, these activists and theorists were left unable to address the complexities underlying her fall. Without the critical means to expose the racialized functions of patriarchal image-making, we settled for burning our memories of the year in the flames of conspiracy theories. *Why was it that a scandal cropped up when a black woman won? Was it just coincidence or expedient that a black woman was also named first runner-up—that way, no one could say that the debacle was racistly motivated, right? How could the pageant officials not know about the pictures before the contest began?*

The existence of the photographs pinned the pageant's liability to the wall and exercised the discretion that contest officials presumably should have invoked. That is, the photographs functioned as a screening committee should have, dividing Williams's present from her past and judging her "fitness" to compete in troublesome accordance with the standards such distinctions imply. However, this break in process and time empowered the images to wreak havoc in Williams's world. The pictures were taken at a moment when, ostensibly, she had no idea that they would overdetermine her career. Once the photos hit the newsstands, their value and meaning transformed not around the fact of her ignorance, but around the *representation* of her knowledge.

The question of whether Williams knew what she was doing is reflected by what it *looked* like she knew: how to eat snatch, how to please herself. It becomes impossible to classify and so withdraw the images as stock stereotypes from straight pornography precisely because Williams was the paragon of American prenuptial chastity; the beauty queen became, irrevocably, the derivative deviant that is the dyke. Though the pictures were taken *before* the pageant, their publication and the consequences they exacted switched the order of the incidents. The staging of the photographs consumed the moment of Williams's televised coronation and replayed the instance of her crowning as the specter haunting the scene. In terms of what caused Williams more trouble, which came first—the crown or the pictures?

The photographs didn't document history (as we might expect), but rather sought to replace it, as they confused temporality as a source causality. The crown, not the representation of the early images, brought about Williams's downfall. The images indicted the pageant as the culprit: if Williams wasn't Miss America, the photos wouldn't matter and would mean nothing. From yet another angle, then, the publication of the photos revoked the pageant's license to moral authority. At the same time, the images challenged feminist arguments promoting the value of sex as labor. The negatives suggest this comparison. In its original state, raw film reverses an image's codes—black objects whiten and white fields darken.

In this way, the sex acts Williams portrayed were inscribed on the film stock in "white" terms—which is how most black folks denied the incident altogether. *Her white boyfriend put her up to it. A white photographer took the pictures. A white woman posed in the photos with her and no one told her name. A white media mogul published them. White folks are freaky dekes, ain't they now?* As a product and form of technology, film replaces the labor of representation. But how does race condition the terms on which representation occurs? How does race effect (and affect) one's agency within the marketplace of sex?

Williams raised these questions herself when she repudiated the photographs as evidence of her abuse. "I feel as if I were just a sacrificial lamb," she explained. "The past just came up and kicked me. I felt betrayed and violated, like I had been raped."[6] With her consent inconsequential to the proceedings—indeed, the value of the pictures no doubt increased to the extent that she couldn't claim ownership—Williams insisted that the positions she took in the photos were "posed" and not "spontaneous."[7] This distinction is remarkable not only because it inverts what the two terms actually mean (posing becomes an instance not of deliberation, but of acting without will; spontaneity indicates the presence, not the abandonment, of intention) but because it opens for view the functions of race in relation to the production of sex.

Williams was in no position to overturn the forces of consumerism that had been stimulated by Guccione's appropriation of the pictures. Nor could she revise the racial symbolism of film and the acts depicted in the images, precisely because the historical construction of black sexuality is always already pornographic, if by pornography I mean the writing or technological representation and mass marketing of the body as explicitly sexual.[8] Public auction ads, bills of sale, notices offering rewards for the return of fugitive slaves, and probate records listing black laborers as "assets" document the fact that, under chattel slavery, black bodies were, literally, capital.[9] To perpetuate slavery efficiently, procreation became necessary, especially after the trade was banned in 1808. Slaves' ability to reproduce compromised the ideal(ism) of pleasure, since black desire was pressed into service to generate wealth. Black babies meant more backs to break over cotton, tobacco, rice, sugar, and indigo, which meant more crop yields, which meant more cash flow. The mere capacity to sire or bear offspring enhanced a black slave's price on the auction block. Mammies and uncles, concubines and studs, breeders all: slavery constituted a form of sex work.

That Tom Chiapel presided over an auction at which he sold the photographs of Williams to the highest bidder; that Williams's body was sold to (re)produce higher profits for her "master," Bob Guccione, recalls not only the legacy of the sexual politics of

*Afrekete*                                                                        *178*

American slavery but also the sex radicals' labor theory of sexual value. To understand why Williams was pinioned between the ideological forces of the Miss America pageant and *Penthouse,* between liberalism and libertinism, we must return to the nineteenth century, to the moment when the terms and limits within which black sexuality was (and continues to be) publicly discussed were articulated and legitimated.

If black sexuality was, in the nineteenth century, the object of property, one meaning of "freedom" was the right to sex. For the fugitive slave-turned-author Harriet Jacobs, this proved to be a dilemma which, if it could be resolved, promised a hope of liberty that rivaled legal emancipation. Barred from pursuing a romance with a black carpenter and torn between yielding to the abusive advances of her master and consorting with another white man who took an interest in her, Jacobs observed:

> It seems less degrading to give one's self, than to submit to compulsion. There is something akin to freedom in having a lover who has no control over you, except that which he gains by kindness and attachment. A master may treat you as rudely as he pleases, and you dare not speak; moreover, the wrong does not seem so great with an unmarried man, as with one who has a wife to be made unhappy. There may be sophistry in all this; but the condition of a slave confuses all principles of morality, and, in fact, renders the practice of them impossible.[10]

In this, her autobiography published in 1861, Jacobs speaks profoundly, right on up to our own age. "The condition of a slave" did influence black "principles of morality," specifying "the practice of them" to be heterosexual. For slavery's logic suggested that

*Queen for 307 Days*

mastery of one's self implied mastery not only of one's sexual desire but one's capacity to reproduce. This ideology privileged and enforced heterosexuality as authentically "black" because the regulation of black reproductive rights demanded this definition.

No wonder, then, that black homophobes characteristically malign black homosexuality as a "white thing," as a relationship that, by definition, reenacts slavery itself.[11] No wonder, then, that black folks use "mama" and "daddy" or "brother" and "sister" as sexual references—"Come on, mama, and give me some sugar"; "Oh, daddy, don't stop now!"; "Brotherman got some boomin' boody"; "That sister is fresh": the alienation of black sexuality gets recuperated by the familiarity of the family, the historically constructed site of freedom.

That the photographs possessed the cultural value to compromise Williams's claims to herself and her authority is implicated in this history. Unlike her victory, it's neither a small nor a peculiar coincidence that she didn't own the copyright to her own image. Without legal standing, Williams couldn't freely choose to reproduce herself and so, again, was figured by the pictures as homosexual. These connections went unexamined, though, because "prosex" within black cultural discourse translates historically as "heterosex." On the other side, "prosex" arguments within lesbian feminist theories provide much-needed space to consider other social categories (in this instance, homosexuality) with which to describe historical experience. However, to the extent that feminist "prosex"-ists undertheorized black history in their various formulations, we were again left without an interpretative means to understand why the images of Williams took on the meaning and force they did.

Hence, Williams had nowhere to go but away. Unable to act on her own behalf, she could not compete against the needs of either the pageant (so she resigned from the throne) or of *Penthouse* (so she retreated from public scrutiny). So thoroughly exploited by the mass culture that offered to proclaim her one of its own, Williams accepted refuge—freedom—in the anonymity of private life.

VI.

Since that time and between her twin triumphs of "Like a Virgin" and "Justify My Love"—between offering herself as a bridal queen and a demimonde dyke type—Madonna has made a whole lot of money doing what Williams was castigated for: transgressing sexual boundaries and flouting gender/racial taboos. I would argue that winning the Miss America pageant defied, however problematically, the cultural maxim that black women are objects of desire meant only for backroom trysts and not living-room-mantel material, and that the *Penthouse* photos publicized the continually denied fact that black women do the nasty among ourselves and with female others. Why is it that Williams paid such a high price for striking her poses, and that Madonna, appropriating the practices of marginal cultures in her stage act, is rewarded so generously?

One reason, no doubt, would be the respective realms in which they work(ed): admittedly, the runway of the Miss America pageant is floodlit by an anachronistic conservatism that stadium rock has always opposed, what with its emphasis on rebellion and hyperbole (how else are you going to reach the cheap seats?). Williams wanted to make it by belonging; Madonna succeeds by refusing her prescribed place in the cultural order. The place where each situates herself, the genre each calls her own, levels the issue of gender with that of race, and it is there where a Madonna-like figure benefits from the sexual SOS sent up by lesbian feminism.

I happen to believe that the sex wars (not to mention the cultural logic of junk-bond capitalism) made Madonna plausible and profitable. As the boy toy turned clit tease, she played out the notion of the gaze (who's looking at and getting off on whom and taking it to the bank?); proselytizing the joys of spanking on Arsenio Hall's show, the material girl got late-night America thinking about the pleasures of paddles and lite s/m, during that same interview thanking the "loose" black girls who encouraged her childhood defiance and, on vinyl and video, ripping off voguing from black gay men. Part of Madonna's glitter and glee is that she's a cultural robber baron, taking what she wants from wherever she roams, incorporating it into her rhetoric of self-presentation, without so much as an ethical doubt as to the political implications of her gestures.[12]

Gazing on the prosex possibilities of a world beat without the Third World, feminist discourses have, ultimately, given Madonna a body politic to deconstruct (and a racial aesthetic to exploit) because they do, in fact, take race as their referential starting point—only they position whiteness as the origin of all theories postmodern, if not the very idea of theory itself. Though other "post" theories (namely structuralism and, now, feminism) are on the politically correct tip since they propose a new rationality based on pluralism, fragmentation, and nonlinear/narrative worldviews, they nevertheless manage to leave race less conceptualized than either gender or sexuality because theorists misconstrue what "race" can mean.

This is why Madonna studies are now a cottage industry in

academia and a figure like Vanessa Williams is shunted to the analytical wayside. Presuming that *racism* is the first and last word bracketing the meanings and experiences of colored politics and culture forgoes understanding the complexities of colored subjectivity. For example, what do I do with the fact that, as I remember them, those photographs of Williams turned me on? I know that part of my excitement came from the shock of (for me, anyway) the new—I had never seen a black woman being made love to by another woman. In that moment—as much as on the night when she won the pageant—I felt affirmed in my womanhood, my lesbianness, which, on both of those occasions, reflected to me a self-image that I needed at the time. And yet, I'm also aware that my pleasure wasn't entirely innocent; that, in fact, it depended on the expenditures of power I've tried to describe in this essay. If we can deal with such complications as they come to us in the figurative forms of a Madonna, why do we shy away from them in the symbol of Vanessa Williams? Accounting for racism is never wrong, but it's necessarily limited and limiting, because it prevents us from seeing how the workings of race are fraught with ambivalences that empower us all, in sometimes discomfiting ways.[13]

There was—and still is—so much to say about the linkages between race and sexuality in American culture. However, our blindness to the political meaning of Vanessa's body, the abysmal silence enclosing her fall, describe this misunderstanding and underscore how the history of black sexuality informed Williams's calamity. It is neither a small nor a peculiar consolation to me that Williams's dark skin was seen and read in such a way that allowed her to pass from consideration precisely because she lay right before our very eyes.

*Queen for 307 Days*

# VII.

As quiet as it's been kept, the (hi)story of Williams's fall from grace should have gotten airtime during the sex wars debate. It didn't, partly because it happened so fast—without warning, without seeming cause, since her term was only weeks from its close. The main reason was that none of us knew how to talk about it, and that preemptive assumption resulted from the legacy of nineteenth-century sexual ideologies about race. If having the right to (hetero)sex constituted a form of freedom, so did the right to keep it private. As long as black sexuality was a market commodity, white voyeurism was an always-present threat, as black sex was subject to public inspection ("interventions" made in the name of rape and lynching). Silence, then, affords a measure of control; a strictly held confidentiality amplifies the pleasures of self-determination.[14] *If no one says anything, then no one will remember. What you don't remember you don't know, and what you don't know can't hurt you.*

If history chronicles the facts and processes of transformation, the history of black sexuality must be written, in order to effect revisionary change. Otherwise, lives will continue to be lost: the silence burying the memory of Williams is the same silence that keeps the mortality rates of black infants, black crack addicts, and black AIDS victims abnormally and immorally high. And this same silence renders black (homo)sexuality invisible both in lesbian feminist discourse and in black historiography.

At the very least, black dykes should have taken up Williams as an ascendant/fallen icon and viewed the episode as a textual moment to be, yes, intellectualized. It was an opportunity for us to create the language and discursive space we need to confront the ways in which sex is illin' our communities. That language and space requires us to specify our sexuality as black and lesbian and to *define* what we mean by those terms; pictures, as the photographs proved, don't necessarily tell the one thousand truths those words can tell. Relying on fiction to do the work of historiography is a dangerous substitution to make, one that the Williams debacle and the novel-into-film projects of *The Color Purple* and *The Women of Brewster Place* demonstrate. While both brought black lesbianism to the Reagan-era masses, while we were right to take measured gratification in these well-meaning translations of our self-images and cultural expressions, the risk of rejection and betrayal was not resolved. Witness the dyke-bashing Alice Walker received on our behalf and the convenient erasure of "the two" from the TV series version of Gloria Naylor's book (black dykes are tolerable for the purposes of a one-shot miniseries but not on a weekly prime-time basis). Even if Spike Lee wouldn't let Opal Gilstrap have it, I took Nola Darling's nipple for my own, but I'd rather not rely on Spike, Walker, or Naylor to realize my desire on-screen or on the page. I don't want to cede that responsibility to others, and I want to pursue other expository forms that require me to claim it all—my race, my gender, my class, and my sex—at once.

VIII.

*Vanessa's coming back. Guest-starring on TV movies of the week. Hosting music-video shows. Starring in her own. Recording chart-*

*busting, Grammy-nominated dance pop with the hottest producers in*
*Hollywood. Marrying a righteously handsome black man with whom*
*she's delivering beautiful children. Posing for the cover of* Ebony
*magazine. Doing all the right things. Consciously.*

Vanessa Williams's return is not—and should not be—contingent on her committing cultural amnesia and forgetting what happened to her. The point is not to remember her reign either as a triumph or as a failure, but to refuse the silence of critical complacency and to claim those parts of our history that are painful or otherwise difficult to account for.

As lesbian identity comes to be understood as a history with its own breaks and continuities, we must consider how race is and is not a seamless narrative as well. I'm trying to imagine how I would've told this story to my mother—she died before the scandal hit. And even if she had managed to live through it, she couldn't have seen it—the cancer had metastasized to her brain and shut down her sight. So I would have had to tell her, in words, that Williams had lost the crown. I would have had to discuss with her, in words, why the pictures banished Williams from further public view. I would have had to assert to her, in words, why what I do in bed with a woman is and is not, necessarily, what Williams did in the photographs. I would have had to risk, in other words, falling from grace in my mother's blind eyes. By writing this now, about us—Vanessa Williams, my mother, and myself—I see myself absolved.

# NOTES

1. Bob Guccione, quoted in Barbara Ehrenreich and Jane O'Reilly, "Sexual Forboding," *The New Republic,* August 27, 1984, p. 11.

2. Vanessa Williams, quoted in *The New York Times,* July 24, 1984.

3. Ehrenreich and O'Reilly, p. 12.

4. W. Plummer, "Haunted by Her Past," *People,* August 6, 1984.

5. Marks's exact words were as follows: "As a man, as a father, as a grandfather, as a human being, I have never seen anything like these photographs. Ugh. I can't even show them to my wife." See ibid., p. 80.

6. "Vanessa's Story," ibid., p. 87.

7. "Ex-Miss America Endures Pain," *Jet,* August 6, 1984, pp. 60–62.

8. Erotica seems to me to be defined by a presumed rarity and ascribed aesthetic of scarcity and restraint. Pornography, by contrast, displays itself as common, abundant, and excessive. Erotica "testifies" and pornography "confesses."

9. Credit for this original insight is due to Ida B. Wells, who advanced this argument in her brilliant report *Southern Horrors: Lynch Law in All Its Phases* (Arno, 1969 [1982]).

10. Harriet Jacobs, *Incidents in the Life of a Slave Girl,* edited by Jean Fagin Yellin (Harvard, 1987), p. 55.

11. For example, the television series *In Living Color* reinforces this assumption through the snapping predilections of the show's gay culture critics, Blaine and Antoine. Whether the men are on film or on the books, they invariably proclaim their lust for white men. They never ogle, for example, Denzel Washington or Wesley Snipes or Kid (of Kid 'n Play).

12. It stuns me that Madonna can brazenly assume, due to the marketability of her name, that the roles of Evita Perón and Frida Kahlo should be hers for the film option taking.

*Queen for 307 Days*

13. For a politically brave and theoretically rich discussion of this point, see Kobena Mercer's essay "Skin Head Sex Thing: Racial Difference and the Homoerotic Imaginary," in *How Do I Look? Queer Film and Theory,* edited by Bad Object Choices Staff (Bay Press, 1991).

14. I want to be clear here: I'm not proposing a "definitive" interpretation of the conditions affecting expressions of black sexuality, nor do I mean to be deterministic. To believe that slavery decided everything closes off the possibilities for—and the truth of—resistance and change. I'm sure that black men and women had pleasurable encounters with each other beyond the master's desirous gaze. Indeed, in my own unsystematic wanderings through academic scholarship and popular culture, I've been amazed at the abundance of joyfully bold depictions of black sexuality in literature, film, music, magazines, and newspapers. My point is that history matters insofar as it constitutes a profound, formative influence which produces the language we use to describe what happens to us, and certain words are given more credence than others.

PAT PARKER

# *Where Will You Be?*

Boots are being polished
Trumpeters clean their horns
Chains and locks are forged
The crusade has begun.

Once again flags of Christ
are unfurled in the dawn
and cries of soul saviors
sing apocalyptic on air waves.

Citizens, good citizens all
parade into voting booths

and in self-righteous sanctity
X away our right to life.


I do not believe as some
that the vote is an end,
I fear even more
It is just a beginning.


So I must make assessment
Look to you and ask:
Where will you be
when they come?


They will not come
a mob rolling
through the streets,
but quickly and directly
move into our homes
and remove the evil,
the queerness,
the faggotry,
the perverseness
from their midst.
They will not come
clothed in brown,
and swastikas, or
bearing chest heavy with
gleaming crosses.
The time and need
for ruses are over.

They will come
in business suits
to buy your homes
and bring bodies to
fill your jobs.

They will come in robes
to rehabilitate
and white coats
to subjugate
and where will you be
when they come?

Where will we *all* be
when they come?
And they will come—

they will come
because we are
defined as opposite—
perverse
and we are perverse.

Every time we watched
a queer hassled in the
streets and said nothing—
It was an act of perversion.

Every time we lied about
the boyfriend or girlfriend

*Where Will You Be?*

at coffee break—
It was an act of perversion.

Every time we heard,
"I don't mind gays
but why must they
be blatant?" and said nothing—
It was an act of perversion.

Every time we let a lesbian mother
lose her child and did not fill
the courtrooms—
It was an act of perversion.

Every time we let straights
make out in our bars while
we couldn't touch because
of laws—
It was an act of perversion.

Every time we put on the proper
clothes to go to a family
wedding and left our lovers
at home—
It was an act of perversion.

Every time we heard
"Who I go to bed with
is my personal choice—
It's personal not political"

and said nothing—
It was an act of perversion.

Every time we let straight relatives
bury our dead and push our
lovers away—
It was an act of perversion.

And they will come.
They will come for
the perverts
& it won't matter
if you're
        homosexual, not a faggot
        lesbian, not a dyke
        gay, not queer
It won't matter
if you
        own your own business
        have a good job
        or are on SSI
It won't matter
if you're
        Black
        Chicano
        Native American
        Asian
        or White
It won't matter
if you're from
        New York

*Where Will You Be?*

or Los Angeles
Galveston
or Sioux Falls
It won't matter
if you're
Butch, or Fem
Not into roles
Monogamous
Non Monogamous
It won't matter
if you're
Catholic
Baptist
Atheist
Jewish
or MCC.

They will come
They will come
to the cities
and to the land
to your front rooms
and in *your* closets.

They will come for
the perverts
and where will
you be
When they come?

MICHELLE CLIFF

# Screen Memory

The sound of a jump rope came around in her head, softly, steadily marking time. Steadily slapping ground packed hard by the feet of girls.

*Franklin's in the White House.* Jump/slap. *Talking to the ladies.* Jump/slap. *Eleanor's in the outhouse.* Jump/slap. *Eating chocolate babies.* Jump/slap.

Noises of a long drawn-out summer's evening years ago. But painted in such rich tones she could touch it.

A line of girls wait their turn. Gathered skirts, sleeveless blouses, shorts, bright, flowered—peach, pink, aquamarine. She spies a tomboy in a striped polo shirt and cuffed blue jeans.

A girl slides from the middle of the line. The woman recognizes her previous self. The girl is dressed in a pale blue starched pinafore, stiff and white in places, bleached and starched almost to death. She edges away from the other girls; the rope, their song, which jars her and makes her sad. And this is inside her head.

She senses there is more to come. She rests her spine against a wineglass elm. No one seems to notice her absence.

The rope keeps up its slapping, the voices speed their chanting. As the chant speeds up, so does the rope. The tomboy rushes in, challenging the others to trip her, burn her legs where she has rolled her jeans. Excitement is at a pitch. Franklin! Ladies! Eleanor! Babies! The tomboy's feet pound the ground. They are out for her. A voice sings out, above the others, and a word, strange and harsh to the observer's ears, sounds over the pound of feet, over the slap of rope. *Bulldagger! Bulldagger! Bulldagger! Bulldagger!* The rope sings past the tomboy's ears. She feels it heat against her skin. She knows the word. Salt burns the corners of her eyes. The rope-turners dare, singing it closer and closer. Sting!

The girl in the pinafore hangs back. The girl in the pinafore who is bright-skinned, ladylike, whose veins are visible, as the ladies of the church have commented so many times, hangs back. The tomboy, who is darker, who could not pass the paper bag test, trips and stumbles out. Rubbing her leg where the rope has singed her. The word stops.

Where does she begin and the tomboy end?

Fireflies prepare to loft themselves. Mason jars with pricked lids are lined on the ground waiting to trap them. Boys swing their legs, scratched and bruised, from adventure or fury, from the first rung of a live oak tree. Oblivious to the girls, their singing —nemesis. The boys are swinging, talking, over the heads of the girls. Mostly of the War, their fathers, brothers, uncles, whoever represents them on air or land or sea.

The woman in the bed can barely make out their voices, though they speak inside her head.

Sudden lightning. A crack of thunder behind a hill. Wooden handles hit the dirt as the rope is dropped. Drops as big as an elephant's tears fall. The wind picks up the pace. Girls scatter to beat the band. Someone carefully coils the rope. Boys dare each other to stay in the tree.

The girl in the blue pinafore flies across the landscape. She flies into a window. To the feet of her grandmother.

Slow fade to black.

The woman in the bed wakes briefly, notes her pain, the dark outside.

Her head is splitting.


She and her grandmother have settled in a small town at the end of the line. At the edge of town where there are no sidewalks and houses are made from plain board, appearing ancient, beaten into smoothness, the two grow dahlias and peonies and azaleas. A rambling rose, pruned mercilessly by the grandmother, refuses to be restrained, climbing across the railings of the porch, masking the iron of the drainpipe, threatening to rampage across the roof and escape in a cloud of pink—she is wild. As wild as the girl's mother, whom the girl cannot remember, and the grandmother cannot forget.

The grandmother declares that roses are "too showy" and therefore she dislikes them. (As if dahlias and peonies and azaleas in their cultivated brightness are not.) But the stubborn vine is not for her to kill—nothing, no living thing, is, and that is the first lesson—only to train.

While the rose may evoke her daughter, there is something

else. She does not tell her granddaughter about the thing embedded in her thigh, souvenir of being chased into a bank of roses. Surely the thing must have worked its way out by now—or she would have gotten gangrene, lost her leg clear up to the hip—but she swears she can feel it. A small sharp thorn living inside her muscle. All because of a band of fools to whom she was nothing but a thing to chase.

The grandmother's prized possession sits against the wall in the front room, souvenir of a happier time: when her husband was alive and her daughter held promise. An upright piano, decorated in gilt, chosen by the King of Bohemia and the Knights of the Rosy Cross, so says it. The grandmother rubs the mahogany and ebony with lemon oil, cleans the ivory with rubbing alcohol, scrubbing hard, then takes a chamois to the entire instrument, slower now, soothing it after each fierce cleaning.

The ebony and the ivory and the mahogany come from Africa—the birthplace of civilization. That is another of the grandmother's lessons. From the forests of the Congo and the elephants of the Great Rift Valley, where fossils are there for the taking and you have but to pull a bone from the great stack to find the first woman or the first man.

The girl, under the eye of the grandmother, practices the piano each afternoon. The sharp ear of the grandmother catches missed notes, passages played too fast, articulation, passion lost sliding across the keys. The grandmother speaks to her of passion, of the right kind. "Hastiness, carelessness, will never lead you to any real feeling, or," she pauses, "any lasting accomplishment. You have to go deep inside yourself—to the best part." The black part, she thinks, for if anything can cloud your senses, it's that white blood. "The best part," she repeats to her granddaughter seated beside her on the piano bench, as she is atilt, favoring one hip.

The granddaughter, practicing the piano, remembers them leaving the last place, on the run, begging an old man and his son to transport the precious African thing—for to the grandmother the piano is African, civilized, the sum of its parts—on the back of a pickup truck.

A flock of white ladies had descended on the grandmother, declaring she had no right to raise a white child and they would take the girl and place her with a "decent" family. She explained that the girl was her granddaughter—sometimes it's like that. They did not hear. They took the girl by the hand, down the street, across the town, into the home of a man and a woman bereft of their only child by diphtheria. They led the girl into a pink room with roses rampant on the wall, a starched canopy hanging above the bed. They left her in the room and told her to remove her clothes, put on the robe they gave her, and take the bath they would draw for her. She did this.

Then, under the cover of night, she let herself out the back door off the kitchen and made her way back, leaving the bed of a dead girl behind her. The sky pounded and the rain soaked her.

When the grandmother explained to the old man the circumstances of their leaving he agreed to help. To her granddaughter she said little except she hoped the piano would not be damaged in their flight.

There is a woman lying in a bed. She has flown through a storm to the feet of her grandmother, who is seated atilt at the upright, on a bench which holds browned sheets of music. The girl's hair is glistening from the wet but not a strand is out of place. It is braided with care, tied with grosgrain. Her mind's eye brings the ribbon into closer focus; its elegant dullness, no cheap satin shine.

Fifty cents a yard at the general store on Main Street.

"And don't you go flinging it at me like that. I've lived too long for your rudeness. I don't think the good Lord put me on this earth to teach each generation of you politeness." The grandmother is ramrod-straight, black straw hat shiny, white gloves bright, hair restrained by a black net. The thing in her thigh throbs, as it always does in such situations, as it did in front of the white ladies, as it did on the back of the old man's truck.

The granddaughter chafes under the silence, scrutiny of the boy who is being addressed, a smirk creasing his face. She looks to the ceiling where a fan stirs up dust. She looks to the bolts of cotton behind his head. To her reflection in the glass-fronted cabinet. To the sunlight blaring through the huge windows in front, fading everything in sight; except the grandmother, who seems to become blacker with every word. And this is good. And the girl is frightened.

She looks anywhere but at the boy. She has heard their "white nigger" hisses often enough, as if her skin, her hair, signify only shame, a crime against nature.

The grandmother picks up the length of ribbon where it has fallen, holds the cloth against her spectacles, examining it, folding the ribbon inside her handkerchief.

The boy behind the counter is motionless, waiting for his father's money, waiting to wait on the other people watching him, as this old woman takes all the time in the world. Finally: "Thank you kindly," she tells him, and counts fifty cents onto the marble surface, slowly, laying the copper in lines of ten; and the girl, in her imagination, desperate to be anywhere but here, sees lines of Cherokee in canoes skimming an icebound river, or walking to

*Afrekete* 200

Oklahoma, stories her grandmother told her. "They'd stopped listening to their Beloved Woman. Don't get me started, child."

The transaction complete, they leave—leaving the boy, two dots of pink sparking each plump cheek, incongruous against his smirk.

The woman in the bed opens her eyes. It is still, dark. She looks to the window. A tall, pale girl flies in the window to the feet of her grandmother. Seated at the piano, she turns her head and the grandmother's spectacles catch the lightning.

"I want to stay here with you forever, Grandma."

"I won't be here forever. You will have to make your own way."

"Yes, ma'am."

"We are born alone and we die alone and in the meanwhile we have to learn to live alone."

"Yes, Grandma."

"Good."

They speak their set piece like two shadow puppets against a white wall in a darkened room. They are shades, drawn behind the eye of a woman, full grown, alive, in withdrawal.

"Did something happen tonight?"

"Nothing, Grandma; just the storm."

"That's what made you take flight?"

"Yes, ma'am."

"Are you sure?"

"Yes, ma'am."

She could not tell her about the song, nor the word they had thrown at the other girl, to which the song was nothing.

She could not tell her about the pink room, the women examining her in the bath, her heart pounding as she escaped in a dead girl's clothes. They had burned hers.

*Screen Memory*

Two childish flights. In each the grace which was rain, the fury which was storm chased her, saved her.

In the morning the sky was clear.


"Grandma?"

"Yes?"

"If I pay for it, can we get a radio?"

"Isn't a piano, aren't books enough for you?"

Silence.

"Where would you get that kind of money?"

"Mrs. Baker has asked me to help her after school. She has a new baby."

"Do I know this Mrs. Baker?"

"She was a teacher at the school before we came here. She left to get married and have a baby."

"Oh." The grandmother paused. "Then she is a colored woman?" As if she would even consider having her granddaughter toil for the other ilk.

"Yes. And she has a college education." Surely this detail would get the seal of approval, and with it the chance of the radio.

"What a fool."

"Grandma?"

"I say what a foolish woman. To go through all that—all that she must have done, and her people too—to get a college education and become a teacher and then to throw it all away to become another breeder. What a shame!"

With the last she was not expressing sympathy for a life changed by fate, or circumstances beyond an individual's control; she meant *disgrace,* of the Eve-covering-her-nakedness sort.

"Yes, Grandma." The girl could but assent.

*Afrekete*                                                                                    202

The woman in the bed is watching as these shadows traverse the wall.

"Too many breeders, not enough readers. Yes—indeed."

"She seems like a very nice woman."

"And what, may I ask, does that count for? When there are children who depend on her? Why didn't she consider her responsibilities to her students, eh? Running off like that."

Watching the shadows engage and disengage.

"She didn't run off, Grandma."

No, Grandmother. Your daughter, my mother, ran off, or away. My mother who quit Spelman after one year because she didn't like the smell of her own hair burning—so you said. Am I to believe you? Went north and came back with me, and ran off, away—again.

"You know what I mean. Selfish woman. Selfish and foolish. Lord have mercy, what a combination. The kind that do as they please and please no one but themselves."

The granddaughter turned away to regard the dirt street and the stubborn rose.

The grandmother didn't dare offer that a selfish and foolish woman would not make much of a teacher. Nor that Miss Elliston—whose pointer seemed an extension of her right index finger, and whose blue rayon skirt bore an equator of chalk dust—was a more than permanent replacement. The bitterness went far too deep for mitigation, or comfort.

"Grandma, if I work for her, may I get a radio?"

"Tell me, why do you want this infernal thing?"

"Teacher says it's educational." Escape. I want to know about the outside.

"Nonsense. Don't speak nonsense to me."

"No, ma'am."

"And just how much do you think this woman is willing to pay you?"

"I'm not sure."

"What does her husband do, anyway?"

"He's in the navy; overseas."

"Of course." Her tone was resigned.

"Grandma?"

"Serving them coffee, cooking their meals, washing their drawers. Just another servant in uniform, a house slave, for that is all the use the United States Navy has for the Negro man."

She followed the War religiously, *Crisis* upon *Crisis*.

"Why didn't he sign up at Tuskegee, eh? Instead of being a Pullman porter on the high seas, or worse."

"I don't know," her granddaughter admitted quietly, she who was half-them.

"Yellow in more ways than one, that's why. Playing it safe, following a family tradition. Cooking and cleaning and yassuh, yassuh, yassuh. They are yellow, am I right?"

"Yes, ma'am."

"Well, those two deserve each other."

It was no use. No use at all to mention Dorie Miller—about whom the grandmother had taught the granddaughter—seizing the guns on the *Arizona* and blasting the enemy from the sky. No use at all. She who was part-them felt on trembling ground.

Suddenly—

"As long as you realize who, what these people are, then you may work for the woman. But only until you have enough money for that blasted radio. Maybe Madame Foolish-Selfish can lend you some books. Unless"—her voice held an extraordinary coldness—"she's sold them to buy diapers."

"Yes, ma'am."

"You will listen to the radio only at certain times, and you must promise me to abide by my choice of those times, and to exercise discretion."

"I promise," the girl said.

Poor Mrs. Baker was in for one last volley. "Maybe as you watch the woman deteriorate, you will decide her life will not be yours. Your brain is too good, child. And can be damaged by the likes of her, the trash of the radio."

Not even when Mr. Baker's ship was sunk in the Pacific and he was lost, did she relent. "Far better to go down in flames than to be sent to a watery grave. He died not hero's death, not he."

> "Full fathom five, thy father lies;
> of his bones are coral made;
> Those are pearls that were his eyes."

The baby with the black pearl eyes was folded into her chest as she spoke to him.

> "Nothing of him that doth fade,
> But doth suffer a sea-change
> Into something rich and strange."

She imagined a deep and enduring blackness. Salt stripping him to bone, coral grafting, encrusted with other sea creatures. She thought suddenly it was the wrong ocean that had claimed him—his company was at the bottom of the other.

> "Sea nymphs hourly ring his knell:
> Ding-dong.
> Hark! now I hear them—Ding-dong bell."

She heard nothing. The silence would be as deep and enduring as the blackness.

The girl didn't dare tell the grandmother that she held Mrs. Baker's hand when she got the news about her husband, brought her a glass of water, wiped her face. Lay beside her until she fell asleep. Gave the baby a sugar tit so his mother would not be waked.

The girl was learning about secrecy.

The girl tunes the radio in. Her head and the box are under a heavy crazy quilt, one of the last remnants of her mother; pieced like her mother's skin in the tent show where, as her grandmother said, "she exhibits herself." As a savage. A woman with wild hair. A freak.

That was a while ago; nothing has been heard from her since.

It is late. The grandmother is asleep on the back porch on a roll-away cot. Such is the heat she sleeps in the open air covered only by a thin muslin sheet.

The misery, heaviness of the quilt, smelling of her mother's handiwork, are more than compensated for by *The Shadow*. Who knows what evil lurks in the hearts of men?

The radio paid for, her visits to Mrs. Baker are meant to stop —that was the agreement. But she will not quit. Her visits to Mrs. Baker—like her hiding under her mother's covers with the radio late at night, terrified the hot tubes will catch the bed afire—are surreptitious, and fill her with a warmth she is sure is wrong. She loves this woman, who is soft, who drops the lace front of her camisole to feed her baby, who tunes in to the opera from New

York on Saturday afternoons and explains each heated plot as she moves around the small neat house.

The girl sees the woman in her dreams.

On a hot afternoon in August Mrs. Baker took her to a swimming hole a mile or two out in the country, beyond the town. They wrapped the baby and set him by the side of the water, "like the baby Moses," Mrs. Baker said. Birdsong was over them and the silver shadows of fish glanced off their legs.

"Come on, there's no one else around," Mrs. Baker told her, assuring her when she hesitated, "There's nothing to be ashamed of." And the girl slipped out of her clothes, folding them carefully on the grassy bank. Shamed nonetheless by her paleness.

Memory struck her like a water moccasin sliding through the muddy water. The women who would save her had her stand, turn around, open her legs—just to make sure.


She pulls herself up and comes to in her hospital bed. The piano in the corner of the room, the old lady, the girl, the jump rope, the white ladies, recede and fade from her sight. Now there is a stark white chest which holds bedclothes. In another corner a woman in a lace camisole, baby-blue ribbon threaded through the lace, smiles and waves and rises to the ceiling, where she slides into a crack in the plaster.

The woman in the bed reaches for the knob on the box beside her head and tunes it in; Ferrante and Teicher play the theme from *Exodus* on their twin pianos.

Her brain vibrates in a *contre coup*. She is in a brilliantly lit white room in Boston, Massachusetts. Outside is frozen solid. It is dead of winter in the dead of night. She could use a drink.

*Screen Memory*

What happened, happened quickly. The radio announced a contest. She told Mrs. Baker about it. Mrs. Baker convinced her to send her picture in to the contest: "Do you really want to spend the rest of your days here? Especially now that your grandmother's passed on?" Her heart stopped. Just like that.

The picture was taken by Miss Velma Jackson, Mrs. Baker's friend, who advertised herself as *V. Jackson, Portrait Photography, U.S. Army Ret.* Miss Jackson came to town a few years after the War was over, set up shop, and rented a room in Mrs. Baker's small house. In her crisp khakis, with her deep brown skin, she contrasted well with the light-brown pasteled Mrs. Baker. She also loved the opera and together they sang the duet from *Norma.*

When she moved in talk began. "There must be something about that woman and uniforms," the grandmother said in one of her final judgments.

Miss Jackson, who preferred "Jack" to "Velma," performed a vital service to the community, like the hairdresser and the undertaker. Poor people took care to keep a record of themselves, their kin. They needed Jack and so the talk died down. Died down until another photographer came along—a traveling man who decided to settle down.

Jack's portrait of the girl, now a young woman, came out well. She stared back in her green-eyed, part-them glory against a plain white backdrop, no fussy ferns or winged armchairs. The picture was sent in to the contest, a wire returned, and she was summoned.

She took the plain name they offered her—eleven letters, to fit best on a marquee—and took off. A few papers were passed.

"Will you come with me?"

"No."

"Why not?"

"I can't."

"Why not?"

"Jack and I have made plans. She has some friends in Philadelphia. It will be easier for us there."

"And Elijah?"

"Oh, we'll take him along, of course. Good schools there. And one of her friends has a boy his age."

"I'm going to miss you."

"You'll be fine. We'll keep in touch. This town isn't the world, you know."

"No."


Now there was nothing on the papers they sent—that is, no space for: *Race?*

Jack said: "And what do you propose to do? Say, hey, Mr. Producer, by the way, although I have half-moons on my fingernails, a-hem, a-hem?"

She was helped to her berth by a Pullman porter more green-eyed than she. In his silver-buttoned epauletted blue coat he reminded her of a medieval knight, on an iron horse, his chivalric code—Rules for Pullman Porters—stuck in his breast pocket. He serenaded her.

> "De white gal ride in de parlor car.
> De yaller gal try to do de same.
> De black gal ride in de Jim Crow car.
> But she get dar jes' de same."

He looked at her as he stowed her bag. "Remember that old song, Miss?"

"No."


*Daughter of the Mother Lode.* The reader might recall that one. It's on late-night TV and also on video by now. She was the half-breed daughter of a Forty-Niner. At first, dirty and monosyllabic, then taken up by a kindly rancher's wife, only to be kidnapped by some crazy Apaches.

Polysyllabic and clean and calicoed when the Apaches seize her, dirty and monosyllabic and buckskinned when she breaks away—and violated, dear Lord, violated out of her head, for which the rancher wreaks considerable havoc on the Apaches. You may remember that she is baptized, and goes on to teach school in town and becomes a sort of mother-confessor to the dancehall girls.

As she gains speed, she ascends to become one of the more-stars-than-there-are-in-the-heavens, and her parts become lighter, brighter than before. Parts where "gay" and "grand" are staples of her dialogue. As in, "Isn't she gay!" "Isn't he grand!" She wears black velvet that droops at the neckline, a veiled pillbox, long white gloves.


She turns out the light next to the bed, shuts off the radio, looks out the window. Ice. Snow. Moon. The moon thin, with fat Venus beside it.

The door to the room suddenly whooshes open and a dark woman dressed in white approaches the bed.

"Mother?"

*Afrekete*

"Don't mind me, honey. I'm just here to clean up."

"Oh."

"I hope you feel better soon, honey. It takes time, you know."

"Yes."

The woman has dragged her mop and pail into the room and is now bent under the bed, so her voice is muffled beyond the whispers she speaks in—considerate of the drying-out process.

"Can I ask you something?" This soft-spoken question comes to the actress from underneath.

"Sure."

"Would you sign a piece of paper for my daughter?"

"I'd be glad to."

If I can remember my name.

The woman has emerged from under the bed and is standing next to her, looking down at her—bedpan in her right hand, disinfectant in her left.

The actress finds a piece of paper on the bedside table, asks the girl's name, signs "with every good wish for your future."

"Thank you kindly."

She lies back. Behind her eyelids is a pond. Tables laden with food are in the background. In the scum of the pond are tadpoles, swimming spiders. Darning needles dart over the water's surface threatening to sew up the eyes of children.

A child is gulping pond water.

Fried chicken, potato salad, coleslaw, pans of ice with pop bottles sweating from the cold against the heat.

The child has lost her footing.

A woman is turning the handle of an ice cream bucket, a bushel basket of ripe peaches sits on the grass beside her. Three-legged races, sack races, races with an uncooked egg in a spoon, all the races known to man, form the landscape beyond the pond, the woman with the ice cream bucket, the tables laden with food.

Finally—the child cries out.

People stop.

She is dragged from the water, filthy. She is pumped back to life. She throws up in the soft grass.

The woman wakes, the white of the pillowcase is stained.

She pulls herself up in the bed.

The other children said she would turn green—from the scum, the pond water, the baby frogs they told her she had swallowed. No one will love you when you are green and ugly.

She gets up, goes to the bathroom, gets a towel to put over the pillowcase.

"Hello. Information?"

"This is Philadelphia Information."

"I would like the number of Velma Jackson, please."

"One moment, please."

"I'll wait."

"The number is . . ."

She hangs up. It's too late.


"She did run away from them, Mama. She came back to you. I don't think you ever gave her credit for that."

"And look where she is now, Rebekah."

"She ran away from them, left a room with pink roses. Sorry, Mama, I know how you hate roses."

"Who is speaking, please?" The woman sits up again, looks around. Nothing.

———

What will become of her?

Let's see. This is February 1963.

She might find herself in Washington, D.C., in August. A shrouded marcher in the heat, dark-glassed, high-heeled.

That is unlikely.


Go back? To what? This ain't *Pinky*.

Europe? A small place somewhere. Costa Brava or Paris— who cares? Do cameos for Fellini; worse come to worst, get a part in a spaghetti western.

She does her time. Fills a suitcase with her dietary needs: Milky Ways, cartons of Winstons, golden tequila, boards a plane at Idlewild.

Below the plane is a storm, a burst behind a cloud, streak lightning splits the sky, she rests her head against the window; she finds the cold comforting.

# *Revelations*

In the May 1991 issue of *Essence* magazine, my mother and I each wrote about my coming out as a lesbian. That article received a tremendous reception—most of it positive—and it remains the most responded-to article in the history of the magazine. Due to the avalanche of mail, my mother and I followed up with "Readers Respond to Coming Out," which ran later that year in the October issue. This article was much more political, allowing me to speak out directly against homophobia in Black communities. Almost overnight, I was unexpectedly catapulted into the public arena, which began a wave of national speaking engagements that left me to cope with both adulation and condemnation.

Before I came out in print, I never had someone tell me I

was going to go to hell. Now people say it to me regularly. When my mother and I addressed a conference of Black social workers about how families may confront their homophobia and accept lesbian and gay children, a sad-eyed man, round-shouldered in a baggy suit, approached me. "I enjoyed hearing what you had to say," he offered, his hand extended. My hand in his, he continued, barely missing a beat, "But you're a sinner. You're going to hell." He said this casually, through a half-smile, as though ready to add, "Have a nice day."

Some people put their condemnation in writing, spitting angry religion-like curse words. These are two of the several letters I received at *Essence*:

*From Smyrna, Georgia:* [Your] behavior is a sin against God that can be forgiven by sincere repentance and turning away from the sin of homosexuality. In fact, the word of God is very clear on the immorality of homosexuality. Read 1 Corinthians 6:9. Homosexuals and the homosexual lifestyle will never be accepted. I believe that sharing the Word with those individuals afflicted with the sin of homosexuality and imparting love and patience, they can receive the loving salvation of Jesus Christ. This is the only way you, and other homosexuals, can become normal, saved persons.

*From Westchester, New York:* [Essence] should be ashamed of itself for having a woman like Linda Villarosa on your staff. Lesbian *[sic]* is not a sickness, it's a sin, and if that woman does not repent, she is going to perish. She should read Mathew *[sic]* chapter 19 verses 4 and 5. Read it and see what it says. Linda, no one wants to know who you are!

The worst verbal attack came at Oregon State University, where I was to address a large group of students about being Black, lesbian, and out. The trouble started before I arrived. I had requested that the organizers contact African-American student groups about coming to my lecture, because I believe that it's extremely important for Blacks—gay and straight—to know that Black lesbians exist and can be happy and out and secure in their identities. A member of the school's Black Women's Alliance (BWA), who was also friendly with the gay group on campus, agreed to make an announcement at BWA's next meeting to garner support and ensure a strong Black presence at the lecture. At the end of the meeting she told the other sisters that an editor from *Essence* would be speaking the following evening. Several women clapped and nodded. "She'll be talking about what it's like to be a Black lesbian," the young woman continued. At that point, the room fell silent. Finally, one woman stood up and said, "Lesbianism is nastiness and they should get a vaccine to make them normal." Spurred on, another declared, "Gays are against God, and because of my religion, I can't hear this woman speak." In the end, another exasperated sister said, "Can we please stop talking about this, I'm getting physically ill."

Thankfully, I didn't know about this backlash or I would've been too freaked to do the lecture. Expressions of homophobia hurt deeply, but coming from other Black women the pain is particularly acute. Knowing that I would be facing such resistance in what was already a largely white audience on a conservative college campus may well have paralyzed me.

The lecture went fine. The question-and-answer period was particularly long with interested students—gay, straight, and of many races and ethnicities—hungry for answers and information. After a while I became tired and announced that I'd answer one final question. A clean-cut white guy wearing a baseball cap waved his hand frantically from the balcony. And there it was:

"You and all gays are going to hell. I'm telling you this because God taught me to love you." Then he cited a Bible passage: "Read Leviticus 20:13."

Bedlam broke out in the room. After several minutes, I got things quieted down and looked out into the expectant faces of the audience. The challenge had been made, and I felt that all of the young, gay people there expected me to defend us all with authority. My voice shook with anger and a little bit of fear that I wouldn't be able to meet this challenge. "Listen, you don't love me, you don't know me, you don't understand me," I said, barely able to remain composed and keep from crying. "You're using religion to cloak your horrible message in the language of love. People like you have used religion to suppress everything you find offensive. In the past the Bible was used to justify slavery and now you're using it to justify your fear and hatred of those of us who are living our lives as gays and lesbians."

The tension broke and the crowd began to applaud, but I felt empty. Even the reporters covering the event saw through my strong front and brave smile. The next day's edition of the *Corvallis (Ore.) Gazette-Times* reported that as I stepped from the podium, I had seemed stunned. It was true: I was stunned. And sad. My words had sounded hollow to me, as though I had been reading from a textbook. I hadn't felt them. My reaction had been a knee-jerk response to being attacked in public; but deep within me, I knew I wasn't so sure about myself. Where do I really stand spiritually? That heckler knew exactly how he felt and where he stands, why didn't I?

Nothing in my own religious upbringing prepared me for these attacks. My family attended an integrated, "progressive" Episcopal church. There were a handful of families of color like us and lots of groovy white people, interracial couples, and aging hippies with their adopted children of color in tow. Our choir didn't sing gospel music, but folky spiritual ballads accompanied by the organ, guitar, and African and Native American drumming.

I don't remember learning many specific religious lessons from our minister. With his long hair flowing over his Roman collar, Father Hammond preached through sleepy eyes, as though he'd been out late drinking the night before. His words were inspirational and easy to understand, filled with references to pop culture. A quote from *Playboy* magazine could seamlessly segue into biblical verse. My mother taught my fourth-grade Sunday school class, stressing discipline and openmindedness. One Saturday morning the group of us gathered for a field trip to a nearby synagogue. We looked like a bunch of "We Are the World" poster children. "It's important to learn about the way other people worship," my mother explained, looking over our group to make sure our two lines were straight and orderly and no noses were running.

To further my religious studies, I attended weeks and weeks of confirmation classes every Thursday night. On confirmation day, I walked down the church aisle, clutching a white prayer book in white-gloved hands. I was wearing a white dress, white lace socks, white patent-leather shoes, and had a white handkerchief pinned to my head. I looked like a brown-skinned vestal virgin awaiting sacrifice. I don't remember one spiritual lesson from that time, but I do remember how hard it was to try to stay clean in all those bleached-white clothes.

We also visited St. John's, my grandmother's Baptist church, on trips back to Chicago, where I was born. Getting dressed for service was a major production. My grandmother had to decide which of her many wigs and hats to wear and whether or not to put on her fur, a decision that had little to do with the temperature outside. After the frenzied preparations, we'd all pile into my grandfather's Electra 225 and float to church in the boat-sized car.

Once inside, I'd always scrunch into my grandmother's side and maneuver a way to sit by her. I knew she was important in this community from the way heads would turn as she led the family—straight-backed—down the aisle to our pew, and I wanted a little of that limelight.

The service really wasn't as fun as the preparation, mainly because of its three-hour length. Until someone got the Spirit. I'd hold my breath as the organ pounded out the same repetitive note and the singing rang louder, rising to more and more tremorous shouts. Inevitably, some well-dressed woman would take to the aisle, chanting and skipping. Then two strong, well-practiced sisters, dressed in white gloves and nurse's uniforms, would walk briskly over and efficiently bring the saved soul back to this world and dispatch her into the care of family members. I would tug at Grandmother's sleeve asking questions about the moment of high drama, but she would slap my Vaselined knees together and hiss into my ear, "Stop-staring-close-your-lips-don't-bite-your-cuticles-put-your-gloves-back-on." The only thing I knew for certain was that no one in our family would ever get the spirit, because my grandmother would die of embarrassment.

From my parents' church I learned about respect for difference and community across seemingly unbridgeable differences, and through my grandmother's church I connected with my Southern Baptist roots. But nothing from my religious past had prepared me to deal with the continued abuse I was receiving from so-called religious people. It was time for me to begin studying the Bible, but, more importantly, it was time to discover my own spiritual core.

First, I dug out the dusty copy of the Revised Standard Version of the Bible left over from my days in confirmation classes, and I looked up the passages that had been thrown in my face. I started with 1 Corinthians 6:9 and 10, which read: "Do not be deceived; neither the immoral, nor idolaters, nor adulterers, nor homosexuals, nor thieves, nor the greedy, nor drunkards, nor revilers, nor robbers will inherit the kingdom of God."

I felt skeptical: had the authors of the Bible really used the word "homosexual" two thousand years ago? No, they had not. The New Testament had been written in Greek and then translated into Hebrew. In 1382 the Bible was first translated into English, and in 1611 came the King James (or authorized) Version. The Bible I was reading had been revised 335 years later. I purchased a paperback copy of the King James Version and looked up 1 Corinthians 6:9 and 10. This earlier version never used the word "homosexual" but listed the "effeminate" and "abusers of themselves with mankind" in its inventory of the "unrighteous," and that had been translated to mean "homosexual" in the revised version. Something had been lost—or gained —in translation.

I decided not to spend much more time trying to sort out what the authors meant and what lessons they were trying to teach about homosexuality—if that's even what they were talking about—in the context of social systems from twenty centuries past. In fact, even after reading Genesis 19 many times, I still didn't see how the story of Sodom had anything to do with gay sex. In that story, Lot, a holy man and resident of the evil city of Sodom, is visited by two angels. Genesis 19:4–8 reads:

. . . the men of the city, the men of Sodom, both young and old, all the people to the last man, surrounded the house; and they called to Lot, "Where are the men who came to you tonight [i.e., the angels]? Bring them out to us, that we may know them." Lot went out of the door to the men, shut the door after him, and said, "I beg you, my brothers, do not act so wickedly. Behold, I have two daughters who have not known man; let me bring them out to you, and do to them as you please; only do nothing to these men. . . ."

Eventually, the angels strike the men blind, and God rains fire and brimstone on the city and burns it down. From this story comes the word "sodomy"—a pejorative term for gay sex. And now, when a city like New York is described as a modern-day Sodom, the underlying assumption is that it's full of sin and sex and gays. Even assuming that the word "know" refers to sex, it seems a stretch to use it to condemn gays and lesbians. Why isn't anyone questioning Lot for offering to turn over his virginal daughters to the mob of men, which is the most obvious aberrance relayed there?

Moving on, I looked up Matthew 19:4 and 5, which says: "He answered, 'Have you not read that he who made them from the beginning made them male and female,' and said, 'For this reason a man shall leave his father and mother and be joined to his wife, and the two shall become one flesh.' "

Upon further reading, it was easy to see that the letter writer from Westchester, New York, had taken these verses completely out of context. The passage had nothing to do with lesbians and gay men but was clearly a condemnation of divorce. In fact, the verses she cited were an answer to the question "Is it lawful to divorce one's wife for any cause?" (Matthew 19:3). Verse 9 says that "whoever divorces his wife, except for unchastity, and marries another, commits adultery." In case there's any question about the seriousness of adultery, Leviticus 20:10 spells it out clearly: "If a man commits adultery with the wife of his neighbor, both the adulterer and the adulteress shall be put to death." What does this have to do with queerness?

Next I looked up Leviticus 20:13: "If a man lies with a male as with a woman, both of them have committed an abomination; they shall be put to death, their blood is upon them." I guess they could be murdered along with the divorced remarried couple from earlier Leviticus verses. At this point, I started getting angry.

It doesn't take a biblical scholar to figure out that people use the Bible selectively. The people who write me letters are not sending hate mail to people who are divorced or to those who have cheated on their spouses. The man who lashed out at me in Oregon is not condemning people who eat pork ("And the swine, because it parts the hoof and is cloven-footed but does not chew the cud, is unclean to you. Of their flesh you shall not eat, and their carcasses you shall not touch; they are unclean to you": Leviticus 11:7–8) or shellfish (". . . anything in the seas or the rivers that has not fins and scales, of the swarming creatures in the waters and of the living creatures that are in the waters, is an abomination to you": Leviticus 11:10).

Neither is he cursing or carrying on about cattle breeders, farmers who grow two different crops, or anyone who wears a poly-cotton blend of clothing despite Leviticus 19:19: "You shall not let your cattle breed with a different kind; you shall not sow your field with two different kinds of seed; nor shall there come upon you a garment of cloth made of two kinds of stuff."

These people are also overlooking beautiful, lyrical passages in the Bible that celebrate same-sex love. In Ruth 1:16–17 of the Old Testament, Ruth says to Naomi: "Entreat me not to leave you or to return from following you; for where you go I will go, and where you lodge I will lodge; your people shall be my people, and your God my God; where you die I will die, and there will I be buried."

David and Jonathan of the Old Testament seem to be deeply in love: ". . . the soul of Jonathan was knit to the soul of David, and Jonathan loved him as his own soul" (1 Samuel 18:1). When Jonathan dies in the war, David writes: ". . . your love to me was wonderful, passing the love of women" (2 Samuel 1:26).

Many so-called righteous people are taking the Bible literally when it suits them, ignoring anything that doesn't easily support their narrow condemnations or calls into question their own lifestyles. And many Black people are using the Bible against their lesbian and gay sisters and brothers just as whites used the scriptures against our ancestors when they interpreted passages such as Ephesians 6:5–6—"Slaves, be obedient to those who are your earthly masters, with fear and trembling, in singleness of heart, as to Christ; not in the way of eyeservice, as men-pleasers, but as servants of Christ"—to mean that our people should remain enslaved.

It is, in fact, a sad irony that the overwhelmingly white Christian Right movement is capitalizing on homophobia in Black communities. Groups like the Moral Majority and the Christian Coalition have never marched side by side with or fought for issues affecting people of color. In fact, the Christian Right has actively lobbied against issues such as voting rights and affirmative action. But now they're recruiting our people, taking advantage of the deep spiritual commitment of the African-American community and distorting Christianity to pass anti-gay and lesbian legal initiatives and turn straight Blacks against gays—similar to the way their ancestors distorted Christianity to justify slavery.


My Bible studies behind me, I felt fortified intellectually but still on shaky ground spiritually. But I knew exactly what I needed to do. I had heard about Unity Fellowship Church and its lively congregation of hundreds of mostly Black lesbians and gay men that worshipped on Sundays at New York City's Lesbian and Gay Community Services Center. Although I had always found excuses to avoid going, now it was time.

When I arrived that first Sunday, the room at the Center was packed with people; in fact, close to one hundred latecomers had to be turned away. The service began with testimonials. Person after person stood up and testified to what had happened over the week: breakups, gay bashing, rejections by parents, eviction from apartments, illness, sadness, loneliness, addiction, sorrow, seemed to silence the news of triumphs and causes for celebration. Pain filled the room, Black pain, gay pain. But when the pastor, Elder Zachary Jones, marched into the room to the tune of "We've come this far by faith . . . ," the mood in the room changed to one of joy.

"It doesn't have nothing to do with who you sleep with, but what's in your heart," Rev. Zach shouted over the low hum of the choir. "Who says God doesn't love gay people? There's love in this room." And there was. A measure of healing had begun. His simple words struck a chord in me, and I felt relieved and then cleansed. As I looked around at the hundreds of other Black lesbian and gay people in the room—who like me had been searching for a spiritual home—I knew I had found a place where I could be comfortable and explore my own spirituality.

Fortified in mind and spirit, from my connection with this community, I felt ready to face the world. And an opportunity presented itself while I was giving a talk at a Black cultural center on the West Coast. After going through my usual song and dance about how it felt to be Black and a lesbian, I began fielding questions. I noticed a woman raising her hand tentatively. She was a sister in her mid-thirties, turned out in an expensive, corporate-looking suit and bright gold jewelry, with her hair freshly done in braided extensions. "You seem like a really nice woman and I enjoyed hearing your story," she began slowly. "But as a Christian woman I need to share this with you. I went through a period in my life when I thought I was attracted to women. But then I discovered Jesus Christ. By reading the Bible, I realized that homosexuality was unnatural and that I was a sinner. If I continued in the life, I would be condemned."

"Where does the Bible say that?" I asked.

Opening her purse, she pulled out a small, worn copy of the New Testament and began to read from a marked passage. " 'For this reason God gave them up to dishonorable passions. Their women exchanged natural relations for unnatural, and the men likewise gave up natural relations with women and were consumed with passion for one another, men committing shameless acts with men and receiving in their own persons the due penalty for their error.' Romans 1, verses 26 and 27."

I listened politely as she read. When she had finished, I reached into my backpack and pulled out my own copy of the Bible. " 'In like manner that the women adorn themselves in modest apparel with propriety and moderation, not with braided hair or gold or pearls or costly clothing,' 1 Timothy, chapter 2, verse 9," I read. "And 1 Timothy 2:11 and 12 say, 'Let a woman learn in silence with all submissiveness. I permit no woman to teach or to have authority over men; she is to keep silent.' I'm sure in your work you have had to supervise men. I know I have. And even by standing up and speaking out today, I guess we're both sinning."

"Wait, that's not fair," she said, her face looking at once confused and angry. "It's not right to take the Bible out of context like that."

"Why?" I countered. "That's what you're doing."

Even as I hit her close to home, I felt sorry for this woman. She was obviously confused and probably a closet case, and I knew I was preying on that, attacking her with scriptures almost as I had been attacked. I was aiming at a place she had only recently uncovered—where she was still vulnerable.

"Listen," I said softly. "I don't want to do this. All of us need to stop taking the Bible literally, and begin to read it critically and intelligently. You know, there are some important messages that we can understand and agree on." I opened my Bible to Leviticus 19:17 and read in a clear voice, "You shall not hate your brother in your heart, but you shall reason with your neighbor, lest you bear sin because of him. You shall not take vengeance or bear any grudge against the sons of your own people, but you shall love your neighbor as yourself." And this time my words sounded strong and confident, and were definitely my own.

CYNTHIA BOND

# *Ruby*

She remembered the sound of bells. All of Liberty did. Real bells,
not the clinking tin kind you buy from Kress's Five and Dime,
but the swelling brass sort that speak of roads taken, of freshly
painted porches and fried catfish and okra in round steaming
platters. The kind that are nailed firmly to ancient chinaberry
trees. The kind that seem to grow like golden pears from the
spreading branches—that sing back to you when you try to lay
your sweaty weight upon the boughs. The kind her grandpapa
had strung like popcorn all about the place the year of his bumper
cotton harvest, when the crop grew so tall and white, folks said it
dusted the heaven with clouds. They said that on a windy day at
picking time, the air would be filled with milky wisps of flying

cotton. It could be seen five miles away at P & K Market. And the sound of bells followed the sailing ivory and settled about the town. Bells that rang with the lightest touch or the faintest breeze. Bells that let folks know in an instant that they were near Belle land. All forty-five acres of it. Mr. Belle ofttimes appreciated the obvious.

When she returned decades later to her grandpapa's land, all but five acres had been parceled and sold and the bells had long since rusted into silence. She was called Ruby Belle by the town, though her step had lost its cadence and her voice no longer held music.

She wore gray like rain clouds, like shapeless rain clouds before the bursting. She wrapped them about her skeleton body, her acres of sheathed legs, her arms swaying like a loose screen. That is how she moved. Her curved bow lips jerking slightly. Her eyes a misting glaze before the storm.

That is how Ruby walked in the crazy years, the years she lived in the splintered lean-to that Papa Belle had left. The years she dug into the Texas soil under starlight and buried the souls of ghost children. The years she wailed under moonlight and sounded like a distant train. The years she shook the top branches of the circle of spring elms. When acorns fell and would not take root, years of dried dead things collecting by her door, only to break and snap and curl about the front porch post like faded ribbons.

In those years, people let Ruby be. They walked a swayed path to avoid her door. And so it was more than peculiar when Ephram Jenkins brought a covered cake to the lean-to and set it without ceremony under the crumbling porch posts.

Ephram Jenkins had seen the gray woman passing like a

haint through the center of town. He had seen her wipe the spittle from the corner of her mouth, run her still beautiful hands through her dirt-caked hair before she turned the corner in view of the town, walking like she had someplace she ought to have been, only to stop five steps away from Peters' Bread Shop, standing pillar still, her rain-cloud body beginning to shake. Ephram had seen Mrs. Peters walk nonchalantly out of the door and say, "Well, child, I was tryin' to find somebody to taste this fresh batch a rolls."

Ephram watched Ruby stare past her as she took the brown sack filled with steaming yeast bread, the tan skin sack so warm it felt like life. Take it and walk away with her acres of legs carrying her, while Sarah Peters said, "You come on back now, Ruby Belle. Come on back 'n' help me out next week if you get the chance."

Ephram Jenkins saw this, had seen it for six years now. He watched the rise of her black-bottomed foot kicking a swirl of dust in its wake. And he wanted nothing more than to put each tired black sole in his wooden cake tub, brush them in warm soapy water, cream them with soft lard, then roll up his mama's knitted wool socks, and lace them into some hard-toed black bear shoes, and then he would talk to her.

He would talk to her of the soft earth and the smell of Rupert Shankle's melons splitting on the vine and how honeysuckle blossoms tasted of sunlight. He would tell her that he had seen a part of the night sky resting in her eyes and that he knew it because it lived in him as well. He would talk until his words entered the clouds surrounding her and stirred her to pour rain out onto the cracked land about her house.

And so because he knew he couldn't, and because he didn't own a wooden cake tub, he asked his mama to make up her white lay angel cake because he needed to carry it to an ailing friend. His mama looked at him out of the corner of her eye but made it anyway.

She made it in that pocket of time before dawn, when the aging night gathered its dark skirts and paused in the stillness. She made it with twelve new eggs, still warm and flecked with feathers. She washed them and cracked them, one at a time, holding each golden yolk in her palm as the whites slid and dripped through her open fingers. She set them aside in her flowered china bowl. Celia Jenkins still cooked in a wood-burning stove, she still used a whisk and muscle and patience to beat her egg whites into foaming peaks. She used pure vanilla, the same sweet liquid she poured into Saturday night baths before her husband, the Reverend Jenkins, arrived back in town. The butter was from her churn, the confectioners' sugar from P & K Market. And as she stirred the dawn into being, a drop of sweat salted the batter. The cake baked and rose with the sun.

Ephram slept as the cake slid from its tin, so sweet it crusted at its crumbling edges, so light little craters of air circled its surface, so moist it was sure, as was always the case, to cling to the spaces between his mama's long three-pronged silver fork. Celia Jenkins never cut her white lay angel cake with a knife. "It'd be like using an ax to skin a rabbit," she'd always say.

The cake was cooling when Ephram awoke. It settled into itself as he bathed and dressed for the day.

Ephram Jenkins smoothed the corners of his great-grand-daddy's hat for the tenth time that morning. His wide square thumbs running along the soft hide brim. The leather so thin in places the sun slanted softly through, filtered like a Chinese lantern, lighting his deep brown eyes.

The magical thing about Ephram Jenkins was that, if you

looked real hard, you could see a circle of violet rimming the brown of his irises. Soft like the petals of spreading periwinkle.

The problem was that no one, not even his mother, took the time to really look at Ephram Jenkins. Folks pretty much glanced past him on the way to Julian's place or P & K Market. To them he was just another thick horse-brown man with a ratted cap and a stooped gait. To them there was nothing special about Ephram. He remained a moving blur on the eyes' journey to more delicate, interesting resting places.

They didn't see his Chinese lamp hat, or his purple-ringed irises, or the way that they matched just perfectly the berry tint of his lower lip. They didn't see the ten crescent moons held captive in his fingernails. They didn't see the left crease near his mouth always ready for his turned smile.

The way he moved, like a man gliding underwater, smooth and liquid as Marion Lake. They didn't notice how the blue in his plaid socks matched the buttons on his Sunday shirt. They didn't smell the well-brushed sheen of Vaseline on his thick hair, soot-black woven with threads of white cotton.

They didn't notice the gracious pause he'd take after someone would finish a sentence, the way he'd give folks the chance to take air back into their lungs, before he'd fill the space up with his own breath and words.

They didn't see the way his pupils got wide when his heart filled up with pride, or love, or hope.

But Ruby did.

Even in the train whistle time, when her life was only a building long scream that faded into night. Even then Ruby noticed Ephram.

———

*Ruby*

The first time Ruby had seen him was three years earlier, after the big Galveston hurricane. It was after the bending of trees, of branches arching to the floor of earth, after Marion Lake had washed away Chauncy Shankle's henhouse, and Clancy Simkins' daddy's Buick, and the new cross for the Church of God in Christ. It was after the great chinaberry tree had split across the red road on the way to Papa Belle's place.

Hurricane Malinda had come in Ruby's third year on the place. And in her third year, she saw Ephram. She saw him when she was fallen rain.

She had lain in the stagnant pools thick with mud and slick browning leaves. She had knelt before the cracked chinaberry tree and lain in the collecting waters, letting the thick fluid cover her like a moving bedtime blanket. She felt her skin melt and slip from her bones; her heart, spine and cranium dissolved like sugar cubes in warm coffee.

She had been muddy waters for three hours when Ephram found her. Her nose rising out of the puddle to inhale . . . and dipping back to release. Out and back. Out. Back. Rhythmic like an old blues tune.

He did not scream. He did not leap over the tree. He did not scoop into her water center to set her free.

For Ephram did not see what anyone else passing down the road would see: a skinny dark brown woman with knotted hair lying back flat in a mud puddle. Instead, Ephram Jenkins saw that Ruby had become the still water. He saw her liquid-deep skin, her hair splayed and cascading like onyx river vines.

And as a gentle noon rain began to fall upon her, Ephram saw her splash and swell and spill out of the small ravine. Ephram Jenkins knew. And in that moment, the two knowings met. That is when Ruby lifted her head like a rising wave and first noticed Ephram.

They stared at each other under the gray dome of the sky with the soft rain and the full wet earth. Then Ruby closed her eyes, concentrated, and melted once again into the pool.

Ephram heard himself asking the strangest questions, heard the questions before they left his berry lips. "Are you married?" But before they could pass into the rain, he saw that she was once again water. And he couldn't ask a puddle, no matter how perfect, if it was married. So he tipped his hat to it, and made his way back down the road.

"Ephraaam! Ephram Jenkins, your breakfast is been near ready! Come in here, boy!" Celia called her eldest boy into her ample kitchen.

As he had every morning of his life, Ephram heard his mother's call. He heard her and was silent as he smoothed the weathered brim of his hat once more and faced his mother's mirror. And this morning, this crisp, end-of-summer morning, Ephram did something he had not done in twenty years. He looked.

He had always straightened the crease in his slacks on Sunday, or picked bits of lint from his deacon jacket. He had held a handkerchief filled with ice on his split chin and lip, the one winter in his life snow had slicked the front walk. He had combed and oiled his scalp and plucked out ingrown hairs. He had shaved and brushed his teeth and gargled with Listerine. But in twenty years, Ephram Jenkins had not truly looked into a mirror.

His greatest surprise was that he was no longer young. He

assessed the plum darkness under his eyes, the grooves along his full nose, the fullness of his cheeks. Ephram pressed a cool washcloth to his skin, then he practiced a smile. He had tried on five or six when his mother launched her final call to breakfast.

He chewed slowly at his mother's kitchen table. Celia Jenkins swept the long hall as he dipped her butter-drenched biscuits into Blue Ribbon cane syrup. She straightened a wood-framed photograph of the Reverend Jenkins as he spooned and licked the hardening glaze. She put *Andy Williams' Gospel Favorites* on the phonograph while he peppered his grits and four scrambled eggs. She sang snatches of "Precious Lord" as Ephram chewed, chewed slowly and waited to begin the day. Waited to walk the red road, to climb over the chinaberry tree and to knock on the door at Papa Belle's place.

Ruby was sleeping. Which was rare. Ruby did not sleep. Much. For her waking mind was full, pressing pushing full. Her mind was full of knowing, and the knowing did not want her to sleep.

For Ruby knew many things. She knew the youth of the world that passed each day before her dim window. She knew the innocence of the trees, still naive enough to lace their branches toward the sun. She knew the hope of the path that wound by her door, still red and dusty and calling for firm feet to track its length. She knew the generosity of the cane fields, the dreams of the stones that lined her worn yard.

She had crept into the secret whispering life of each of these. She had become the puddle, the tree, the cane, the lake, and the stone, like a child dressing up in her mother's clothing. These were the rare moments when her wit did not slip and scatter, like milkweed in a strong breeze.

For ofttimes now, in her waking, Ruby would forget the meaning of the aching pressure above her groin. She would forget until the yellow liquid ran warm down her legs. She was often impervious to her monthly blood as it collected in the tangle of her hair and dried in fresh smears on her thighs and knees. She left dark maroon droplets in the arches of her torn slippers, on the graying sheets and faded chairs and worn steps; they dotted each sanded oak floor in the small house. Vomit dried in forgotten corners of the kitchen, until driven to hunger she would crouch and scrap at her own remains. Often now she caught herself snarling for hours at a time.

And so one late August afternoon, four years ago, in search of a refuge from the pelting storm behind her eyes, she had grown roots.

She had been standing in the waist-tall grass at the edge of what had once been a mite-sized field of blue ribbon sugarcane. Ruby stood in the memory of the cane field; she was kissing close to the old chinaberry tree. A few mulberry-colored stalks remained.

She had dug her bare toes into the soil, and pressed her thick eyelashes together, lid to lid, and concentrated. That is when she felt her toes stretching, running wide along the topsoil. Her toes were thin tendril roots that wrapped like yarn about the thickness of the chinaberry. Her skin became purple and hard, her body narrowed and stretched. She felt sweet syrup thick within her. Her breasts and buttocks became gentle knotted swells in the sugarcane's stalk. She felt the dripping-wet strings encased in brittle darkness. She felt them playing a delicious melody that scented the golden August wind and called striped bees and hummingbirds and curious dragonflies.

Ruby had felt it then. The audacious hope of rooted things. The innocent anticipation of the shooting stalks, the quivering stillness of the watching trees.

Next, she lived two days as a stone. Ruby had felt their smooth rocking willingness when she had lain curled in the front yard one long morning. Just as she had felt her arms weld to her abdomen, her calves affix themselves to her thighs. She felt her skin and teeth and limbs fossilize and gray.

She had heard it then. The leaping expansive dreams of the stones around her. Ruby felt the stones' love of the winding road, and so for the next five days she became the road. She felt herself stretching from the dusty passageway which ran through Liberty, Texas, and her grandpapa's five acres, to access roads, to paved yellow-lined promenades with streetlamps, to Berkville, to Prairieview, to Katy, to Houston, to Austin, to Galveston and beyond.

She left her porch each morning and walked the few yards to the red earthen thoroughfare before her home. Few traveled that back path so she wasn't disturbed. But what she felt as her skin and flesh turned to dust and swirled in the passing wind was joy. She tasted it and was seasoned by it. She could feel a pair of soft child shoes stepping five miles away in Neuton County, ten miles down in Berkville the thick callused feet of cane field workers at dawn. Faintly she heard the skipping step of a man who still had the sweet ripe smell of woman on his fingers. Far away the hushed step of two teenage braided cousins rustling skirts and practicing kissing one another against a shaded tree. She felt the rumble of diesel engines, and a hundred pairs of black rubber wheels barely touching asphalt.

Ruby remained red road long past the owl call of midnight.

She slept with gravel for a twining mattress and woven cotton and starlight as her covering quilt.

She had slept and awakened on that same road for four mornings until dusk of the fifth day when Chauncy Shankle's horse Millie almost kicked her in the head. She rose, covered in dust and straw, to his cursing crazy women left alone to get themselves killed. She turned to enter her yard as he slid from his worn saddle. She stepped slowly from the red dust as he covered the distance between them and turned her about. His thick brown chin folded as he studied her blank eyes. Her eyes still holding the road. He called her. He jostled her. He shook her. He turned his nose at the smell of her. Then Chauncy Shankle spit into her face. Her face remained vacant and still. He saw flecks of his saliva dot her dust-covered cheek. The thick fluid slid down her face revealing feather brown skin. He took his shirtsleeve, licked the corner and began wiping. He then began patting dirt and grass from her dress, her arms, her buttocks, her stomach, her legs.

He peeled off her gray dress and rubbed at her nakedness. Wiping her with the wet edge of the shirt. He felt himself rise in his stained trousers, tent the looseness by his zipper. When she was sufficiently clean, he half carried, half dragged her to a ditch only three feet from the open road. His swollen belly distended above her as he globbed saliva into his palm, wetted his penis and crammed into her.

And yet to Ruby, her dress empty and flat two feet away, the small of her back scraping on a smattering of pebbles, her pelvis and ribs crushing under a sweating full weight, this was a mere irritation. Like a fly landing on freshly buttered corn bread before being flecked away. Like trooping ants on the kitchen counter.

Chauncy Shankle could not know that he was only a cinder

in her wandering eye. Much more preferable to what lay coiled in the plate of her memory.

For what was poised for remembrance had razor teeth and a rotted breath. It growled and licked decaying bones. For Ruby, men were a slight discord that she waited to pass. She simply kept her limbs numb and her eyes empty as she had since she was fifteen. Since she was twelve. Since she was seven, four, two. One. Eight months, when the first man had pulled her pink and white plastic rattle from her drooling mouth, and placed his penis there instead. When the first man had held her nose so she would cough and cry and gag to intensify his pleasure. The first man who had shaken the rattle in her ear as he groaned and jetted semen in acrid smears down her small throat, across her cheek, filling her released nostrils. The first man who had wiped her vomit and mucus from his penis before zipping and reading the *Austin Sunday Herald* in the next room.

When Chauncy Shankle finished he patted her head absently as one would a stray dog. He nudged her to movement. Then kicked her. Then left mumbling a stale warning about lying in roads that grown men had to travel. He climbed on the old horse and trotted down the road.

The road held him as it had the children and the cousins and the hundred spinning black wheels. It did not buck him, or open up and chew him to pieces. The betraying road held him in its open palms. It led him home. It led him to his bed. It led him back to her door whenever he cared.

It held him as the first man had been held by earth, had been shaded by tree, had slept under stars and ripped apples from branches and devoured them in his sharp teeth.

When she was young, Ruby had hated the spinning earth for this betrayal. But in time, as her mouth and vagina and anus were filled again and again, she grew to know that that much malice could not exist in a splashing circling globe. Ruby came to understand ignorance. Ruby saw the young heart of the world and was patient. As a mother watches a toddler gurgling and balancing on chubby new legs.

She kept her horror entwined within her. She did not release the undulating slickness up from her bowels, through her throat and forking past her lips.

Instead, Ruby waited. She waited for the branches to burn to cinder, for Marion Lake to creep over her banks and to steal the calling length of the road, for the ground to split in smoldering cracks and swallow the dreaming stones.

In her waking, Ruby waited for all of these things to come to pass. She waited for the young, young world to discover its nakedness without her, and fall, crouching on the ground heaving and wretched, with knowledge burning in its eyes.

But in her sleep she was a poet. In her sleep she breathed out words like sweet bubbles under a clear sea. They rose to the beamed ceiling of the shack and collected like foam in the wooded slats and waited to be strung together upon her waking. Strung together as delicately as glass beads on a rope silk string.

But Ruby awoke each morning with a guttural start, a wild leaping jolt that shook the morning stillness of the air. And the startled air burst each glossy bubble, leaving only a misting rain to fall upon her twisted face, where it lingered for a heartbeat.

And in that brief space of time Ruby's face would calm, the storm in her eyes would still. In those moments Ruby would look down at her hands and see the dirt caked thick under her nails, and her eyes would spill over with tears and she would remember.

She would remember the sleek maroon leather of the train car that had brought her south to Liberty. Remember the cupped warmth of her lover's bed and the calm of Kara's breath. Remember the faces of friends like planets ringing her. Remember the dripping sink in her old New York, East Side flat and the loose rubber fitting on her refrigerator. Remember jabbing broken glass into her own flesh to keep from feeling the splintering pain inside. Remember the wrenching of her spirit and the binding, jarring pull toward home. Home where it had all begun. Where an old woman with withered fingers had pried into her soul and sold pieces of it like chewing tobacco.

She would then remember the traced softness of Kara's lips and what it had taken to leave her. Ruby would glimpse what it had been like before her own creeping madness made her fear for Kara's safety and she would lift her hands and weep into her creased palms. She remembered Kara sitting in the wideness of their New York bed. It had been an ocean. It had rippled foam blue under them. Swimming, they had met in the center, surrounded by the lapping of tumbled sheets. They had both been dripping and wet. They'd held fruit between them. Pockets of burgundy sweetness surrounding each seed.

"Look, it's you," Kara had whispered. "The color . . . like jewels . . . like rubies . . . like you."

And she'd flicked one of a hundred pomegranate seeds from its fleshy resting place and between two cream-colored fingers, placed it in Ruby's dark mouth, her velvet ribbon mouth holding the fullness of this gift, wrapping it in her bow of a mouth. Kara held her finger like a prayer against Ruby's lips while she chewed. Ruby remembered chewing the redness, the seed, that shone like a million sisters in the palm of Kara's hand.

But in a breath, the memories ended, as the fallen mist evaporated like fine dew in the rising sun.

Again, Ruby's coal-brown eyes filled with horror. Her

mouth bent and warped into a gnarled gash. Her skin carved deep like welted wounds. She grunted, and then fell to the floor and beat her forehead rhythmically until she broke skin and bled.

No . . . not then . . . not then could she remember just two hours earlier, whispering behind sleeping eyes, "Hold me like a crescent moon. Gently, not to wake too soon."

Or the name, "Kara."

Or a few notes of a bell-toned song.

Ruby could not remember. But the old house did. And it gracefully, gratefully held each sound like a lullaby. Drinking in the music of the words. And as Ruby drifted into her after break-fast slumber, the cracked house sang them back to her, with long rolling creaks and the rustling of worn brocade curtains in the eastern sun.


The same sun warmed the back of Ephram's neck as he began his journey. It glowed against his dark skin and called forth a thin sheen of sweat. Celia Jenkins had been fussing before he left about children who were set to spark some ole gal and had to lie to their mamas to do it. She had been talking to the air just outside of Ephram's door as he had laced his shoes.

It did not occur to Celia Jenkins to speak to other than the door frame and the broom handle and the empty long hall. Just as it did not occur to Ephram to form an answer.

He kissed his mama on the cheek as she mumbled into the glass-topped sitting table. He said good-bye as she began convers-ing with the plastic covers on the gold-leaf sofa she was dusting. Andy Williams' "Closer My Lord to Thee" and the rise and fall of Celia Jenkins' tremulous voice followed him down the walkway onto the road.

Ephram could feel the warming sun rising behind him as he walked. The faint scent of Mennen antiperspirant, Pullman shaving cream, and Colgate toothpaste kept him company. He watched his shadow stretching before him. It grew shorter in increments as the sun climbed in the sky and he came closer to Belle Land. He thought of the house holding Ruby. He thought of the curved piece of earth between them and walked carefully. Careful of the cloud of sweetness he carried on fine gold-rimmed porcelain, careful not to let the September breeze blow twigs and dirt under the cotton cover, careful not to get the red road on the polished black of his boots. Careful not to hope. He walked and thought and held his mama's cake.

The old Belle house had stood there for nearly a century. Had been nailed board by board by Ruby's granddaddy. The planks hewn and planed by his sure hands. Its chimney still a jutting angle. Its steps still a little slanted. "To keep out them shaky, crooked folks," he would say. "Straight-minded folk can walk up any kinda stairs."

And sure enough, many's the day folks ended up in Mama Belle's sugar snap beans just to the right of the porch. They'd be brushing off earth and twine and sweet beans torn from the vine and grumbling, while the inside of the house would be catching and tossing full round laughter.

He laughed quite a bit, Mr. Belle did. He laughed at things that no one else found funny. He laughed at funerals. He laughed at hurricanes and floods. He didn't laugh at the loss or misery, but at the way the hand of nature spun the world about like a woman at a square dance. He laughed at the foolishness of folks who kept getting huffy and indignant at the way they were getting spun.

He sat each evening with fresh tobacco filling his yellow pipe, and his back firm against his rocker. He would puff deep and long. Then he'd put down his pipe and take out his curved amber fiddle and bow. He'd play the sun a going-away tune. Then he'd stitch a patch of song into the night with his flying horsetail needle, threading the twilight sky with music. The night looked kindly upon him and flung the brightest, highest stars to his piece of the horizon. It was the only welcome she knew to offer, as he tipped his hat like a courting gentleman before disappearing into the slanted house.

The proud evening found herself blushing a deep indigo. She pressed against the clean smell of the wood. She lay her ear to the silent earth. She listened. She heard the hollow of a waiting womb. She felt the brittle anger of the wife who slept beside him. The gentle night opened her dark hand and released two of her favorite stars. She pressed them palm flat, through the sky, through the wooded house, through the layers of cotton nightdress and woolen underpants, through the firm, round tan belly, through the hot rush of blood and flesh. She planted them in the womb of this woman, Ruby's mother's mother. A star, within a star: first one daughter, then the daughter of a daughter. A generation of starlight to twinkle like diamonds in the old man's eyes.

But in her fervor to gift the man, the night forgot to look into the eyes of the sleeping woman. Forgot, in fact, to see what lay behind the oiled lids. And when the woman started and sat bolt upright in the bed, the night saw, and was chilled. For the woman drank life in the dry well of her eyes. The woman drew breath from kittens and the small mossy tops of growing new things. The woman placed her tight fist over the rise of her belly and involuntarily struck. The night bowed with the weight of regret.

No more did the young night leap glistening and wild from the edge of the setting horizon, to splash her darkness across the sky. Now she strained as she traveled the stretch of land with the slanted steps and the chinaberry tree. With each passing year she hung even lower, and walked a bit slower, until the hem of her wide skirt dragged and caught and tore. Ruby arrived in Liberty when the night was in tatters, like an old lonely woman.

Ephram moved as slowly as a turtle down the red road as his shadow disappeared under his feet. He thought of the time Ruby had first arrived in the town fresh from New York. She had worn city shoes with thin straps and height. She had carried five bags, a portable typewriter and a square camera case. She had black lines framing her questioning eyes and currant-colored lips that smiled quickly and nervously. She had wanted to know how to get to the old Belle place. She said she was Papa Belle's kin and had spent some time there as a child, and that she wanted to capture the "essence" and "charm" of the place before it disappeared. She carried disdain and desperation into the store like an unpleasant scent.

Ephram had been getting his mother a Sunday paper when he heard her. Saw her. Saw the circles of sweat under the crisp blue of her sundress. Saw her pointing first this way and that, trying fruitlessly to follow Harold Perkins' spoken map, cutting him off tersely and then offering to pay Harold Jr. to drive her out back that way without an inkling that she was insulting both the family and the man.

Ephram had seen all of this and did not know why he felt his heart pierced with a crushing sorrow. He avoided her as he laid the dime and nickel down on the counter. He was careful not to brush her as he swept silently from the store.

Ephram kept to himself very much of that day. He did not even notice his yellow cat, Kitten, when she pressed herself against his ankles in the evening time, as was her custom. He forgot to wish his mother a pleasant sleep. He did not brush his teeth or put on fresh pajamas. He lay in his thin bed, fully clothed, staring into the ancient night. He did not allow himself to sleep until dawn.

Six years had passed since her June arrival, three since he had seen her as fallen rain. Now he approached the leaning slant of the house to the right of the road. The stone well sat boarded and covered and dry.

Ephram could hear the crunch of his boots in the silence. He could feel the brittle crisp of the grass and the worn slope of the stairs. He felt a prickly heat above his full lips. His heart rang like a cowbell in his chest. Ephram stood under the splintered porch awning, took off his hat, and knocked. Silence. He knocked again. Silence. Again. Again. Again.

Tentatively, cake in hand, he circled the house. Several times he cleared his throat and said, "Excuse me." He knocked again on the door. Then he leaned on the rusted screen and looked at the day fading to afternoon.

Here he was, waiting in the shade of the porch. The sugar sweet rising like cane through the blue plaid cake cover. And since he couldn't find her and since she didn't answer, he gently placed his hat back on his head, dusted off his polished boot tips, and sat down on the lanai, to the right of the cake, and waited to greet her—to greet her with the welcome of her first birthday in six years. Although he had chosen the date from his calendar.

He waited as the sun slipped low in the sky. He did not know until after that he had fallen asleep.

He woke when he heard the midnight wailing.

Ephram Jenkins walked around the leaning shadowed wood with his covered cake in hand. There he saw her digging in the dry cracked earth with her bare hands. He saw Ruby jerk and rip at a solid root. He walked silently closer and saw that in the impact, one of her nails had peeled back and hung by bloody cartilage and mud made by the wet smear of her own red wound. He saw her bury her wound deeper into the soil.

She dug with a fury. A whipping wild might and she wailed until the roots and branches shook. And her tears streamed like lava as she cried in words scratched like charred wood, "My babies . . . Jesus! Jesus! They pulled my babies out my womb . . . Jesus Lord they pulled them out . . . They pulled them out and ate them whole! Jesus Lord! Jesus Lord!"

Webs of saliva spewed from the twisted knot of her mouth and she spread her acres of legs and pressed into the shallow grave of earth and released the hidden soul of yet another of her murdered children.

Ephram watched her bury it and consecrate it with her tears. Ephram knew that he had seen the breaking of the storm. He held his white lay angel cake like a waiting moon against the flat blackness of the night.

Ruby bled into the earth. She bled onto the rooted earth. She held onto the root to keep from spinning off into space and stars. In the holding came a knowing, an understanding that the root she held belonged to the fallen chinaberry tree.

Before the hurricane, the tree had lived on the land for four long centuries. Its roots hollowed to underground rivers and tunneled through Ever-Lawns cemetery. They grew through the splintered wood of waiting coffins. They wrapped about silent blanched bones and offered lost spirits a home.

Upon the roots rested houses and secrets stitched into handkerchiefs. The chinaberry tree held much in its knotted arms. The tree's snaking roots held Ruby.

And in that moment Ruby was graced with the knowing of the old bloodstained root. The knowing of the old bloodstained root. She felt her fingers, limbs and sternum harden and grow thick and gnarled and reaching. Ephram looked and saw her becoming. Once again, the two knowings met. And Ruby, who had become the root of the chinaberry tree, heard the whispering of women and the scream of their young.

The roots told her of black folks: black, brown and yellow, and some passing white, but black folks all the same.

The marrow of the tree remembered what had never been told. What no woman would ever tell, what they didn't dare tell themselves. Of breasts ordered cut off by mistresses. Of the wombs pierced with hot pokers through twelve-year-old vaginas . . . more . . . more . . . A drunken white man splitting his one-year-old daughter in two after shoving his penis into her . . . After taking his knife and cutting to make her opening large enough. About the mother finding the child laid open like that.

The roots cradled her as they told her that this mother was her kin, generations old, Ruby's great-great-great-grandmother, who had taken her next baby and held the back of her thin neck and cut with a sharpened knife over a newly dug hollow of earth; she did it to release, to save, to protect. She did it in love.

For she had wanted the child to warm her sleep bed. She had wanted the child to make her smile in the death of her life. She had wanted the child to hold to her beating heart, to suckle at her heavy breast, to love. But Willa knew the price of such luxury.

She had paid it before, and would not again. So when she killed the child she did it in love.

And she did it in prayer that if she offered the blood of her baby, her dear moving smiling one, that God might spare her other five, two of them girls, might spare them. So she cut. And the blood collected in the well of earth. And she lay there all night with her daughter's lifeless form wet in her arms. She prayed her spirit home to Afrik. She prayed her spirit home.

When the men heard what Willa had done, they called her crazy. They spit at her in the fields and hung crow's feet on her door. But after a time it took root in the rotting marsh that can grow in the mind of all powerless things. In time the men started meeting, started digging earthen wells, at night, once a year, to send another spirit home. But it was no longer that. No. It had started by then. By then it was grinding down all the hatred they could find and then looking for more. And babies were not freed, they were snatched and ripped from gagged mothers' wombs. And it was their own men who tortured and murdered in the silence of southern nights while their masters slept a hundred yards away.

The whispering root took a deep breath. In its release it trembled, and the world seemed to shift, and one and a half miles away the split thick trunk of the chinaberry tree swayed. The rusted bells rang on the fallen branches.

Ruby sobbed into the hole of earth. She held to the solid root.


Ephram Jenkins saw Ruby born of the tree's anchor. He saw her emerge from the pit of fiber and soil she had dug. He saw the hem of her graying dress. A corner had been ripped away and a clean fold of pale blue cloth lay gently across her legs. And he realized that he could not ask this root daughter, this passing storm, this act of nature, if she wanted white lay angel cake. Or a picnic lunch next Sunday after services. Or to cross the threshold of his home as his bride. No. He could not. But he could feel her might and her beauty, her truth and pride. He could help her to her feet.

Ephram reached out for the first time in his forty-three years. He reached out to smooth down her dress bunched high about her. He took a folded handkerchief from his left trouser pocket and wiped her face and tried to wrap it about her hand.

And with her face still wet with tears, she lay on down, down on the hard brown grass, she opened her legs again and expected.

Ephram could not know that they had been coming by, Chauncy Shankle, Gilbert Fillers, Moss Reyfolk and more, twisted and broken as she was, for months on years to push into her. He could not know that they had always come, to leave her filled with their congealed waste, that clung like Elmer's glue to her thighs. The creased hatted men who entered and left like thick black ghosts, with midnight claw hands and Crisco wrapped in wax paper so they could slide in and out of her rectum.

He could not know that to Ruby Belle, he was only one more, and for her the swifter he finished the better, and he had brought what looked like a cake, which was more than most, more than all. So when he smoothed Ruby's skirt again, she snarled at him. Because if he didn't want to rip into her openings, he must want something more vile.

She snarled and her legs and firm feet kicked him. Kicked the waiting moon cake. Kicked his bluish full lips and bent back one of his strong bone-white teeth. She crouched like a wet possum, her tail wrapped about her gray heaving form, prepared for his redirected anger.

And this is when Ephram sat on Papa Belle's land and began sobbing. He sobbed into the smashed splayed whiteness that had once risen cane. And his crying entered Ruby. His crying spirit entered her like the spirit of a child yet to be born.

And she sat with him and cried anew, surrounded by the circle of spring elms, the rise of the rooted chinaberry and the small pregnant hills filled with the souls of her murdered children.

And she told Ephram how they had done it. How it had happened on this land after her grandpapa had died. How her grandmother had given her over again and again to the dead-eyed men. How they had bound her arms and mouth twenty years before. How they had scraped into her young sixteen-year-old body and retrieved an eight-month-old moving being. How they had laid it upon her belly. How they had pierced its abdomen with a steel knife. How it had slipped upon her. How they had not cut the cord. How they had sought to consume the spirit of her child. How all of her babies had died in the teeth of black-eyed haints, of ghost men still roaming her body searching for hidden souls. She told how she hid them in the womb of earth. How the earth was nursing them to the warm beat of her red mountain heart.

Ephram stared at this woman, who held the ocean in the shore of her eyes, who was as still as stone, as proud as cane, as dark as this hush of twilight. And that was when he realized that he did not have to ask the universe that was Ruby to love him. And so together, like small ashy-kneed children they stared into the sweep of sky.

*Afrekete*                                                                 252

Ephram spoke into the womb of velvet night and said that soon her babies would emerge like turtles from eggs and head for the sea of stars.

Ruby looked at this gentle man, who seemed like forgotten kin, and felt their souls braiding with that of the tree and rising to meet the arch of sky. Ruby circled her lips and let out a breath of awe. The deep night tied the silvery braided rope about her soft dark waist, shifted her horizon and contemplated the kindling of dawn.

Ruby and Ephram sat in wonder. They sat in silent sacred reverence while they ate the most amazing white lay angel cake and bits of dirt and grass upon the spinning pregnant earth.

MELANIE HOPE

*Dare*

As a child my mother taught me to stretch my arms above my head and say, "Good morning, world," at the beginning of the day. I remember this ritual making me feel like the world was welcoming me to it. Now I walk through the world as an African North American lesbian whose lover is a white woman, and I still find myself saying "Good morning, world" on days when I need to reassure myself that this world wants me here and that this is where I belong.

This childhood memory has stayed with me like so many others that skip, rattle, and jump through my head. Memories and voices filled with lessons and rules that I was always to abide. Some of these rules I have followed loyally while others I proudly have betrayed. My celebration of each day is an example of the former response. My lesbianism exemplifies the latter.

The one rebellion against family lore that I found to be very difficult was having a white lover. We were given very adamant messages against interracial love. I was taught to look down on Black people who had either married white people or had intimate relations with them.

My family came to the United States from Guyana and Nevis. I am of the second generation to be born here. Like many people of their time, my grandparents went from Ellis Island to Brooklyn and settled there to begin their new lives. They cleaned the homes of white people, worked in factories owned by white people, saved their money, and prayed in churches run by white people. They hoped their children's lives would be easier, meaning they would have more opportunities to prosper and jobs where they didn't have to get their hands dirty cleaning up after others. They wanted their children to own their own homes and cars and they saw that the way to achieve this was by getting as much education as possible.

None of my grandparents are alive now and I often wonder how they would fit into my life if they were still here. I wonder if I would be "out" to them, or take my new girlfriends to their homes hoping for their approval. In their lives they didn't have intimate ties outside of their own racial community. Although they went to school with the white children of other immigrants, those relationships didn't transcend school grounds. My parents, like my grandparents, didn't have white people they called friends. Their relationships with them were limited to either school or work environments. Unlike my parents and grandparents, I have always had non-Black friends, and those friendships are intimate and they extend into my private life. I was born in the late sixties and came of age in a time that allowed these types of relationships to form.

My parents met in church in their early teens, dated until their early twenties, and got married. Then they made what was considered a great journey at that time and moved from Brooklyn to New Jersey. Although their move was unprecedented, there were no protests or disappointments about their choice. By getting married, they were doing what their families and communities expected.

My mother has told me many times the story of how after I was born and she made sure I had all my fingers and toes, she began to map out the events of my life. She knew, before taking me home from the hospital, what I was going to do and when. In her plan, I was essentially a newer version of herself. With more freedom and more options I would be able to do anything her class, sex, or race may have prohibited her from doing. She saw me in school, working, growing into an independent woman, choosing a nice man from a nice family, and settling down according to heterosexual tradition. Needless to say, there have been things that I've done that my mother failed to include in her planning, many of which have left her feeling disappointed and even hurt. My being a lesbian wasn't even in the dimmest, dustiest corner of her mind.


My family has always been small in links of blood but large in links of friendship and love. Our home is the meeting place for holidays, birthdays, doing homework, or just hanging out and talking. There is always plenty of food and a welcoming vibe and a cultural union of the West Indies, the South, and Harlem. Our home is a place where Blackness is celebrated. My brother, myself, our cousins, and others who lingered there had daily confirmations that being Black was, is, and will always be beautiful. It was in the music we listened to, the books we read, and the positive images that surrounded us. I didn't grow up thinking my lips were too big or my hair too nappy. No one ever told me my nose was too wide, that I shouldn't stay out in the sun too long, or not to eat watermelon on the front stoop. It was never questioned that we would embrace our natural selves: smells, textures, and all. Every time we left home, we left that celebration of Black in some way, but we also learned how to carry it with us, wherever we went.

Very often the places we were going were predominantly white. Places like church, school, or the doctor. They were predominantly white because, like their parents before them, my parents wanted only what was considered the "best" for their children, and white people had access to what was "best." So there we were, in the "best" private schools and in the waiting rooms of the "best" doctors. In these places I often felt isolated, as if I wasn't where I truly belonged.

When we came in contact with this whiteness, we were somehow supposed to know where to draw the line of intimacy. As children we were to know that it was okay to have slumber parties with white friends and go to each other's homes for dinner, but that an interracial couple in the street epitomized betrayal of the entire race. Everyone thought the Black girl with hazel/green eyes was pretty, but somehow the union of her white mother and Black father could not be tolerated or imitated. We were coming of age in a racially mixed time and place but we were still given the rules of segregation that our parents knew to live by. My brother and I came of age as middle-class Black children, the notorious "bourgeoisie," with new privileges and choices. It was up to our generation to determine how those new options would be integrated. Our parents wanted us to have options, to be free, but still not to wander too far from them. The message was that it was okay to have white friends but not white family.

We were taught that interracial love was a false love and doomed to fail. "He better not bring no white girl home" was a familiar refrain, one that I heard so often I cannot name the voice. But the voice was a strong one that lingers in my memory. "Home" was for family, where we were safe, and white people were not family. One cousin brought his white girlfriend home from college and the way condolences were paid to his mother, it was as if he had died. "Well, at least he didn't bring home a man," I remember a voice saying. This was another important piece of information to take in and integrate into the contradictory rules of the game.

There are many contradictions for me between what I was told to believe about interracial love and what my experience has shown me. Neal was the exception that proved the family rule. He was a Jewish man and a very close friend of my parents and a sort of big brother to me since his age fell somewhere between my parents' and mine. He was welcomed to every family occasion, even if it meant going to church. He was also known to only date Black women, which in his case, made him more accepted in the family. Had he not been part of the family and was seen on the street with one of his girlfriends, he would have been subject to those same judgments. If he had been a Black guy who only dated white women, he would not have been seen as an appropriate role model for me, let alone my brother. Years later I remember learning that a friend of my parents, whom I'd always assumed was single, had been in a closeted heterosexual relationship with a white woman for over twenty years. No one, including my parents, ever spoke about this. More information for me to take in. I decided that no matter what I chose to do with my life I would never hide. I would never do anything I felt obviously ashamed of. The messages, you see, were often mixed. There were rules and there were the exceptions. And there were the revised rules. It was obvious to me that I wasn't determining any of them but was expected to live my life according to them.

Finishing high school was a symbolic transition into young adulthood and I was on my way to college like every other student from my private high school. I was taking the expected next step by going to another private institution where people would assume I was on scholarship, even though I wasn't. More than anything I was waiting, wanting, to be far enough from home to "come out" and deal with the lesbian inside of me that wanted very much to be acknowledged. My first day on campus I met the androgynous, unshaven, short-haired woman with no bra that I had imagined a lesbian was supposed to look like and I was immediately attracted. I had found what I thought I was looking for. However, in my pre-college fantasies I hadn't considered the challenges of her being white. With all the warnings from childhood I had never actually been intimate with a white person.

The first time we made love, the first time we lay breast-to-breast, it made so much sense to me, it felt right. I was too young to be afraid of falling madly in love and so that's exactly what I did. She was the first person to hold me through the night, and she was the first person who truly made love to me. It was a new world opening up to me from that day forward and I was loving it too much to care that she was white. I didn't care initially because I was finally acknowledging and releasing my lesbianism. It also didn't matter that she was white because I was taking such great care to be sure that no one knew what was really going on between us. And it was easy to hide the fact that my lover was a white woman when I was hiding so many other things about myself.

Soon it took too much to let myself love her. Soon I wanted to stop hiding my lesbianism and I thought I was ready to begin the process of coming out. What I realized very quickly was that I was not ready to come out about being in an interracial relationship. I was afraid of being left out even more than I already felt. I was searching for a place that would be accepting of me, and I knew that being in an interracial lesbian relationship wouldn't get me in anywhere. Eventually the racial conflicts became too much for me to deal with and I left the relationship. I had to leave; all those old voices from childhood had conquered me. I later felt like I had given in too easily because of what I feared other people were thinking. I regretted leaving.

When I decided to come out, the one person in my family I felt I had to tell first was my mother. She was the person who really mattered. I thought that if I could tell her and she could accept me—which I was sure she would—then it wouldn't matter how anyone else felt. It was the first summer I was home from college and one evening I asked her to come into my room. She sat down and I remember sweat dripping off me as I told her I was a lesbian. Everything went better than I thought it would and I went to bed that night feeling relieved. But about two days later, everything that seemed calm exploded. I wasn't at all prepared for the backlash of my mother's response. By having gay friends, whom she herself helped to deal with their parents' homophobia, she had given me a different impression of who she was. Her only explanation was, "You're my daughter—it's different." From that day forward my relationship with my mother was never the same. We looked at each other differently, spoke to each other differently, and avoided any reference to my homosexuality. There emerged between us a tense silence that I have had to battle continually.

I waited an entire year before coming out to my father and brother, and this time I chose to do so in a letter. They seemed to take it all in stride, at least in relation to how my mother had responded. I believe part of my father's ability to remain calm and be supportive has to do with the fact that his role as a primary male figure in my life was not being threatened. I think if someone were to be seen as worthy of blame for my lesbianism, it would be my mother. She was the one who had failed; as the same-sex parent, she had obviously forgotten to do something which allowed me to stray from the heterosexual path.

Experience taught me to be much more careful of exposing my "deviant" sexuality. I relearned to be silent about my true self, and as a result I was left feeling like an outsider much of the time. In college the safe lesbian places on campus were predominantly white, while the Black places were heterosexual. I didn't feel I fit in anywhere, but from my "outsider" perspective I finally began to see the distorted vision of the world—in terms of interracial love—that had been handed down to me. These new insights turned the sadness of not being able to keep the first love I had found into anger. The contradictions that had always been floating harmlessly around me began to turn on me. I wanted, for the first time ever, to be someone other than who I was. I started to question who was making the rules of this game I had been forced into. I kept asking myself why I was trying to live by standards of people who didn't want to have anything to do with me.

Around this time of heightened confusion and feelings of isolation I heard a tape of Pat Parker reading her poem which begins, "My lover is a Woman." In this poem she writes about her personal, familial, and societal struggles as a result of having a white lover with blond hair and blue eyes. For her there were conflicts, and consideration of how her ancestors may feel concerning such a union. Here was a woman who had felt what I was feeling.

Now Pat Parker is dead. She has moved on to be with the ancestors, and I think, "Well, at least she loved who she wanted to love in the time she was here." I question whether or not I am brave enough to do the same. What if she hadn't taken that dare? What would her life have been worth if she had shunned the one she truly loved because of race? What does it mean now that she's gone? I wonder if there were disapproving friends who now see the absurdity of their judgments? I wonder.

I don't think it was a complete coincidence that my next serious relationship was with a Black woman. I was seeking affirmation through likeness that I thought would be possible with her. Through her I found a community of other Black lesbians outside the insular college scene. Finally I fit in—and I thought I could rest awhile. I had found a new home. Yet, in that home, like all others, there were rules to live by. That particular group of Black lesbians enforced the rule that it wasn't acceptable to "deal in snow," which meant it wasn't cool to be involved with white women. Although I was involved with a Black woman at the time, I was not willing to make assumptions about other Black women who were not. I still remembered what it felt like to be looked at as being on the other side of the proverbial fence. My initial feelings of comfort didn't last for long in this community, and that relationship ended for reasons other than race.

There aren't many role models to be found for interracial love. Not in lesbian, gay, bisexual, or heterosexual worlds. There aren't people demonstrating in the street or demanding more respect and visibility for their interracial relationships. There are few formal networks of support, so I have found some of my own role models.

Audre Lorde was another Black lesbian whose writings I had been introduced to in college. I learned she had also dared to love across racial barriers and written about it. In her book *The Cancer Journals* she writes about realizing how in the moments she felt herself closest to death she saw how pointless her silences were. Times when she was silent out of fear, and out of wanting approval of others. I suppose in such moments much of how we have lived our lives becomes more clear. Her words have forced me to look at how I have lived and want to continue to live. There are some regrets, but there are also many triumphs and reasons for celebration. The celebrations are for times I have stood my ground or spoken out for something I believed in. Or when I have conquered a fear that had once seemed insurmountable.

James Baldwin once wrote: "People pay for what they do, and still more, for what they have allowed themselves to become. And they pay for it simply: by the lives they lead." He is another role model for me for many reasons: as a writer, as a proud gay man, and as a fierce thinker. He was also in a long-term intimate relationship with someone who was not Black. When I assess my life in my last days, if I am given that chance, I hope I am able to feel content with the life I've led. I hope there are not too many regrettable silences. I hope there are not loves that I've not let myself embrace because of societal limitations that attempt to control me and the power of my love.

Pat Parker, Audre Lorde, and James Baldwin are all people that have had a tremendous impact on the lives of others. Their ability to see the importance of honesty in who they were above their fears will continue to be as inspiring as it was the first time I encountered their work. Their love for non-Black people did not inhibit their vision. They are all important African-American writers of their time. And in no way did their concern for the world's treatment of Black people lessen because of the intimate relationships they shared with people who are not Black. I think the high level of their creativity and the words their literary selves dared and the ways they transcended those boundaries involve the same forces it took for them to catapult over boundaries in their personal lives.

I met my lover in New York City in front of the Lesbian and Gay Community Services Center in 1991. We are intimate in ways our ancestors could not have dreamed of. Not solely because we have crossed the boundary of heterosexuality but also by virtue of the fact that we are loving across race and not hiding. There has been a noticeable increase in the level of intimacy between Black people and white people in the last two generations. But regardless of these changes, messages persist in our society that say we should not be loving each other the way we do. By doing so we are breaking two significant taboos.

*Dare*

On my desk there is a picture of my lover and me. She is kissing me. We are smiling. The color difference is as clear as the different textures of our hair. We are daughters of two very distant tribes yet we are drawn to each other by an unnamable force we usually understate with the word "love." When I started to fall in love with her I was guarded. I tried to be aloof. I thought she was charming, warm, and beautiful—but she was white and I did not want to get too close. I had already been through that with the first woman I was involved with. I was already a lesbian, and I kept telling myself, that was taboo enough. I didn't want to threaten the place I had established in my new community of other African-American lesbians. I was afraid of all the feelings that drew me to her.

It has been frightening at times for me to love her. I sometimes think the history is too thick and the language too polluted. Then I remind myself that I am not every Black woman in history, nor is she every white woman. But there is the bloodshed of racism under each step we take together and under every place we lay our heads. There were times when I felt bombarded by inner conflicts, when I needed to go outside of myself and find other people, books, any resources available to help disentangle my thoughts and feelings. There were times I felt like I was going crazy trying to sift through all of this alone. Again and again I would realize that the conflicts were based on the messages from family and the outside world that I digested as a child.

My fears were not that a mob would attack us in the street, but more about being rejected by my family, friends, and other Black lesbians. It was difficult for me to be intimate or vulnerable when we were in public. I know my lover, and I know the work she's done on her own on issues of race, class, and sexuality. But the person who sees us together on the subway doesn't know that. Even the lesbian who sees us out at a bar doesn't know anything except that we are Black and white and obviously together and in love. They don't know my struggles or hers, they don't know us, they don't know who we are. It reminds me of how unfair I always thought it was when, as a child, I heard people being judged based on whom they were walking down the street with. I remember arguing, "Maybe they're just friends," in some meager attempt to save that Black person from being condemned. It was clear also that more emphasis was put on Black men who had married white women rather than the other way around, as if the Black women were somehow more disposable and less important to the race. I suppose there was just part of me, in my childhood innocence, that wanted to protect all of those people from unfair judgment.

After many rounds of internal fighting, several nights lying awake debating whether I could acknowledge my feelings, I gave in to my desire for her. Once I entered, just as I knew all along, I didn't want to leave the connection that had quickly formed. Unfortunately I was still afraid and this fear manifested itself in the form of petty arguments, distancing myself emotionally, and trying to hide my relationship from others. I spent a lot of time unsure of what I felt; even in the morning when I reluctantly unraveled myself from around her I questioned the validity of my feelings. I convinced myself whenever we had a difficulty that it just wasn't meant to be, that it would never work, that we were from different places and obviously wanted different things. My favorite mantra was, "We're going to break up eventually, so we may as well break up now."

I had walked for a long time with internal fears of disapproval both by people I loved most and by strangers. I had walked around ready to fight anyone who dared me. Then one day it occurred to me that no one had approached me on the street, or in my home, or at a party. No one had said any of the things that I imagined they were waiting to say. And as I began to look at myself I began to see that many of my fears were coming from inside me. And when I became aware of that, I was able to begin to release them. I turned off those voices of disapproval, my own voices, that were scrambling in my head for my attention.

There were breaks, there were silences, and tears, but the more I settled down internally and shut out all the voices of disapproval, much of the drama was shut out too. With each step out of silence and hiding I felt myself treading more stable ground. I still overprepared myself for the possibility of conflict, but not to a point of becoming an incubator for unexpressed rage. I got to a place where I could give myself permission to fully love my lover, and the power it gave both of us shattered those old fears and silenced those old voices.

When I looked to role models and I looked to friends for support, it came, many times from unexpected people. When I was able to introduce Catherine as "my lover" with certainty, people respected it. I find the more time she and I spend with my family, the more comfortable we all become. She is no longer just a white woman, but a person who is very important to my life. While there are still many conversations that need to take place, I feel I have, with family and friends, reached a point of mutual respect and peace.

Through these struggles I have come to know everything can't be okay all of the time. I also know that no one is accepted everywhere all of the time. By affirming myself and following my feelings I have been able to have my whole self in my relationship for the first time ever. I want most of all to be free. Free to be a lesbian, and free to love my woman even if she is of a different race than I.

Although our struggles are different, we walk through them together. For her, race was one of many ways we were different and would not be one that determined whether or not she stayed in the relationship. At the same time she was able to stand with me through my process of coming to terms with our racial difference and listen and talk when I needed her to.

Now when I wake up next to my lover and I reach my hands toward the sky and say "Good morning, world," I can feel just as sure that this world is welcoming me to it as I did when I was a child. Our love is as real as it could possibly be. I have not lost myself. I am still Black woman me. I never wanted to lose my place in my tribe and now I know that I won't.

The most intense love in my life has come from a place I was taught to not expect or receive it. And I know that I am not the only Black lesbian who has had this circumstance to deal with. I know there are other sisters out there feeling nervous about taking their non-Black girlfriends certain places, feeling ashamed and angry. I know there are some of us who feel excluded from certain crowds because of our non-Black girlfriends. But I am here to testify that there is a place for all of us out here if we demand it.

I have come through this process a more affirmed and confident African-American lesbian. I was forced to expand my vision, and in doing so all kinds of new information has been allowed to slip in. Even if people make negative assumptions about my lover and I when they see us together, as they may, I know that they are only seeing the cover to the book on our love. We continue to grow together, nurturing our relationship, each other, and our-selves. In our growth, like all change, there is some fear, but we've learned to step through that as well. We continue to dream, imag-ine our future and create it as it comes. I am daring to love the person I want to love.

SHAREE NASH

# Take Care

*I seemed to go from nags to bitches. I allowed them to wail in my face until it was spackled with the textured spittle of rage, their eyes, lips, teeth, tongues whirling like a bright carousel of fire, whirling and spinning and spinning and whooshing into a blinding white chimera. Tirades, damnations, invectives. I couldn't ignore their baiting and chanting, so I would, once again, pack my existence with all of its longings and quietly leave those lovers behind.*

It was true that I had spent a magnificent part of my life as a fugitive. Raised on the fruit of divestment and learned in the nature of self-elation, displacement was my form. And so I would run from one to another in need of contact, but always expecting indifference.

Owning precious and little—a battered hide sack full of magical elixirs, substantial, well-worn boots that carried me in a supernatural manner, and my self-worth thrown hastily over my shoulders—I could flee at any moment's notice.

I would leave, sometimes at the very height of distress, because bliss had spun wildly out of control. I'd arrive numb, on blue-black nights, secretly knocking at dangerous doors, empty and dismal, and desperately seeking shelter. I'd softly plead with strangers to open up their doors and spare me a tiny, simple place to be. So I was invited into placid and mannered homes that carried the aroma of pity and changed them. Once inside, I would pull out my elixirs and cast a spell and soon I'd be kissing thrilled lips, holding thankful bodies, and stroking weary heads. I, foolishly, gave them something to believe in. Sweet, gentle lovers who would soon go mad when they realized that I could not believe in anything.

They always sat back in gratitude and watched as I pulled all kinds of healing ointments from my sack. They would watch uneasily as I moved around. Did they know that I was always moving away from them? They hoped that I might offer my self-worth in exchange for their stability. And sometimes, senselessly, I would surrender because I did not know the value of my own self-worth. Always gaining little or nothing from such exchanges, I would leave for another city and new strangers. It never occurred to me that what I needed was a belief in something, a faith in someone compelling that might make me stay.

I was lured to the next town by softly throbbing lights, the clatter of heels against concrete, and the rousing tempo of distant voices.

In those towns I gambled lavishly with my precious possessions, because they were all that I had and they deserved every chance at extravagance.

In those towns, I was shrouded in the night, excited by the delicious amber liquors, the pipes with plumes of smoke from herbs and opiates, the aromatic breads and meats and oils and spices. The nights would turn out hoarse, saxophones and clarinets mingling with the sultry thumping on drum skins.

I would languish in the night's vast lap, and listen to stories —tales told by degenerates/devils/hustlers/lovers/adventurers/angels. I would close my eyes and listen to stories about plump anonymous rumps pressed against steamy, steady grinding hips; smooth mounds sizzling under the kiss of moist mouths; firm, insistent hands entering the two-halves of natural design, beautifully caressing swollen flesh.

This would send my mind reeling and I would leap from that lap and join the story makers.


I ordered another coffee, lit a cigarette, breathed air, heard music. And then I saw her. She was having a coffee and a snifter of Sambuca delivered to her table. I watched her wrap a large, amber-colored hand around the round-bottom glass and pour the clear liquor into the black coffee. Then she brought the empty snifter to her lips, closing the dark lids over her eyes while drinking.

Her neck was massive, packed with luscious muscle. I wanted to put my lips on her shoulders and climb that mighty neck kiss by slow sweet kiss until I reached her colossal mouth.

I wanted her to look up from the pages of her small,

hardbound book. I ordered a whiskey for my own coffee and watched. I could see the last three letters of the gold-engraved title of the small book—*gic.* Was it *Magic?* Or *Tragic?*

I took a cigarette from the case, just as she pulled a chubby little smoke from the pack lying on her table, never taking her eyes off the pages of her book. Maybe *Logic* was in the title.

We began to mirror one another: she would turn a page in her book just as I turned a text-filled page in my notebook; as I went for my coffee mug, she would just be placing her bulky cup back down on the wooden table.

When her waiter came to her to refill her cup, she ordered another Sambuca. Then I saw, clearly, her lovely face. I ordered another whiskey.

Her eyes were big brown tarnishes with wild heavy black lashes, and swirling above those eyes were two black thickets of brow. Her short hair was parted loosely up the middle and curled into the air like sooty, smoky wisps.

When my whiskey arrived, I took a sluggish draw from the glass while I watched her roll a glistening tongue over her lips to taste the Sambuca.

One black clog clung loosely to the beige sole of her foot like a clump of dark, damp sod from the earth.

All around my body was this sense of mysterious satisfaction. My eyes followed one of her amber-colored hands, one finger adorned with a polished silver ring that held two great pieces of moonstone in its middle. That hand lay upon the rich mahogany tabletop and I watched her begin to unconsciously stroke the heavy wood, gently fingering the smooth veneer. I reflexively began to caress my shaven head, stroking the plushy velvet, black hairs.

I lit another cigarette and drank more whiskey. Her cigarette lay burning in the ashtray. She lifted it to her lips, lips like two purple plums; ripe and tumescent. She was a slow and affectionate lover to her cigarette, guiding the tan filter tip to those voluptuous lips, parting them with uncomplicated consent, taking deep pulls that stirred the cherry to crackle and glow as flecks of ash shot off, savoring the inhalations of blue-gray smoke loitering deep within her chest, exhaling billows of smoke, bringing the cigarette to repletion.

Our smoke mingled and filled the air of Daza. My reason was lulled by the liquor, and I was in the mood to take myself in her direction. But I knew how easily I could squander the whole of my self-worth on such dazzling caprices. I knew well how easily I could be put in the mood, and how disruptively I could be thrown out of it, so I decided to pray about it, lie about it, deal without it. I decided it best to just gather up my things and get gone from that café.

Her voice was like old, bartered coins rustling in a dusty leather pouch. This I knew because she whispered to me as I passed out of the café, *"Cuidaté . . ."*

## TOP SEEKS TOP

There are loves that I had accepted out of reckless curiosity and there were loves that I had endured out of hazy ambivalence. What I truly sought to find was a love ingested for divine intoxication.

There had been too many bizarrely twisted instances when I allowed myself to be led to some sultry sea of despair. Duped by beauty and convinced that my only true pleasure and my only great purpose was that of retrieving some fatal lover from the

*Take Care*

abyss of self-loathing, down I would go, splitting depths to love a decomposing soul.

But these days my demons could only be satisfied with one exploit: the precious act of being caught up.

I wanted rapture: a giant of a lover parting my thighs, moving them like mountains. Smothering my ginger flesh and gentle bones with quiet desire, entering my needy mouth, soaking my tongue with a savory sap. Full lips crashing against mine, stinging, dissolving me into fog. Storms and fogs. Yes, these were the queer days when I was in a constant state of aching. Just walking around felt so intense. My need was so raw that I began combing the classifieds:

AFFECTIONATE HAPPY PUPPIES TO GIVE AWAY

LOVING KITTENS IN SEARCH OF HOME SWEET HOME

COAT CHECK DIVA WANTED FOR HOT NEW NIGHTCLUB

YOUR FABULOUS DREAM HOME ON THE JERSEY SHORE!

BREATHTAKINGLY BEAUTIFUL PILLOW PRINCESS
SEEKS SEXY TAKE-CONTROL TOP

1-800-HOTT-SEX
1-900-LES-BIAN

But nothing like this would do. I did not want anything that could be bought, nothing that could be won from insincere charm, no stealing of only a moment to enjoy forbidden pleasures. I was in need of something that had always been treasured, something ancient and saturated with wisdom.

So I did the only thing that I could do that might ease my

yearning. I made my way over to Daza for some music and some liquor.

## DAZA

Fermina Daza did not return the love of Florintino Ariza for fifty-one years, nine months, and four days in Gabriel García Márquez's *Love in the Time of Cholera.* The café was named after her. I took myself to Daza as often as I could, because she inspired patience. It was to her I went when I needed to understand that my desires might only be contented from a cocktail and some cigarettes and some music. It was at those moments when I was struggling to believe in something that I would fall into the lap of Daza and feel a serenity reiterating like warm, fragrant breath blowing a sacred and enduring mantra in my ears. Daza was the acceptance of nature's temperament. Daza was to endure without complaint. And at the very least, she would provide the loveliest of distractions, the most peculiar of conversations and music to fill the creases of the heart.

> ♫ *You give me attention, you're someone who understands my needs, a man who is sensitive . . . you give me everything I miss at home. You know how to love me and do all the things I want to feel, inside of each tender kiss you're giving me everything I miss at home . . . things I miss at home.* ♪

My friend Gabriel was sprawled at a table off in a corner sipping an extra thick Bloody Mary, and I stopped to say hello to him. Gabriel had just finished the last leg of what he called "three

*Take Care*

nights out" and he was anxious to tell about it. So I sat down. Some friends had taken him up to Harlem, to a luxurious four-story brownstone on a prosperous block. This brownstone served as a safe-sex club on Saturday nights.

"A bordello, honey! Filled with the most gorgeous Black and Latino boys. And get this, you check your clothes at the door."

"What does that mean?"

"That means that you can't go up into the party with any clothes on!"

"No clothes." I mused. It always seemed to me that queens would not go anywhere without the grandest drag as a defense against the viciousness of being seen as flawed. "What did they leave you with for protection?"

"I was fierce! I stripped down to just my work boots, a black velvet thong, and black leather wristbands."

"And you didn't feel defenseless?"

"Oh, there was plenty of protection . . . bowls upon bowls of condoms. Sizes, textures, flavors, colors!"

"Four floors filled with naked bodies ready for play, Gabriel?"

"Romper room all night long and some of the hottest bodies, in so many hues." By this point, Gabriel had no more time for my questions. He rolled himself up to a sitting position and gave details about the first episode of the evening.

"After I got inside, I headed for the bar—the drinks were included in the price of admission—and I ordered a drink and stood in a corner because I knew I would need to ease into that groove. Then some big, thick man came and pressed his crotch against my ass. Now, I had seen him when I was peeling off my clothes at the door; he was behind me in line. Anyway, we didn't speak a word, we just started grinding into each other to the music. Then he led me to one of the private rooms on the first floor . . . The particulars of what went on in that room I cannot disclose, but whatever you can imagine is pretty close to it."

I could only imagine Gabriel's big, brown body tangled with other boy bodies in dark corners, on stairwells, in hallways, in front of small salacious crowds waiting for their chance. I was imagining hot, thick lips pressed against burning, purple mouths, stroking hands, searching fingers, cadent gyrations.

"Honey, there was no limit to my transgressive acts! I had willing men in front of me, unseen faces behind me, eager boys to the left of me, and rainbow bowls of condoms to the right of me."

Then I had to go. I had to get a table and think about the boys and Gabriel and their escapades. I wanted to be left alone to fantasize about the constant, abundant, orgiastic anonymous sex among men; and then to speculate on the sheer exhaustion of sex without love among men. How would it alter the state if women were to carry on that way, away from the "bad girls" back rooms where so much was staged? Loving a nameless, faceless body full with lust? Instant intimacy without endless pity? Feeding the body the sin it deserves?

I sat at the most isolated table in Daza and tucked my head into an eccentric book on the paradoxical relationship of sluts to saints.

"Mi mártir bella." Her voice rose like the vapors from a thick, grainy salve, soothing everything around me. "May I sit and have a cigarette with you?" She had just quietly appeared at my table.

A lovely stranger at my table? I loved strangers. Friends were not always as compelling. So I cleared a space for her.

She sat, folding her long, chunky legs under the immovable wooden table, and opened my cigarette case. She took two, lighting both between her plump lips, then handing one to me.

"It's Spring," I said, after releasing a cloud of smoke.

"Yes, it might as well be spring," she replied.

"No, my name is Spring. You called me something else before you sat down."

She directed the flow of smoke from her lips toward the ceiling. I needed to kiss those lips. But I had always kissed lips with the desire for nothing more than that but had ended up with more than all the trouble I needed.

*"Ah, tú habla español?"*

*"Sí, pero un poquito.* Why do you call me martyr?"

"I called you 'beautiful martyr.' " She smiled, and I wanted to press my lips against her cool, ivory teeth.

"Why?" Who had she been talking to, what had she heard?

"That is how I see you."

"Tell me why."

"I don't want to explain now. *Pero digamé.* Why Spring?" She was not interested in telling her story. She had given me her full attention. I felt awkward with that. I had seen that look of fascination stretch across faces and had felt the repulsive strain of self-indulgence. But that didn't matter at this moment. I was gazing into luminous eyes that bobbed like pitch-filled moons.

"I was born in the midst of a frozen season. My mother thought the pregnancy unending and wildly emotional, and the winter almost unbearable. She longed for the time when the thaw would come and bring new life to her emotions and warm the land. She told me all she wanted was my life and the coming of spring."

"Then it might as well be spring," she sang. "Should we

have some wine? I'll ask Ramone to bring us a bottle. A nice Spanish red wine?"

She hadn't told me her name, but I was in the mood for red wine. "Yes" was my answer.

She motioned for Ramone and when he came near she drew him close to her mouth and talked softly into his ear. Ramone smiled and headed down the cellar to find our bottle of wine.

"Tell me your name." I had to at least know what to call her.

"Evangelista."

Ramone reappeared and opened a bottle. He poured a taste for me and I sampled. He filled my glass and then Evangelista's.

I watched her sip her glass of bloodred wine, and when she smoked those cigarettes of mine, I was savoring the way she made so much of them.

Her untamed, inky black hair absorbed the scent of frangipani floating in the café's air. I sat in a golden limbo, watching the yellow flicker from the ivory candles saturate her burnt-amber skin. Around her shoulders, and her chest, and her arms the many textures of the clothes on the walls gathered. In the time I sat with her, she seemed to entice everything from the margins to come to her.

"You're a Pisces, aren't you? I see now," she said, fixing her eyes on my face.

"Yes, I am." I pulled myself upright. "Who have you been talking to?"

"No, no one. It's very simple. It's those big, beautifully tragic eyes you have. They are the trait of a particular Pisces and that is why I realized you are a Pisces. I have seen you often, so aloof and gliding serenely as if through water, in no direction and with no intention. And I would just enjoy the fantastic length of your body. How fluid your fingers are! How thin and winding your

*Take Care*

torso and hips, and how perpetual your legs are. But I most enjoy your flawless, round head. I want to stroke it. You go about so calm and still, yet every slight disturbance brings on a hurricane. That is why you are my beautiful martyr." Now she was revealing my own self to me, with the help of the nice bottle of red wine.

"But I don't see how that all makes me a martyr." Though someone once told me that Pisceans have a martyr complex.

"Because it's easy to see pain in you and it's so easy for you to accept pain. Distress is so familiar to you." She knew too much.

"So, is it that you study the signs of the zodiac?" Maybe now I could get something out of her about herself.

"No. Not really. I like to know different things to make reason for everything." She swallowed the last of her glass of wine. "I'm a coffee maker at a café and also I perform." She poured each of us another glass of wine.

"What do you perform?"

"Some friends have a small restaurant/cabaret, and I sing there three nights a week."

"What kind of songs do you sing?"

"Torch songs, songs of love and misery."

"In Portuguese?"

"Yes, some Portuguese. My father was Portuguese, but I did not know him. And my mother was the mulatto—Black and Italian. I sing some in French."

"I would like to come and hear you."

"Sure. It's what you would like, melancholy and hushed and smoky. If you come soon, I have a song that I will sing for you."

"How do you know me?"

"By the ways I have watched you and the ways I have heard

your body speak." The words floated from her big chocolate mouth.

Suddenly I realized that I wanted her desperately, so I had to leave her and that café. "I have to go," I told her, as I gathered my things and handed her a sheet of paper with a bit of prose I had written. Never had I given my work to someone that I did not know. It was risky, just when I had vowed to myself not to take another risk.

"Of course you do. I saw it in your wandering eyes. But will you have lunch with me tomorrow?"

I smiled "yes" and left her to read a bit of prose born one night of a wonderfully boozy solitude:

> Our understanding of our comfortability was extraordinary and delicious, but it seemed so routine. Was it that we had known one another in some past life? No. Your smell was not the reminiscence of any that had ever passed beneath my nose. I had never known a mouth shaped like that of a stealthy submarine. I had never been so blessed as to hear a voice so strong and steady aimed at my whole body. And your body, I have never been wrapped in a fine blanket of supple lambskin.
>
> No. We had never known one another.
>
> It's that we had strayed into deep burgundy smoking parlors. Someone sat in a blue-lit corner articulating sorrow on a simmering saxophone. We sipped spirits while a generous ivory pipe passed from your hand to another then to another and then another until it was pressed into my indulgent hand.
>
> We had sat in boxy, eggshell-colored rooms, on creamy overstuffed sofas and in deep-seated faux-velvet chairs, with candles blazing from every available space, and the haze of burning incense guarding over the room. A lethargic, thick-haired pussycat brushing against lazy calves. In the background Teena Marie sang of a Portuguese love on the "Quiet

*Take Care*

Storm" while we all tried to concentrate on the tales being told by a talker. And we smoked stubby Gitanes, drank cold white wines, you holding your lover as I held mine.

We were guests at great gatherings in boundless town houses. You floated out of a barroom that was crowned majestically with a gorgeous chandelier, carrying your crystal goblet full of red wine, I drifted past you.

You sank into a high-backed, gold-loomed, red tapestry banquette, surrounded by soldiers of admirers, politely disengaged. I sat in the banquette next to yours, crushed in by lovers, patientless with the boredom, longing for some uncommon intoxicant.

We danced on the glimmering ballroom floor, with our poorly acknowledged lovers, to all of the same songs that could move us to meaning.

Yet we had never known each other, had never wandered a path together as we traveled to the kinds of ways we liked to pamper our passions.

This was our very first time together.


Neither of us had said where and when we would meet for lunch, so I assumed it would be at Daza. But I had accepted work for the day so I had to miss that lunch. So I wouldn't have to face the dread, anger, and the desire of waiting for a new lover.

I took this tedious job writing copy for the day, and afterward, I took myself to this bar that always gave me a sweet vibe. I knew the woman who worked there. Euclid was her name. I liked to call her liquid because that's what she gave me. She made these weighty, symbolic silver rings and performed exotic dance at a club on Wall Street, and tended my vibe bar. She was so scandalous, with her British superfunk clothes, heels-closest-to-heaven, hotpants showing off her sickle moons of flesh, tossing her massive braids behind her ample shoulders. She would tell bawdy tales and never believed that they should not be told. Her breasts were glorious—breasts of exceptional sympathy. Her laugh was an echo to bounce off buildings. She was a great big mess. Euclid was always sleeping with someone, but no one in their *right* state of mind would sleep with her, so naturally most of her encounters were too terrifying to tell. But she had to tell someone, and I was always willing to listen.

I walked into the bar and there was Evangelista, sitting at the bar. She was such a bold sight. I was pulled toward her as if by the will of a surging current. And there seemed to be no need to struggle against this current, because I knew I was not moving toward any rocky cliffs of despair.

"Hi, Beauty." She pressed her plum lips into my forehead and I breathed in her scent. I expected something heady, something smoky, because that's how she made me feel, but she smelled like air, like the air I imagine whipping through when I think of myself swinging from purple-fruited trees. "What are you drinking?"

"I could not make it for lunch."

"But you are here now. So what would you like?" Her words laying down the tar that would seal away my confusion.

I turned to Euclid. "Hello, love, how are things?"

"Delicious!" Euclid flashed a tasty smile. "What would you like?"

"Scotch, rocks."

"E, another?" She knew Evangelista.

Evangelista nodded and Euclid poured our drinks.

"So you know Euclid?" I lit a cigarette and took a swig from my glass.

"One for me, too." Evangelista motioned as I took that first drag, and I gave her mine and lit another. "She pours me good drink, arouses me with laughter, and I speak with her of my need

*Take Care*

for the perfectly imperfect lover. And you, how do you know Euclid?" she asked, pushing smoke from her lips.

"I met her and her boyfriend at a Pride parade one summer. She knew friends that I knew so we all rode that love roller coaster together. By the end of the day she was trying to get me home for her and her boyfriend."

"Did you go along with them?"

"No. I was the wrong person for what those two wanted."

"Why is that?"

"I've played that game before and ruined some beautiful memories. Euclid is much more intriguing to me when I can just sit back and hear all her talk of her calamities and her erratic interludes."

"The fish as voyeur." She amused herself with some kind of thought on that statement. Then said: "Because, you know, the fish is an exhibitionist."

"I think the fish has the power of supreme flotation, swimming in its oasis, not really needing anything but naive to everything intriguing. That's when someone dangles a hook full of hazardous bait and wrecks the whole balance with temptation."

"Yes, because how else can one have the pleasure of taking part in your tranquil state? Do you want to be alone?" Evangelista leaned into my face and felt the warmth of the waters I always felt I had been taken from.

"Sometimes I want to be left alone. But I do not want to be alone for all times."

"Yes, the fish. Spring, how is it that you are the color of a sweet potato's skin?" She caressed my face and ran her big hand over my head.

"I don't know. I'm Creole."

"It is the most brilliant color for you. You must absorb sunshine. How dry you must feel when there are only clouds in the sky. By the way, I think you are positively right and very tender!" She took my hands.

Impulse had taught me to try and ignore the elation of having my hand in another's. A hand in mine would be soft and needy, when I wanted it to be willful and guiding. "Right about what?" I asked, deciding to ease my hands away from her.

She let them go with understanding. "We have always been mysterious angels for many lovers, but have never loved one another."

"Ah, you read my piece of prose."

"Why do you think that you left it for me?"

"It was all that I could offer to you that made sense."

Evangelista nodded. "Extraordinary and delicious! It excited me! How were you conceived?"

"Yes, excite me with questions," I thought to her.

"One night, two lovers, feeling nothing particularly fancy, are suddenly overwhelmed with the thought of kissing the flesh of some other body. Overcome with the desire to just close their eyes to each other while letting the hands hold genitals, caress blood-rushed muscles, enter them irrationally. Laughing wildly as their bodies collided, all traces of jagged edge gone due to the constant smoothing of their copulating bodies. Two lovers felt like making love."

"Then that is how you like to make love. Wonderful!"

Sitting there, thinking how she made assertions that you had to believe, I had not realized that she was up and almost out of the bar, saying something about us needing dinner. I followed. Did we leave money for Euclid? Did we say good-bye? "I want to find a bosom of a restaurant and eat there with you."

I remembered what Euclid had said to me a few days before

*Take Care*

as she poured me cheap champagne and tossed quarters into the jukebox to play slow love music. She had stretched across the bar and said to me, "If you want a woman, I'll send you a woman."

Evangelista and I walked the streets in silence, headed toward food, and found that we had crushed our two long bodies behind a scanty table in Miss Rose's Little India restaurant. Cramped and smaltzy, just right.

Our Black bow-tied waiter came over to open the bottle of wine I stopped to bring along.

Evangelista took over, ordering quite a few starters and entrees all at once, insisting that everything be brought to our table together so we need not be disturbed.

I started a cigarette and leaned back. "You're a bit pushy." I blew out with my dirty smoke.

"I was going to say that I thought you were being too much the good girl with me," she announced with excitement.

"I'm being on my best behavior since I don't know you."

"But you know you. You must say what you want before and not after you go along with something." Shrugging those heavy shoulders of hers.

"So what are you?"

"A problem for you."

"No. When were you born?"

"I am a Scorpio."

Glad I didn't have to hear myself say "What's your sign?" I said, "Oh, I don't really know what it means." I didn't, but after her I would be more aware of what it might mean.

"The scorpion and the fish are like this." She dipped one of her enormous fingers in her wineglass then daubed my lips with it. The wine stung my lips a bit and I ran my tongue across them for soothing. I grasped her hand as she was moving it away and pressed it to my face. Her hand had the smell of a long day and a faint hint of sweet perfume.

Evangelista held my face in her hands. "No. Don't you think about leaving." She was right. At that moment I wanted to say that I was drunk and uncomfortably full from food and I had to go. "When did you give up on love, Spring?" She lit two cigarettes and refused the man who had come to clean off our table.

"I'm the fish, I swim with my variety and enjoy my life of buoyancy and liberation, I don't know about loving another." Love was the weight of a sinker.

"My martyr, don't you feel like making love? Right now, if you forget to think about your fright and your vow to not love, wouldn't you want some love, if only for tonight?"

I sat back and said nothing, lit another cigarette. The wine was all gone.

"Don't you want to make love?"

"No. I want to be caught up in something so fantastic that it will explode from the earth and is remembered only in the realm of the senses. Let me take you someplace."

"Someplace to make love, any kind of love."

I took her to an after-hours Afro-Latin dance club. SalSoul was private information to devotees of rhythm and late nights. You didn't need a membership, entry was granted by instinct or the familiarity of your face. Down the interminable stairs of one building Evangelista and I went, following the passageway under the belly of stuffy offices closed by night, and into an elevator that would take us to the top floor of another building and open us onto the dimly lit, salsa-blaring private room. While going through the passageway Evangelista pushed me against a cold wall and kissed me firmly in the mouth. "We've just made more love," she had said, with a closed-eye smile of pleasure. She was determined to lay me open.

I liked to drink rum and Coke when I listened to salsa, so I ordered one for me and one for Evangelista. We sat at a table farthest away from other people. She didn't care to dance, preferring to drink her cocktail and smoke her cigarettes. I danced with the crowd of boys and girls on the dance floor. Evangelista watched me, she and I both teeming with desire. I took her by the hand and led her away.

"Someplace else now?"

"My place. I want you in my bed." But not the way I had taken others to my bed. With the others, I wanted to ease their small bodies into my arms, caress and exalt their sexuality, delight their senses and not make it a matter that I would feel danger if they wanted to take me into their arms. But Evangelista, she had the strength to hoist me to the peaks of airy ecstasy.

The streets were abandoned for us and so we walked in harmony. Evangelista and I slipped into a bodega for an overnight supply of cigarettes, water, juice, an avocado, and, against our will, canned fruit because it was just too late for any fresh fruit. And then on we traveled. Evangelista's gait was even and mesmerizing. I fell into syncopation and nearly passed the building where I lived.

Carefully we padded up the stairs. The rustle of our plastic shopping bags wasn't enough to cause a stir, the heavy click at the turning of the lock was not remarkable enough to announce our entrance, but the soft blast as the bulk of our two bodies hit the wall was the demolition of some ill-crafted barriers I had built up as defense against intimacy. I pressed my lips into her mouth and she tasted of curry and peppers. She crushed her monumental body firmly against my quaking body. Her thighs moved to steady my aching legs. With her pelvis securely fastened over my pelvis she rocked me mercifully. Taking my face into her hands, this Evangelista planted soft, hot kisses on cheeks, temples, bridge, tips, lips, chin, lobes, hairline. In blindness I groped for the heavy, silver belt buckle anchoring her hips.

This intricate buckle captivated me the very first time I looked up to find her standing there at my table in Daza. In those moments before going off to sleep at night I would open my imagination to that silver splendor, imagining the world that would be opened the instant I eased the sterling catch from the black leather strap.

The intensity of her lust must have been restrained by that silver belt buckle. My head was whirling as I took hold of the black leather strap and eased it away from the silver hook to liberate her bulky hips.

My lips and tongue were tangled up in the billowing black of her curls, the curls everywhere on her body. Her kisses landed in the crook of my arms, my neck, the sweep of my shoulders, the tautness of my buttocks; they sprang back from the tight curls of my hair and they lifted the sweat from my palms.

I stood strong, held tight to her body, every moment it felt as if I were clinging to a tree. A sturdy, thick, ginger-colored tree with a tender bark, creases to finger and sweet-filled crevices to taste.

And on into fresh light we traveled and conversed and wept and scandalized.

As we pulled ourselves awake, Evangelista mixed up orange juice, ice, milk, and vanilla in the blender. "This is called *morir soñando* . . . to die dreaming."

*Take Care*

"It's very tasty." My voice was still weary from traveling through sleep and my body was still wandering in the forest of her vast and enchanting body.

I scrambled some spicy eggs and served the avocado with a little lemon juice and olive oil.

"Who is your mother?" she asked.

This was a very amusing question for me. I laughed a gut-wrenched, nervously loud laugh. "That's a good question!"

"Are the two of you friends?" This one liked to make points. Points about other people's notions.

"Yes, I think we are friends."

"Does she love you the way you want to be loved?" Why did she need to ask so many questions?

"Is this leading to an implication that I'm loving women because I want my mother's love?"

"Then your answer to my question is no?"

"No, she doesn't. But I don't blame her." I shrugged.

"No blame, just pain. You've decided to love her and you want her to love you. She is your place of pain."

"My place of pain? Is that the place where the heart should be?"

"It is the heart. *Y eres todos corazón.*"

"You're attracted to pain," I say.

"Yes, because it's beautiful and because it's passion."


Everything Depends on You

What had once been a private social club for men of means and leisure was now Vibration Café.

The first-floor parlor was sparsely occupied with hipsters

lounging in profoundly deep-seated smoking chairs. Conversations passed around polished, mahogany cocktail tables. I could hear Nina Simone singing about a sinner man.

Paintings of café-society big ladies in dark suits puffing on pipes and shooting billiards, loomed around the heights of the starched walls and amber ceiling fixtures.

The bar was a golden shimmer of detailed craftsmanship and it seemed to go on for some distance; I moved to the middle of this bar and perched on a bar chair and ordered a Scotch, neat.

I had come to see her. I was told that she performed in the third-floor parlor. So I sipped my Scotch and smoked a cigarette before I went upstairs.

It seemed to take me forever to climb those crimson, deep-pile carpeted stairs that reached up through the ceiling and seemed to shoot straight to the moon.

Reaching the second-floor landing, I stopped to look into a room of downy lights, velvet, blush-colored sofas and settees of gold lamé. Queen-size, satin deluxe pillows were piled in the corners of the room. One provocative melody after another seeped out of the big black boxes hiding in the corners. Figures hovered coolly, overseeing the sluggish bodies as they fused in mass on the dance floor, administering grooves to those writhing on the satin pillows. I leaned lightly against an abandoned wall; I had the feeling that I just might disappear if I put my full weight against it, and watched the divinity spin hot sex from his platters.

Watching all of this filled with so much lust, I seemed to float up the staircase to the third floor. What I thought would be an anonymous experience was not: I knew a few too many of the people meandering around the third-floor parlor. I had hoped this would be a night of absolute anonymity. At least Evangelista had no idea that I had come to hear her. I said warm hellos to the

*Take Care*

friends I knew and took a tiny table in the dimmest corner. The cocktail waitress was a very lovely animal and I ordered a Scotch, thrilled with the thought that I would see her smile at my solitary table once again.

Cascades of chatter and gales of laughter randomly punctuated the sounds of the horn and the bass and the drum that sprang from the jazz trio playing center stage.

This was a blue room, a cobalt blue, illuminated only by creamy, beige candles set in sapphire-blue glasses. Suddenly there was silence. Then I heard a guru begin to tinkle his piano ivories. Sweetly audible, only the fleshy pads of his fingers patting the keys, he created a hollow yearning. He seemed to haunt the room.

"Good evening to you and yours." The voice of a seraph. And then she appeared, moving into the tranquil, yellow lighting, wearing a metal-gray evening gown. This was no angel.

Instantly her eyes were on mine. She smiled, her sultry eyes folding beneath her eyelids, giving me only a glimpse of the pale powder that colored them.

"I have a special listener tonight." Evangelista turned to the piano guru and the bass player, who began to pluck gloomy notes. She turned to the microphone and began her song.

> I could sing a new song, never sing a blue song
> Everything depends on you.
> I could end my dreaming, lonely nights of scheming
> Everything baby, everything depends on you . . .

I left when the song ended with a hush. What could depend on me? Who could depend on me?

EVELYN C. WHITE

# *Ode to Aretha*

The last time I talked to Aretha Franklin we exchanged a few words about Coretta Scott King. It was in the fall of 1981, after Aretha had given a spine-tingling concert at Radio City Music Hall in New York City. By telling the security staff that I was Martin Luther King's daughter, I had gained entry to the back-stage room where the Queen of Soul stood in a muted black tuxedo and fluffy pink house shoes.

I stood at the outer edges of the love-drunk throng that circled Aretha and waited patiently for my turn to pay homage to the Queen. Aretha politely greeted each admirer as she puffed languidly on a menthol cigarette. Although gracious, she definitely gave the impression that she would rather have been in a setting more in sync with her shoes. Rising like luscious brown dinner rolls from the tube top she wore under her tuxedo jacket, Aretha's breasts, like her feet, seemed to be begging to go home.

After a few minutes I was ushered to the front of the crowd by a towering Black man who proudly introduced me to Aretha as "Martin's daughter." Taking a deep drag on her cigarette, Aretha smiled demurely, looked me in the eye, and gently asked, "How's your mother?" Festooned in a yellow bandanna, a paint-splattered sweatshirt, and bright red parachute pants, I met Aretha's gaze and calmly replied, "Fine." Before she received the next person, the Queen of Soul turned back toward me and said, "You look different, but then again, it's been a long time."

It's been nearly thirty years since I first heard the electrifying shouts and moans of Aretha Franklin. Since then, I've bought just about every album she has recorded, seen her perform live whenever I could, and filed every scrap of paper bearing her name that I ever found. And while I would never engage in such tomfoolery today, I am not ashamed to fess up to the schemes I concocted to meet Aretha—all in the spirit of reexperiencing that experience of my past that so strongly informs my identity today. I am willing to reveal my passion for the Queen of Soul because she has always been willing to open her heart and let listeners feel her joys and pains. In a culture where Black women are taught to numb, blockade, detour, stifle, dismiss, and ignore our feelings, Aretha Franklin has shown us how to open ourselves and be free. Her expansive and unbridled bosom says it all.

One of my most vivid childhood memories is of my mother and her friends sitting in our living room talking about Aretha. The scene is Gary, Indiana, in the late 1960s. Back then, Gary was a flourishing steel town flanked by the sand dunes of Lake Michigan on one side and the hip grandeur of Chicago on the other.

The perpetually burning furnaces at the mill released a fiery orange smoke that enveloped the city and ultimately became Gary's most famous landmark. But we were not worried about air pollution, toxic waste, or protecting the environment back in those days. As a child, I loved looking up into the shimmering orange haze the steel mill had painted against the blue sky. It was like finding dreamsicles in heaven.

For Blacks fleeing the hardships of the South, the mill provided a pathway to their dreams. With the hearths going full blast twenty-four hours a day, 365 days a year, the mill offered steady jobs for Black men without high school, let alone college, diplomas. On the paychecks they brought home from the mill, the men in my neighborhood were able to keep dinner roasts on the table and car notes for Ford Galaxies and Chevy Impalas paid. Their labor bought Easter clothes, *Ebony* subscriptions, hula hoops, chemistry sets, and piping-hot bags of popcorn from Sears. Thanks to a strong economy, the term "female-headed household" was nonexistent during my childhood years. An "absentee father" was a man who worked holidays or a double shift at the mill.

It was during the late-night hours when the menfolk were at the mill that I recall my mother and her friends gathering to talk about their lives in spirited and sensual conversations during which they often shared their feelings about "Sister Ree." While other neighborhood women dropped in from time to time, the group that usually came to my house included: Mrs. McCann, a large, fun-loving mother of ten, Mrs. Henry, a salty-tongued woman whose right side had been paralyzed by a stroke, and Mrs. Smith, a Seventh-Day Adventist who had a shiny black myna bird named Duchess that mimicked every word we said.

With regard to Black music in the late 1960s, The Word was

*Ode to Aretha*

definitely Aretha Franklin. In soulful arrangements that blended her gospel roots with the driving funk of rhythm and blues, Aretha released a series of hits for Atlantic Records that put the "H" in holler and the "G" in get down. Along with the James Brown tune "Say It Loud—I'm Black and I'm Proud," Aretha's "Respect" had become an anthem of the Civil Rights movement. With its plaintive and sassy lyrics, the song had also emerged as a bold commentary on relationships between Black women and Black men. Twelve years old when it was released, I remember feeling a sense of triumphant elation whenever I heard Aretha belt out "Respect." "Here's a sister who ain't taking no mess," I'd think to myself as Aretha wailed. Her impassioned, soulful licks and sly innuendos about sexual pleasure made me feel good about myself both as a Black American and as a young girl about to discover sex.

My feelings about Aretha were validated by the voices I heard as I stood pajama-clad in the hallway, eavesdropping on my mother and her friends. With the ink-black darkness of the bedrooms at my back, I'd lean against the furnace room door, my right ear pressed against its slats. I would pitch my left ear out toward the living room where an amber pool of light put a loving glow on the words that drifted back to me.

"Girl, have you heard Aretha's new record?" That was usually the voice of Gerri McCann, who lived three doors down in a red house that was the closest to the highway entrance if you were driving to Chicago. Her proximity to the big city and the fact that she had more children than any other woman on the block gave Mrs. McCann an earthy "worldliness" that both attracted and intimidated me. I thought she was cool because one afternoon when I was visiting her daughter Yvonne, Mrs. McCann put Marvin Gaye's "Hitchhike" on the record player and danced—her

fleshy body flailing wildly around the room. But she also un-
nerved me because I figured a mother who would "shake it" in
front of neighborhood children was liable to say or do anything—
like ask me in broad daylight if my period had started or if I was
wearing a bra.

Her question hovered in the living room air for a minute as
my mother and her friends geared up for the conversation. "Girl,
I heard it on the radio just the other day, and I went right to the
record shop and bought it," Mittie Smith would say. "You know
Aretha can't sing unless she's in pain. She must really be in bad
shape 'cause this song is just too tough."

"We . . . ll, I re . . . ad in the *Jet* that her hus . . . band
beat her up," said Mrs. Henry, whose Mississippi drawl crawled
heavily since her stroke. "I wish a nig . . . ger would try to go
up . . . side *my* head. I'd knock him o . . . ut."

"Myra, you know you ain't got but one good arm left," my
mother would say, prompting affirming guffaws from Mrs. Smith
and Mrs. McCann. "You best be trying to keep it."

With that the whole group would fall out in a burst of
laughter that rolled down the hallway, accented by the clinking of
ice cubes in their Bacardi-filled glasses. "They're having fun," I'd
think to myself happily. "They're having a good time."


It was thus through the prism of Aretha Franklin that I first came
to see my mother and her friends as Black women with lives
outside of cooking, cleaning, taking care of husbands and kids. As
I stood in the hallway, held by their conversation, I realized they
had feelings, opinions, and interests in matters outside of their
homes. I came to understand that the women who laughed and
cussed about their thighs getting stuck to our plastic-covered sofa

*Ode to Aretha*

had not always been mothers and wives; I began to see glimmers of them as young Black women who'd once dressed up and stayed out late finger-poppin' at parties. I pictured them as being bashful, raucous, giddy, vulnerable, and timid. I also imagined their aspirations and dreams.

Years later, I realized that my innate physical and emotional desires for women were likewise being shaped by the moments I spent bearing silent witness to the interactions among my mother and her friends. I longed for the sister love that filled our living room.

One night they were talking about "Ain't No Way" and that high note Cissy Houston hit ("and held, baby") singing background. Then the discussion shifted to a topic that nearly caused me to blow my cover in the hallway. As usual, it was Mrs. McCann who got things rolling: "Sometimes, when Ezra and I are screwing, honey, it feels so good. I just wanna scream."

"Girl, I know exactly what you mean," Mrs. Smith quickly added.

*Screwing? Ezra?* That was Mr. McCann, a tall, light-skinned man who was always smiling and appeared totally nonplussed by the fact that he had a dozen mouths to feed. Caught off guard by Mrs. McCann's comments, I immediately flashed on the box of small silver screws my father kept in his toolbox. With his maroon-handled screwdriver he'd twist and grind the screws into place as he fixed broken pot handles or assembled Christmas toys. I was deep in thought about the matter when Mrs. McCann began to pant and make mock sighs of pleasure. I got the picture. I'd seen enough Troy Donahue movies to know exactly what they were talking about.

"Sex," it dawned on me with such force that it seemed as if

I'd bellowed the word out loud. "Mrs. McCann is talking about doing the nasty."

Once I got over the shock of hearing this mother of ten talk dirty, I was mesmerized by the conversation which, other than the initial comments, I can only remember in muted tones and impressions. I do know that I was not ashamed, embarrassed, or upset about the words or images that drifted from the living room down the hallway to me. I sensed no hurt or pain in the sentiments my mother and her friends expressed about sex. On the contrary, I remember the ease, excitement, and openness with which they talked to each other. They shared an intimacy and closeness that defined Black sisterhood for me for life.

The "Ain't No Way" sex conversation was also important because it distinguished my mother and her friends from Donna Reed, June Cleaver, and the other television moms who'd been a part of my upbringing. Like many Black children of the era, I secretly longed for a family that was as ordered, polite, and stable as the Cleavers and the Reeds. I wanted a dad like Ward Cleaver who carried a briefcase and wore a suit and tie to work instead of a blue work shirt. I wanted a perfectly coiffed mother who peeled potatoes wearing high heels, a dainty apron, and a tasteful strand of pearls.

But after the "screwing" discussion I began to see the shallow emptiness in the lives of the white television mothers. The "perfect" TV families against which many Black children unfairly measured their own, lacked the warmth and spontaneity of the homes in which they were raised. I could not imagine June or Donna uttering a syllable about sex, let alone using the delightfully graphic terms and descriptions that rolled so easily off Mrs. McCann's tongue. The sex conversation made me feel proud of my mother and her friends for being passionate and sensual women. Standing in the hallway, I was happy to hear them talk about desire and their appreciation of husbands who, in the words of Aretha, gave them their "propers" when they got home from the mill.

Of course, on the flip side of passion there is the possibility of heartache. And the Queen of Soul has always given Black women an effective remedy for romance gone down the tubes.

Despite her well-documented history of man trouble, Aretha is never downtrodden, pitiful, or defeated when she sings. Take "Don't Play That Song for Me," her signature tune about a troubled love affair. Far from playing a victim, Aretha delivers an assertive, power-packed directive making it clear that she doesn't want to be reminded of the smooth-talking man who did her wrong. Calling her lover on his false pledge of devotion, she counters his every "Darling, I love you" with a soulful "Baby, baby, you lied." Even in pain and heartbroken, Sister Ree stays in charge.

Truth is, regardless of the turmoil in her love life, Aretha's artistry makes it impossible to feel sorry for her. You just can't imagine her depressed, blowing her brains out, or overdosing (a la Billie Holiday) over a man. Not the Queen of Soul.

Setting a healthy model for other sisters to follow, Aretha opens her mouth, sings about her misery, and gets it out of her system. And when she's finished shouting and screaming, you know Aretha is heading straight for the kitchen. You can picture her at the stove in her fluffy pink house shoes, puffing on a cigarette as she checks on her pot of greens. Heartbreak notwithstanding, she's made it clear that no man is going to stop her show.

My mother died just as Aretha was hitting her disco phase.

The McCanns moved to Chicago. Two of Mrs. Henry's daughters got murdered, and Mrs. Smith's husband went to his shoe repair shop one day and never came home. When I cajoled my way into that dressing room at Radio City Music Hall, I was searching for a path back to cherished childhood memories. More than anything, I wanted to recapture the warm love and joyous laughter that was shared between four Black women and filtered to me through a soft, amber light. I hope that Aretha and the King family don't mind.

*Ode to Aretha*

AUDRE LORDE

# Today Is Not the Day

*I can't just sit here*
*staring death in her face*
*blinking and asking for a new name*
*by which to greet her*

*I am not afraid to say*
*unembellished*
*I am dying*
*but I do not want to do it*
*looking the other way.*

Today is not the day.
It could be

but it is not.
Today is today
in the early moving morning
sun shining down upon
the farmhouse in my belly
lighting the wellswept alleys
of the town growing in my liver
intricate vessels swelling with the gift
of Mother Mawu
or her mischievous daughter
Afrekete Afrekete my beloved
feel the sun of my days surround you
binding our pathways
we have water to carry
honey to harvest
bright seed to plant for the next fair
we will linger
exchanging sweet oil
along each other's ashy legs
the evening light
a crest on your cheekbones.

By this rising
some piece of our labor
is already half-done
the taste of loving
doing a bit of work
having some fun
riding my wheels so close to the line
my eyelashes blaze.

*Afrekete*

Beth dangles her stethoscope over the rearview mirror
Jonathan fine-tunes his fix on Orion
working through another equation
youth taught as an arrow
stretched to their borders
the barb sinking in so far
it vanishes from the surface.
I dare not tremble for them
only pray laughter comes often enough
to soften the edge.

And Gloria      Gloria
whose difference I learn
with the love of a sister      you      you
in my eyes bright appetite      light
playing along your muscle
as you swing.

This could be the day.
I could slip anchor and wander
to the end of the jetty
uncoil into the waters
a vessel of light      moonglade
ride the freshets to sundown
and when I am gone
another stranger will find you
coiled on the warm sand
beached treasure      and love you
for the different stories
your seas tell

*Today Is Not the Day*

and half-finished blossoms
growing out of my season
trail behind
with a comforting hum.

But today
is not the day.
Today.

*April 22, 1992*

# Biographies

**JAMIKA AJALON** is a freelance writer, poet, and performance artist and a film- and videomaker. Her latest completed piece, *Cultural Skit-zo-phrenia,* has had screenings from coast to coast in various film and video festivals. "Kaleidoscope" is a short story adapted from a feature script for a film in progress. She graduated with a B.A. in film/video from Columbia College in Chicago. She currently resides in London.

**CYNTHIA BOND** attended Medill School of Journalism at Northwestern University before transferring to the American Academy of Dramatic Arts in New York City, where she received the Drama League Scholarship. She worked for many years on the New York stage with notable talents, including Pulitzer Prize–winning playwright Charles Fuller and Academy Award–winning director Mike Nichols, and was also a repertory member of the acclaimed Negro Ensemble Company. She has worked extensively in television and has won critical acclaim for her film and stage work. Because Ms. Bond suffered extreme sexual and physical abuse as a child, she has developed a healing creative writing program for at-risk teens entitled "Words Changing Worlds," and is working with UCLA's program Community Based Learning. She is currently working on her first novel, *Ruby,* from which her short story is excerpted.

**MICHELLE CLIFF** is Allan K. Smith Professor of English Language and Literature at Trinity College. She is the author of the novels *Abeng, No Telephone to Heaven,* and *Free Enterprise,* the collection of short fiction *Bodies of Water,* and *The Land of Look Behind,* prose and poetry.

**MALKIA AMALA CYRIL** was born in 1974. She has lived her twenty years in the Bedford-Stuyvesant section of Brooklyn, New York, and has been writing poetry since she was six. An earlier version of her poem, "What Is Yet to Be Sung," was written and read at the memorial service for Audre Lorde held at St. John the Divine in New York City. Today, her writing and community work, both at Sarah Lawrence College, where she is an undergraduate, and beyond, are reflective of her belief that poetry is allowing language to examine the many layers between struggle and liberation, between freedom and death.

**L. JOYCE DELANEY** is a graduate of Sarah Lawrence College. She presently works at a nonprofit agency assisting homeless families with children. An aspiring screenwriter and filmmaker, she lives in Los Angeles.

**ALEXIS DE VEAUX** is a poet, fiction writer, and essayist whose work is nationally and internationally known. Born and raised in Harlem, New York and the author of several critically acclaimed books, she has a Ph.D. in American studies and currently resides in Buffalo, New York, where she is on the faculty in the Department of American Studies at the State University of New York at Buffalo.

**JACKIE GOLDSBY** is a writer and former editor at *Out/Look, The National Lesbian and Gay Quarterly*. She is a doctoral candidate in American Studies at Yale University and also serves on the Board of Directors of the Center for Lesbian and Gay Studies at the City University of New York.

**JEWELLE GOMEZ,** originally from Boston, is a poet, critic, activist, and author of the novel *The Gilda Stories* and a collection of essays, *Forty-Three Septembers,* both published by Firebrand Books. After living in New York City for twenty-two years, she resides in San Francisco, where she is working on the adaptation of her novel for the stage.

**CAROLIVIA HERRON** is a novelist, scholar, and computer game maker now living in Brighton, Massachusetts. She is currently the visiting scholar at Hebrew College in Brookline, Massachusetts, and has held professorial appointments at Mount Holyoke College and Harvard University. Her novel *Thereafter Johnnie* was published by Random House in 1991.

**MELANIE HOPE** was born in 1966 under the sign of Sagittarius. She is a poet and playwright living in New York City.

**HELEN ELAINE LEE** grew up in Detroit, Michigan. She was educated at Harvard College and Harvard Law School. Her first novel, *The Serpent's Gift* (Atheneum), in which "Water Call" first appeared, was published in 1994. She lives in Washington, D.C.

**AUDRE LORDE** (1934–92), internationally recognized activist and artist, was the author of ten volumes of poetry and five works of prose, including *Undersong: Chosen Poems Old and New, Our Dead Behind Us, Sister Outsider,* and the autobiography *Zami.* Lorde's honors include the Manhattan Borough President's Award for Excellence in the Arts (1988); in 1991 she was named New York State Poet.

**CATHERINE E. MCKINLEY** is a writer and freelance editor. Her work has appeared in *Black Women in America: An Historical Encyclopedia* and numerous magazines and journals, including *Ms., Emerge,* and *Essence.* She lives in Brooklyn, New York.

**SHAREE NASH** was born in St. Louis in 1967. "Take Care" is an excerpt from a novella in progress.

**PAT PARKER** (1944–89), Black lesbian poet, feminist medical administrator, mother of two daughters, lover of women, softball devotee, and general progressive troublemaker, died of breast cancer on June 17, 1989, at the age of forty-five.

**MICHELLE PARKERSON** is a writer and independent filmmaker based in Washington, D.C. Her poetry is anthologized in

*Fast Talk, Full Volume* and *In Search of Color Everywhere.* Her films and videos include *Gotta Make This Journey: Sweet Honey in the Rock,* the sci-fi short *Odds and Ends (a New-Age Amazon Fable),* and most recently, the documentary feature *A Litany for Survival: The Life and Work of Audre Lorde.*

**SAPPHIRE** is a poet and writer. Her volume of poetry and short fiction *American Dreams* (Serpent's Tail) was published in 1994. She lives in Brooklyn, New York.

**JOCELYN MARIA TAYLOR** is a videomaker, performer, and activist from Washington, D.C. After moving to New York in 1989, she became involved with DIVA-TV (Damned Interfering Video Activists), an affinity group of ACT-UP (AIDS Coalition to Unleash Power). Her videos *Father Knows Best, Looking for La-Belle, 24 Hours a Day,* and *Frankie & Jocie* explore issues of coming out, sexuality, and eroticism. Currently, Jocelyn works as the screening director at Downtown Community Television Center, where she develops and promotes three yearly video festivals and a weekly screening series. She has also produced art and calendar segments for the cable television program *DYKE-TV.*

**LINDA VILLAROSA** is executive editor at *Essence* magazine. She is the editor of *Body and Soul: The Black Women's Guide to Physical Health and Emotional Well Being,* published by HarperCollins (1994).

**EVELYN C. WHITE** is a reporter for the *San Francisco Chronicle.* She is editor of *The Black Women's Health Book: Speaking for Ourselves* (Seal Press) and coauthor of the photography book *The African Americans* (Viking). A new edition of her book *Chain*

*Chain Change: For Black Women in Abusive Relationships* is forth-coming.

**JACQUELINE WOODSON** is the author of *Autobiography of a Family Photo* (Dutton) and five young-adult novels. The winner of the Kenyon Review Award for Literary Excellence in Fiction, two American Library Association Awards, and an American Film Institute Award, her work has been widely anthologized. She lives in Brooklyn, New York.

# Acknowledgments

Grateful acknowledgment is made to the following for permission to print their copyrighted material:

Ajalon: "Kaleidoscope" printed by permission of the author. Copyright © 1994 by Jamika Ajalon.

Bond: "Ruby" printed by permission of the author. Copyright © 1994 by Cynthia Bond.

Cliff: "Screen Memory" reprinted from *Bodies of Water* by Michelle Cliff (Dutton Books, 1990). Reprinted by permission of the author. Copyright © 1990 by Michelle Cliff.

Cyril: "What Has Yet to Be Sung" printed by permission of the poet. Copyright © 1992, 1994 by Malkia Cyril.

De Veaux: "Dear Aunt Nanadine" first appeared in *Essence* magazine in

July 1982. Reprinted by permission of the author. Copyright © 1982, 1994 by Alexis De Veaux.

Goldsby: "Queen for 307 Days: Looking B(l)ack at Vanessa Williams and the Sex Wars" reprinted from *Sisters, Sexperts and Queers,* Arlene Stein, ed. (Plume Books, 1993). Reprinted by permission of the author. Copyright © 1993 by Jackie Goldsby.

Gomez: "Wink of an Eye" reprinted from *Forty-Three Septembers* by Jewelle Gomez (Firebrand Books, 1993). Reprinted by permission of the author and Firebrand Books. Copyright © 1993 by Jewelle Gomez.

Herron: "The Old Lady" printed by permission of the author. Copyright © 1994 by Carolivia Herron.

Hope: "Dare" printed by permission of the author. Copyright © 1994 by Melanie Hope.

Lee: "Water Calls" reprinted from *The Serpent's Gift* by Helen Elaine Lee (Atheneum, 1994). Reprinted by permission of the author and the author's agent, the Faith Childs Literary Agency. Copyright © 1994 by Helen Elaine Lee.

Lorde: "Tar Beach" reprinted from *Zami: A New Spelling of My Name* (The Crossing Press, 1982) by Audre Lorde. Copyright © 1982 by Audre Lorde. Reprinted by permission of The Crossing Press and the author's agent, The Charlotte Sheedy Agency. U.K. rights granted by permission of Sheba Publishers and the Abner Stein Agency, London. "Today Is Not the Day" reprinted from *The Marvelous Arithmetics of Distance* by Audre Lorde (W. W. Norton & Co., 1993). Reprinted by permission of W. W. Norton & Co. and the author's agent, The Charlotte Sheedy Agency. Copyright © 1993 by Audre Lorde.

Nash: "Take Care" printed by permission of the author. Copyright © 1994 by Sharee Nash.

Parker: "Where Will You Be?" reprinted from *Movement in Black* by Pat Parker (Firebrand Books, 1978). Reprinted by permission of Firebrand Books. Copyright © 1978 by Pat Parker.

Parkerson: "Odds and Ends" originally appeared in *Waiting Rooms* by

Afrekete

Destined to become a classic in the tradition of the best-selling *Black-Eyed Susans/Midnight Birds* and *Erotique Noire/Black Erotica*, *Afrekete* gives collective voice to the tradition of black lesbian writing. In the vast and proliferating area of both African-American and lesbian and gay writing, the work of black lesbians is most often excluded or relegated to the margins. *Afrekete* meshes these seemingly disparate traditions and celebrates black lesbian experiences in all their variety and depth.

Elegant, timely, provocative, and inspiring, the fiction, poetry, and nonfiction in *Afrekete*—written in a range of styles—engage a variety of highly topical themes, placing them at the center of literary and social discourse. Beginning with "Tar Beach," an excerpt from Audre Lorde's celebrated memoir, *Zami: A New Spelling of My Name*, which introduces the character Afrekete, the collection also includes such prominent writers as Michelle Cliff, Carolivia Herron, Jewelle Gomez, and Alexis De Veaux. Other pieces are by Jacqueline Woodson, Sapphire, *Essence* editor Linda Villarosa, and filmmaker Michelle Parkerson, with other contributions by exciting new writers Cynthia Bond, Jocelyn Taylor, Jamika Ajalon, and Sharee Nash.

*Afrekete* is a collection whose time has come. It is an extraordinary work, one of lasting value for all lovers of literature. A fresh, engaging journey, *Afrekete* will both inform and delight.

**Catherine E. McKinley** is a graduate of Sarah Lawrence College, where she and L. Joyce DeLaney began their creative collaborations. She is a writer whose work has appeared in *Black Women in America: An Historical Encyclopedia* and various magazines and journals, including *Essence*, *Emerge*, and *Ms.* She lives in Brooklyn, New York. **L. Joyce DeLaney** is a screenwriter and independent videomaker. She lives in Los Angeles.

COVER PHOTOGRAPH BY LORNA SIMPSON
COVER DESIGN BY MARIO PULICE

0595

US $14.00 / $19.50 CAN

ISBN 0-385-47355-9

51400

9 780385 473552